SWANSONG OF A CHILDLESS PEOPLE

SWANSONG OF A CHILDLESS PEOPLE

SIMON LENNON

Pine Hill Books

Swansong of a Childless People

Fiction (Speculative, Dystopian)

Published by Pine Hill Books

ISBN 978-1-925446-24-1 (electronic)

ISBN 978-1-925446-25-8 (paperback)

75,000 words

The characters in this novel are fictitious. Any similarity to specific real people, alive or dead, is coincidental.

Cover image: South Park, Darlington, 2006, used with permission

To my eldest daughter

A LITTLE TIME FROM NOW

The days were peaceful, summers warm. Gerald Keaton thought it mattered.

At only twenty-nine years of age, he and Alec Frewer were among the younger Englishmen around, although they knew nothing of each other as they knew too little of themselves. Darlington was the most populated place in County Durham but there were next to no children, not that people noticed. Each for his or her own reasons and without reasons at all, Europeans had stopped bearing babies.

The market town centrepiece was a nineteenth-century market hall, crafted with Gothic whimsies the English no longer wasted time to make. Its Victorian clock tower was an amenity of Gerald's inherited prosperity, although he checked the time from the latest electronic gadgetry he carried in his pocket. Good living had made his face quite full, with his steely, bluish eyes and jaw so resolute. Hairdressers had cut and styled his short fair hair to look like other businessmen, while he thought most about the bars, restaurants, and shops where he bought gifts to his girlfriend and himself.

When Gerald's work was a chance to be near Newton Aycliffe or Vanessa's work brought her to Darlington and they could both afford the time, they ate their lunch together. Thus there came the day, a Thursday, they strolled along High Row, Darlington, holding each other's hands. She was two years older than he was, with brunette hair, complexion like the whitest portions of a lily, and eyes of green in blue.

Walking ahead of them, near the waters falling down the sculpted steps, were a man and woman with large packs on their backs. Sewn to their packs were American flags almost as large. "Mum and Dad honeymooned in America, Gerry," remarked Vanessa. She was the only person to call him by that name. "They rented a cottage near Newport, Rhode Island, towards Providence."

"I'd like to see America."

Vanessa stopped walking, causing Gerald to stop. She turned to him. "You haven't forgotten they invited you to Sunday lunch?"

He looked at her, her eyes. "How could I?"

Their eyes lingered upon each other, before she smiled, reached up, and briefly kissed him, as familiar English couples did. She pulled away, drawing his attention to a rather telling likeness of the most familiar face in Britain, the King, partly drawn on the paving stones and looking past them to the sky. Kneeling on a blanket, a long-haired artist with several sticks of coloured chalk toiled through his task.

"It's a shame the rain will wash it away," said Gerald, studying the colourful chalk art.

Vanessa took ten pounds from her purse and offered it to the artist. "May I please borrow your chalk?" she asked him.

Away from the artist's effort and with a single stick of chalk, Vanessa drew a box on the ground. She filled it with the number "1." She then drew two boxes above it, numbering them "2" and "3." She drew a fourth box she numbered, as Gerald slowly realised she was drawing a hopscotch court in the middle of High Row. She drew eight numbered boxes across the ground, closing with a semicircle.

"I hope that's legal," said Gerald.

Vanessa returned the chalk to the artist, giving him five more pounds, before returning to her handiwork. "Don't you like children's games, Gerry?"

"Who has time to think of children?"

"You and I do." Her long heels can't have been the best shoes for hopping, but Vanessa raised her left leg and hopped onto the first square. "We'll see what you have to say after Sunday." She jumped to land her feet in the next two boxes. She hopped and jumped through all the boxes before stepping into the semicircle and turning back to Gerald.

"What would your business associates think to see you hopping?" asked Gerald.

"They haven't seen."

After looking around to see that he didn't recognise the people watching him, Gerald stepped before the first box on the ground. He raised his left uncertain leg. She laughed, as he hopped. Each hop and jump was easier than the last, his knees loosening and legs lightening a little. He jumped into the last box and fell forward into her. Their arms held each other, standing close together. "What might I say after Sunday?" he asked her.

She smiled. "Mum and Dad like their lives, but they've lots of friends with long regrets. They want you to be aware."

"I've got parents, too."

"My parents suggested you invite them."

Their close affection becoming too close, Gerald turned, leaving one arm around her. He led them into a man wearing a red cap and holding a camera, energetically bouncing up and down.

"You're a very beautiful couple," the man told them. Gerald tried to lead Vanessa around him, but he stepped in front of them again. "I want to take your picture."

"No, thank you," said Gerald.

"You don't have to buy anything."

Gerald and Vanessa posed, smiling for the camera, until the camera clicked. Their chore complete, they started to walk around the photographer.

Again, he stepped in front of them. "Have a look at you," he told them, holding the back of the camera towards them. The image of them smiling filled the little screen. "Didn't I say you were beautiful?" Gerald tried again to move away. "Ten quid gets you two prints."

Paying him would be the easiest way to pass. "For that much money," said Gerald, taking his wallet from a pocket inside his jacket, "we must be beautiful."

The photographer pulled a small notebook and pen from his trouser pocket. "I need your name and address," he told Gerald.

Gerald wrote his name and the address of the Stafford Joinery offices and factory, before parting with his pounds. The photographer bounced away, stalking other couples and tourists wearing packs or holding maps. "We might never see the photographs," Gerald told Vanessa.

She looked up at the tower clock. "Time we both nipped back to work, Gerry." She again reached up and kissed him.

Soon enough, Gerald was at his office desk. There he heard, as he often heard, Niles Stafford's bark: "Keaton!"

Nineteen years older than Gerald but seeming much older, the owner of Stafford Joinery was an austere man, with a long face and nose, thin moustache, and forceful chin. Thoughtful and intense, his voice was deep and resonating. Gerald hurried to his office, expecting another perfunctory meeting about the work he'd done, was doing, or would do.

Stafford sat in his dark leather chair behind his dark timber desk. Memoranda spread around were interspersed with samples of new cornices, skirtings, and other timber ware, replacing whatever styles people no longer wanted. Hanging from the walls were the classical pieces his company used to make, between framed photographs of Stafford receiving business awards and, in the largest frame of all, a page from the *Northern Echo* newspaper featuring an article about him. The motifs on his computer screen were of more timber products.

In the low chair facing him, Gerald sat upright, leaning forward. Gerald was still below him.

"You're a single man, aren't you, Keaton?" Stafford hadn't asked Gerald about his personal life since interviewing him before he joined the company.

"I have a girlfriend."

"Serious?"

Gerald knew the answer Stafford expected. "No, sir."

"Good, Keaton, good." Stafford lived alone, but he worked late at night and through most weekends so that his home was unimportant. "I'm looking for someone to be my special projects manager, Keaton. You'll answer only to me, and I'll pay you for the privilege."

Gerald struggled to comprehend what Stafford said. The older man would work until he died and mightn't die for another thirty years or more, but his invitation was a chance to sit eventually at his desk with all his life entailed, the power of command. "I'm honoured, sir."

"You should be honoured, Keaton, damned bloody honoured. You can start by joining me for lunch, Sunday, at my club." Stafford picked up a letter from his desk and began reading it, in the sign that Gerald was excused. Gerald quietly departed.

In the privacy of his office, Gerald pretended to read memoranda. His desk and office walls glowed that day and Gerald glowed with them. He held his open hands before his face to see the light against the patterns in his palms, trusting the future.

That evening, Gerald stood at the wide window of his second-storey apartment in the well-to-do West End, among the trees and four-storey blocks in brick along the western side of Marlborough Drive. The window was just a little open, affording him a hint of breeze and the sounds that slipped inside from passing cars.

Save only for his jacket hanging in a wardrobe, Gerald remained in his business shirt and wear. His patterned porcelain plates rested in the kitchen warmer. Slices of fresh veal in their red wine marinate lay cooking in the oven. Sliced carrots and broccoli in pots of salted water were almost boiling on the stove. An untouched glass of dry martini stood on a coaster on the sideboard. Another glass was in his hand.

Soft music plying from his sound system was interrupted by a short repertoire of tones from a small speaker on a wall. Someone, Vanessa, was pressing the button marked for his apartment outside the building doors. While she made her way through the communal entrance hallway and up the stairs or lift, Gerald had time to close the lounge room curtains. She soon reached the door to his apartment he opened to see her dressed out of her business clothes into a casual blouse and skirt. They kissed.

"Ooh, nice," she smiled, "martini."

"We're celebrating." Gerald retrieved the second glass to give her. "Niles Stafford wants me to become his special projects manager," he told her, as they sat down together on the cream-coloured leather sofa, his arm around her. "I'll be involved in everything important: developing new product lines, dealing with the factory."

"My parents'll be thrilled!"

His arm stopped moving. "Stafford's invited me to lunch on Sunday."

Her shoulders straightened upright and forced his arm away. "You told him you were busy?" she said, as much a statement as a question.

"That's no way to make the right impression."

"Is this what life with you will now be like? Where does your evolving life leave us?"

He studied her eyes of green in blue and small pupil to her mind, uncertain what she was asking, hoping to find a clue. "I'll see your parents again another time."

Her voice became slow. "Will we ever see America, Gerry, rent a cottage outside Newport on the road to Providence?"

"I'll need to check with Mister Stafford about my holidays."

She laughed at him, before her voice became pensive. "When all I considered was my ambition," she explained, "then I'd have sold my soul for a job like yours. If someone offered it to me today, so starkly, then I'd decide whether I wanted to be another Niles O Stafford, while I have the chance to choose."

If Gerald sensed righteousness in her, then he didn't know that she was right. Were the chance to succeed in a career so obviously hers, then he wouldn't have let her forsake her chance. "I can't refuse a promotion," he told her, "not without leaving the company."

She sipped her martini, staring through his eyes, until the sound of the oven clock alarm broke the mood between them.

Gerald returned to the kitchen while Vanessa remained on the sofa. Speaking only as loud as she needed for Gerald to hear, she asked, "Do you love me, Gerry?"

Gerald ceased preparing their dinner. "Yes," he replied. Whether she believed his answer mattered less than whether he believed it.

He slowly resumed tending to the broccoli, giving himself time to think and her time to not. He might've loved her, although loving her might've made their relationship more challenging. If his love for anyone were the one thing that could unsettle him, then he would fare better not to love her and keep his perfect life intact. He might've feared the pain of parting less than other risks in loving and being loved.

Vanessa opened a sideboard drawer, from which she removed stainless steel cutlery for two. She laid out the settings facing each other, across the dining table. He paused to smile, before she watched him serve their dinner. "Were you being truthful when you said you loved me?" she asked him.

"Do you love me?"

"Can't you tell?"

"Can't you?"

The sounds of him pouring wine into the glasses were never louder than they were that night. "Thank you," she said, as she might address a waiter. When Gerald finished, he stood the bottle on the table. They sat in their chairs in uneasy unison.

Gerald and Vanessa rarely spoke during the meal. He watched her, waiting for her to say something or look longer at him than she did, while her cursory words reverberated in his head. Sometimes, when she was looking at him, he smiled. Her eyes quickly looked down again. The words of persuasion and negotiation that served him well in his working life weren't serving him well then.

If he gave his heart free rein then he might love her, without knowing if he would. If she drew him into loving her or if time together would be enough for her to let him love her, then she made loving her more difficult. Without knowing what the risk of love implied, it seemed she'd risk too much. He wouldn't let her tempt him into doubting his dear ambitions, pushing him somewhere he didn't want to go. They'd premised their relationship upon silence above dishonesty, except perhaps earlier that evening, which might've been a failing.

They finished eating. Vanessa picked up her plate from the table.

"I can take that," said Gerald.

"I can do it." She carried the plate into the kitchen and placed it on the sink near the dishwasher.

Gerald laid his plate and soiled cutlery beside hers. "Can I get you some coffee?"

"Not tonight." She walked slowly back to the dining table and picked up her half-drunk glass of wine.

He poured the last wine from the bottle into his glass. He stood in front of her.

"Gerald," she said. "You don't have to do anything differently because of me; I'd feel terrible if you did."

He tried to place his hand against her cheek, but she stepped away. If she were deliberating about whether to end their time together, he didn't know what to think. He'd previously ended short and long relationships when choice was imposed upon him. Without choice, there could be no regret.

"Relationships can make people want to do things they otherwise mightn't have wanted to do," explained Vanessa. "People can make each other change what they want, without meaning to."

She stepped forward and raised her free hand near his face. He could see what she was doing, believing all the feelings that might arise within him he threatened to deny. She placed her palm and long soft fingers against his cheek.

Gerald leant closer to her, concentrating upon her. His wine glass neglected in his hand, he softly kissed her lips. His touch was his best persuasion, trying to keep her life in his as it already was. She slowly closed her eyes, threatening to bring him into her life as it could be. Still kissing her, Gerald placed his glass on the dining table before gently drawing her glass from her hand. He placed it beside his and, wanting her to feel more than she could think, wrapped his arms around her.

They continued kissing for several moments, without her

holding him. She made him feel unconvincing, but he'd already said too much.

Gerald slowly pulled his face from hers. Her eyes opened and he saw her uncertainty, without wanting to hurt her. Standing face to face, his hands against her sides, their lives remained unresolved. If she kissed him, then he would know he had persuaded her to accept the life he wanted. She didn't move.

If she imagined she could persuade him to share her visions for a life, then he knew that she was wrong. He wouldn't compromise their careers to let her try. Her face before him could not deter him from the noble task of doing so. If he tried again to kiss her, then he expected her to interrupt to tell him of the choice for him to make. "Whatever Niles Stafford wants me to do," he told her, with a formal tone of officialdom holding them apart, "I'm going to do."

"What you do is your decision," Vanessa sighed, "but I don't want to be a widow without ever being a wife."

His hands fell from her sides, while he tried to think so far ahead. Turning away from him, she collected herself together. Gerald watched her, resigning himself to what had always been. She was beautiful, he liked her, but she might never have been his for him to lose.

"I better go now," she said.

"Do you want some port?"

"I'll have some at home." She kissed his lips more fondly than lovingly, but she seemed uncertain about kissing him at all. "Thank you for dinner."

Gerald couldn't recall if she normally thanked him for the meals he cooked. She checked the reflection of her mouth in a small mirror near the door to see her lipstick wasn't smudged, while he opened the window curtains to the night and brazen lights from other homes before opening the door from his apartment to the corridor. "I'll come down with you," he said.

She glanced at him, as if about to say he needn't do so, and stepped onward. Gerald followed her to the closed lift door, where he stepped past her to stretch his hand out to the wall. He pressed the button summoning the lift to take them downward.

The sounds of the coming lift broke the silence in which they stood, while Vanessa stared forward at the closed lift doors.

"It's normally slow," said Gerald.

Vanessa turned and walked briskly down the stairs, while the lift slowed and stopped behind them. Glass-panelled doors separated the building entrance hallway from the ramp and few steps down to the street, where her car was parked. She stopped to face him. "I hope you're happy, Gerry." Her eyes had never been tenderer than they were tender then.

"I'll call you tomorrow."

"Not tomorrow." She turned and opened the building door before Gerald could open it for her.

They shared so many passions, but not a passion for themselves. "Give my best to your parents," said Gerald.

She turned around again to face him. "Do you know what *I* want, Gerald, since you never asked?" She spoke with all the force that parting words could be. "I want to marry and have children, who might play hopscotch and grow up to eat lunch with my husband and me some Sundays." She started to turn away again.

"Wait!" said Gerald. Many things he might've said flew through his mind, but none of them meant anything. He dared not speak words that meant too little or too much. He moved towards her, grabbed both her arms with his hands, and held her as he pressed his lips against hers. His eyes were closed, but he thought of hers wide open and surprised. It was all he knew to do.

He let her go. His eyes opened.

She briefly continued looking at him, before turning away. The heels of her shoes pattered against the steps as she scurried down them to the pavement. Gerald heard her start to cry, as she opened her car door and stepped out of sight. Standing alone too early and late at night, the glass-panelled building door closed and locked in front of him.

2

A YARD OF ALE

The Monday after he last saw Vanessa, with Gerald settling into his new role, an envelope with a handwritten address arrived at the Stafford Joinery offices. Marked for Gerald Keaton, it enclosed two copies of the photograph of him with Vanessa in High Row.

Placing his hands over the faces, Gerald tore up one photograph. He dropped it in the wastepaper basket beside his desk. Placing his hands over the second photograph, he hesitated. Interrupting him from his office door was Niles Stafford. "What have you there, Keaton?"

"Nothing, sir." Gerald slipped the photograph back into the envelope and the envelope into his pocket.

Gerald worked away each week, becoming familiar with Stafford's private club. Outside, few people noticed England fading away. Anything English was old-fashioned.

The last Darlington town crier in colourful uniform became too sick to perform for the few interested passers-by. The crowds upon the Market Cross cobblestones no longer cared.

Festivals became fewer and weren't for everyone, but for their few participants. The last Morris dancers perpetuated a little English culture from one dance to the next, if only for themselves, before finally folding away their folk dress.

A minor icon from the long-gone Middle Ages, St Cuthbert's Church ceased being a church, without losing its name. What once dominated Darlington and the countryside no longer did.

Refusing to fade were the actors, actresses, and other performers parading on red carpets laid out too long before them, although Alec Frewer only paid attention if he was nearby anyway. He looked away when they were mentioned in the news.

Places for people and parades had become places for politics, marshalled by police maintaining their thoughts of law and order. Sometimes they struggled to restore it. A demonstration disturbed the traffic in which Alec travelled. A rally interfered with him hurrying past.

Alec was his youngest self with his thick blonde hair waving from his head, striding over stairs he didn't pause to touch. The rows and wynds led him from one appointment to the next, where tasks he called important wouldn't wait. He was his oldest self in guises in which he sat through conference meetings; his well-pressed suits and shirts held his sturdy frame.

There were times, not often, that Alec boarded his bus home to West Park of a weekday evening or to the office of a morning without work to finish or to plan. The morning of his thirtieth birthday was such a time, a time to contemplate, rolling gently with the motions of the bus, but thinking about his birthday of itself didn't teach him much. His eyes began to drift about the other passengers, dressed in working suits.

They pushed their way aboard so serious and concerned. They jostled for the places they preferred near the front or rear, beside a window or an aisle, or just anywhere. Finding respite in a seat, some hid behind their books, magazines, and newspapers. Some sat with small computers on their laps, reading electronically what they could've read in print, without ever looking up. Some simply sat, gazing nowhere at the backs of heads in front of them or through windows at whatever passed them by, lulling them in their insecurity.

A man wearing a gabardine suit clutched a bottle of wine to

his side. Alec thought he recognised the man and suit, if not the wine, from prior trips.

A woman opened her handbag as soon as she sat down. She pressed her fingernails through a foil metal sachet, popping a white pill she quickly swallowed. She saw Alec watching her, and quickly turned her head away.

A man in a dark woollen pullover examined a colour chart for paint. He held a piece of aubergine fabric against shades of purple barely distinguishable from each other. Alec glanced at the fluorescent lights inside the bus that shone each night but not that morning, and wondered if the lights in that man's home could be so bright.

One well-dressed woman studied a House of Fraser catalogue as if it were too important to be enjoyed. When the well-dressed woman beside her also tried to read it, she pulled the catalogue close to her face, caring only to claim the fashions for her own. The second woman scowled, but Alec guessed she would've done the same. He imagined them sharing what they had to see, but knew they never would. The women could've smiled and commended each other for being beautiful, but he suspected the only thoughts they ventured of the other were cruel comparisons they didn't need to speak aloud.

The bus stopping along its route briefly broke some passengers' concentration. They left, or realised it wasn't their stop to leave.

The only person watching them was Alec. Nobody talked except to someone he or she already knew; that was only one or two. No one was really quite awake. In such a crowd, they were alone and had been for a while.

Grey speckles in the hair of men whose hair was not yet grey were only visible to people near them; grey slips of hair were dignity in men who thought they didn't age while they wore their sleek apparel. Women were less forgiving of the changes in themselves, and masqueraded before anybody noticed. They wore white powder and red gloss convincing each other and themselves that they were young, amidst other men and women also aging. Life bubbled through their veins, but they were getting old behind their eyes.

If Alec told them what he observed, they would've said that they were tired, but tiredness only made the unexplained more inexplicable. The expressions of their faces didn't change with anything they saw, or read, or seemed to think. Neither did Alec's. They were people he was becoming more alike each day.

His time to contemplate ended before he entered the Northern Lights Company offices at around about eight thirty. It always did. There were too many other things to think about and do: too many meetings.

By the time for lunch, when other people leisurely wandered High Row, Alec was rushing back towards his office. Roaming the Row, as he often roamed public places in County Durham, was a thin lanky man with dried beads around his neck. "Love everyone," he told the men and women he accosted, presenting to them a tray hanging from his neck. The small sign he'd affixed to it that day wanted money to help victims of an earthquake in Peru. Most men and women donated something.

In too much of a hurry, Alec merely shook his head. In his distraction, he crashed into someone.

"Hey," she screamed, as her cup of coffee sprayed from her hands.

"Sorry."

Alec stopped to face a woman of about his age, with shining round blue eyes. Against the monochrome skirts and slacks of other women, she wore a loosely fitting, flowery blouse and long brown dress. A floppy straw hat stood atop her long blonde hair; the only hat he'd seen worn for a while. They made her seem careless, frivolous, and poor. Her face and figure were surely thin by her accident of life without thought of her appearance. Her coffee was a puddle on the ground, the fallen cup beside it.

"I'll give you the money," Alec told her.

"Look where you're going!" She walked away, shaking her head. He watched her leave, before rushing not quite so quickly to his office.

Early that evening, Alec and his colleagues gathered in the smallish Hole in the Wall pub on Horsemarket. They often gathered in public bars, of which there were several to choose in Darlington, although that day they gathered for Alec's birthday.

Birthdays of young men and women were the only birthdays anybody mentioned, and thirty years of age was young among a people getting old. Older people didn't talk about their age and thought still less about it, subscribing to their name days every year if they subscribed to anything so personal at all.

Recorded music played from speakers on the walls, overwhelming nearby conversations. Only people standing alone, and only some of them, paid much attention to it. Most men and women stepping between each other with fresh glasses of liquor in their hands excused themselves, if only to reduce the chances that anyone would knock and spill their drinks. A muted television set in one corner of a ceiling broadcast a football match from Ireland, which men watched drinking beer and eating potato crisps. Small pockets of men also commented upon it, loudly, sometimes raucously. The few people smoking cigarettes did so outside.

"Happy birthday, young Alec," smiled Rupert Phipp, as he raised his beer-filled glass. Fifteen years older than Alec, Rupert was large and proudly rotund, with several chins below his bulbous cheeks and a thick white moustache to compliment the thick white hair across his head. "Baby Alec Frewer," he added, teasing Alec as he teased anybody younger than he was.

The men and women raised their glasses of beer, spirits, and wine in unison. "Congratulations, Alec," said one.

"Well done," said another.

Alec smiled. He raised his gleaming glass of beer.

"Not so fast, young Alec," Rupert interjected, leaning forward and taking the glass from Alec's hand. He placed it on the bench behind them and waved his hand, ushering towards them a pretty waitress waiting patiently. Her crimson cheeks and platted hair commanded Alec's interest, until her hands holding a yard-long glass filled with beer confronted him. People laughed to see the smile slip from Alec's face, charged with conquering it.

The yard of ale glass contained two and a half pints of amber hops and bubbles: two and a half times the biggest mugs of Darlington Pale Ale that Alec slowly drank on other nights his colleagues led him out. Normally, the yard of ale glass stood as an ornament mounted behind the bar: a point for conversations among people inspired and those unsettled that any man could drink so much in one long open swallow. Whenever the long glass came from the wall, other patrons in the bar and bar staff not otherwise engaged watched the minor spectacle, speculating what might shortly happen, dissuaded from drinking smaller glasses in their hands.

Occasionally, somebody invited the bar men or maids to fill it with draught beer for someone else to drink, promising to pay for the ale if he drank it in one mouthful. "Now, Alec," said Rupert, "you don't want to pay for this!"

That wasn't Alec's thought. Reluctant so much as to touch the intimidating vassal, Alec stared apprehensively at the beer. "I'm not as young as I used to be," he told them.

"You are!" laughed Rupert.

Rupert held the glass as did Tarpin Hobbs, a tall and almost gangly man not long past his thirty-third birthday. "Come on, Alec," said Tarpin. "Do it for us!"

"Alec! Alec! Alec!" chanted Rupert, driving him onward.

Others joined him in a growing, laughing chorus: "Alec! Alec! Alec!"

Alec breathed deeply, settling the last cup of coffee he'd drunk at his office into his stomach. Bracing himself, he placed his hands on the condensed glass, wanting to control the fluid coming towards him as much as Rupert and Tarpin wanted to ensure he couldn't.

"One swallow," said Rupert, interrupting his chant.

Alec looked at him. "I like to taste my beer," he told him.

"Taste the one after."

Alec looked back at the daunting glass, while people around him continued chanting boisterously: "Alec! Alec! Alec!" None of them had tried to drink it.

He wondered whether to take the chance to try something he'd never before tried. If he failed to drink the beer in one mouthful, then at least he'd tried to drink it. The worst that could happen was that he spilled the beer over his pinstriped suit. The best that could happen was that he suffered the pain of holding his throat open, to become intoxicated without any pleasures along the way. The only reason to swill it in one swallow was the opportunity he might never have again. Besides, the mob pressing down upon him was hard to refuse.

Alec pulled the heavy glass towards his mouth. The chant rose still louder around him: "Alec! Alec! Alec!" The smooth, round lip of the glass touched his taut pursed lips. Chanting as they did, Rupert and Tarpin carefully raised the far end of the glass.

The beer soaked the skin around Alec's mouth. His lips remained closed, preparing his mouth and throat.

"No cheating, young Alec," said Rupert, his face close to Alec's lips.

Alec opened his mouth, accepting the beer. Some men cheered and laughed, as the muscles in Alec's throat opened to allow the beer its passage. His muscles tightened, holding his throat open as he continued gulping down the beer continuing to come. Alec concentrated on his lungs, breathing as best he could. His throat drew the beer downward.

Rupert and Tarpin gently raised the far end of the glass pouring more into him. "Alec! Alec! Alec!" people screamed, from the clouded daze around him.

The beer gushed through Alec's mouth, leaving only a small sense of its taste before flowing to his stomach. The end of the glass might be nearing, he thought, although he couldn't think too clearly.

The last of the beer drunk, Rupert pulled away the glass. "He did it," yelled Rupert, "our hero, young Alec!"

The muscles in Alec's throat relaxed and he breathed through his mouth and nose again. People clapped their hands and cheered, while Alec felt the struggling weight in his drowned belly. He clenched his fists and held them high in the air like the champion he was, while his head and mind began to hurt.

"Fantastic," said Tarpin, patting his back.

Other colleagues shook Alec's hands. "You're a legend."

Alec grinned, gazing dazed around at them. Slowly, he slipped back onto a stool.

"Another one?" asked Tarpin.

Alec shook his head.

The laughing waitress took away the yard glass to be cleaned before it returned to the wall behind the bar. She might've been impressed by what he'd done, but Alec couldn't yet speak with her about it.

"How are you feeling, Alec?" asked Rupert.

"Not bad, but that might change."

Men and women who'd watched the stranger resumed their usual conversations. Some talked briefly about the yard glass, before they talked of other things. "Do you think you'll get the new account?" Their short attention passed, men again watched the football game, still not listening to the music.

Alec's colleagues prepared to eat, while he tried ignoring the weights in his brain and belly. He wandered away from them, up the stairs to a quieter, more spacious, place.

Against the wall by the bannister was a long dark leather lounge, at which three women sat. Among them, reclined with her stocking feet resting against a low table on which her floppy hat lay, was a blonde woman he slowly recognised. In her hands was what appeared to be a milkshake she was drinking through a straw; two metal beakers also stood on the table. Beside her were two other women of around about her age, one of whom wore a similarly lazy shade of comfortable brown dress. The other wore an unconvincing business suit.

"I'm sorry again about the coffee," Alec told the blonde woman.

"Was that noise because of you?"

Alec slumped down in a chair facing her, if only to avoid returning to his colleagues. "The yard glass of beer."

"Did you spill it?"

He smiled. "I drank it."

Her blue eyes studied his suit and bad condition more than him. "You should've spilled it."

The people he'd left behind doctored their thoughts before speaking, but she seemed so unashamed. "I'm Alec, Alec Frewer."

"The Yard of Ale is a brewery, isn't it?" asked one of the other women.

The blonde woman placed her lips on the straw, sipping the last of her drink while her eyes looked around. She made everything seem fancier than Alec had realised a pub could be. "I don't normally come here," she told Alec.

"I probably shouldn't."

She looked at her friends and their empty glasses on the table, and slipped her feet back into her shoes. "Shall we go?" she asked them.

They also slipped their feet into their shoes. The three women stood up and left.

3

JOSEPH PEASE

The day after his thirtieth birthday, wearing another of his usual suits and jackets, Alec's head was still a little sore. Not feeling hungry through lunchtime, and a little full from all the coffee he'd drunk that morning, he wandered away from his office and people he knew.

Spaced neatly about Darlington were parks and greenery: the softening leaves of pretty trees refreshing the already clean county air. Small brown squirrels hopped across a street-side patch of ornamental grass upon which the Darlington Borough Council forbid people walking, less they might damage it. Some lawns mattered more than men or women enjoying them underfoot.

A reticulating fountain plied its waters among people strolling leisurely about, with only Alec paying attention. A brass plaque was no longer legible, but would've honoured someone who did something.

Near the High Row steps down which more water fell, two violinists played tunes of love, behind their violin cases lying open on the flagstones. Doing just as well, a budding opera singer sung sounds only she comprehended. A mime entertained people with time to stand and watch. Passers-by enjoying the performances and people hardly noticing them dropped loose coins from their pockets and purses, without breaking their gait. More people gave more money to the busking artists than gave it to an old man without legs, sitting in a wheelchair with an up-turned bowler hat in his lap.

Collecting the most pounds and pennies was the thin lanky man getting in people's way. He bathed enough to keep his long hair clean but left his face unshaven for several days. Cloth sunflowers he'd sewn into his drooping flare-sleeved shirt and faded bell-bottom jeans were slowly peeling off. Attached to his brown lattice-leather belt holding up his jeans was a plastic water flask, from which he drank sporadically. He often stood at public thoroughfares in Darlington, proffering to anybody coming near him the far-flung social smile that stretched across his face.

Putting money in the tray hanging from his neck, without looking at his eyes and face, were people thinking they were noble for their donation and people who just wanted to escape the stares of other people watching them until they gave. Most people didn't care why they gave, but gave anyway.

"Thank you," he responded, as he turned towards another person. "Love everyone."

Alec didn't give the collector money for people in Peru; he wasn't in the mood. He dropped a few loose coins he hadn't noticed in the up-turned hat for the man without his legs.

Standing before a statue atop a block stone pedestal was the blonde woman he'd seen twice the previous day, wearing a wide straw hat and long deep red dress. She studied the blackened bronze figure of a man larger than the man had been in life, dressed in a Victorian-age suit and coat with his left hand to his side and right hand resting in his waistcoat.

"Not many people look at statues anymore," Alec said to her.

She glanced at him and his suit. "It's my job," she said.

"Now that's a job everyone should have."

"It's mine," she told him, as she walked away.

Alec watched her walk, until she'd walked far enough away not to return. Stripped of other thoughts, his gaze drifted back to the figure in antiquated garb, standing in statue. The inscription in the stone called him Joseph Pease: a name a little bit familiar. Alec stood in Pease Place.

His birthday celebrations had distracted Alec from dwelling upon his age, which that man long passed away brought to sharp relief. The statue was of a man not much older than Alec would soon be, but much younger than Alec would become. The eyes, face, and form were of a man with thoughts, hopes, and fears who might once have stood where Alec stood, but the man aloft was a stranger to him. There seemed so many strangers.

A woman's voice interrupted him. "I work for the borough council."

Alec turned around. Standing again before him was the blonde woman with a hat. "Why did you come back?"

"You stared so long at Joseph Pease; I can't have you taking my job."

Her words seemed to tease him. "Can I buy you that coffee I spilt?"

She glanced up at the time on the clock tower. It was after one o'clock.

"We can have lunch," Alec added, although he'd probably just eat salad, "at Maxine's."

"I don't know you. I don't know Maxine's."

"In the Bannatyne Hotel," said Alec, "on Southend Avenue."

"I can't afford it."

"I can."

She shook her head. "Look at you, your suit," she said, stepping back and opening her arms. "Look at me!" She looked down at her long dress dowdy by comparison: the sorts of clothes she could wear as readily away from work as at it.

"Here," said Alec, as he whisked off his jacket and began to put it around her. She stepped back, but the jacket caught her shoulders.

She laughed; that the jacket was much too large for her only made it comfortable. It made her dress seem colourful. "Why me?"

"You don't need me to entertain you."

"That makes you want to give me things?"

"It makes me want to be with you."

She looked at him as if he was rather strange, in his white business shirt and suit; perhaps he was. She pressed her hands against his jacket she wore, finding a padded weight against her chest. She reached in her hand and pulled from it his black leather wallet. "Come with me," she said and walked away, holding his jacket to her shoulders so it wouldn't fall. Alec followed her to a coffee shop, where she opened his wallet and removed five pounds. "How would you like your coffee?"

"Espresso," said Alec.

The barista dealt with other orders, conversing with cafeteria dwellers about boiled beans with the wisdom of wanting more. The woman turned back to Alec. "I only had that coffee from a voucher," she told him. "Do you want apple juice?"

She used his money to buy two cups of juice, returned the change to his wallet, and handed it back to Alec. His jacket was still around her shoulders when he pushed his wallet into his trouser pocket. "What is this job of yours?" he asked her, preparing to sip his first taste of apple juice.

She swallowed her first mouthful. "I assist the conservation officer, cataloguing and curating art works in the council's custody."

"You get paid to do what you'd do anyway?"

She laughed. "They're not all statues displayed in public places. Some are paintings piled ten deep against the walls in dark spare rooms. Gifts to councillors from other councils are in the studies of their homes, where only they and I can see them."

Alec smiled, not really listening so much as watching her. "Have you any greater ambition than to do what you're already doing?"

"I'm thirty years of age, and I've explored palace museums throughout Europe." She could've been ready to break into dance, but Alec's jacket would've fallen from her shoulders. "I've seen most important works of art, but I haven't painted any."

"You haven't told me your name."

"Hollie Mayfield." She finished her cup of apple juice. "We're even now," she said, striding away with her new jacket flowing from her. "I'll keep the coat."

"Maxine's for dinner," called out Alec, "now that you've got the clothes."

She walked a few more paces before spinning around with barely a break in her stride. She called back to him, "seven o'clock."

The Bannatyne Hotel occupied a nineteenth-century townhouse, with suitably styled furniture, at least in part. Patrons to Maxine's bar and restaurant drank wine from crystal glasses and ate food from English porcelain, in comfortably cushioned chairs and tables under elegantly fashioned lights. They chose and ate their meals for the tastes those meals afforded them; eating merely for being hungry would be crass. Public food and beverage were staple points of conversation, as the meals heated in people's homes could never be.

The best chefs in the best restaurants made the bread and butter they served their customers. Bread rolls at the Bannatyne were warm, baked each morning in the kitchen. The small clay bowls of butter accompanying them had been churned from sour cream. Removing the side plate from a patron who'd finished eating the bread and butter at Maxine's restaurant, a waiter or waitress then used a sterling silver brush to wipe away the crumbs from the tablecloth. The service could be slow, but getting good staff was difficult when the most diligent of people were waiting to be served.

Alec arrived a little before seven o'clock that evening. Leaving his jacket with a waiter and ordering two glasses of freshly squeezed orange juice, he sat down in the rest of his suit at the table he'd reserved in both their names, facing the entranceway. When his yellow tie fell on the tablecloth, he brushed it back to his white shirt.

A little late, she appeared, dressed in a long black woollen dress, surely her most elegant attire. Alec stood up to face her before she'd seen him. She refused a waiter's offer to take the shopping bag she carried, before he led her towards Alec. She saw him, he smiled, but she didn't acknowledge him.

"You're not wearing your new jacket," said Alec, as she reached the table.

"I couldn't match the colour," she said, offering him the shopping bag. "You better have it."

Alec took the bag, in which his folded jacket lay, while the waiter pulled out her chair and she sat circumspectly down. Sitting down too, Alec rested the bag on the floor by his legs, while she looked around them. She drew him into watching the people sitting at the tables around them too, listening to them.

Most of them sat alone, reading something, staring into their glasses, or eating. Four tables hosted pairs of people, talking between themselves. "Trade between North America and Europe declined by one percent last year," said one businesswoman to another.

A man at another table wiped his napkin around his lips after each mouthful of his meal, before resuming his dissertation. "Megganini's new film lacks the depth, the essential validity, the sincerity of his earlier works." The man sitting with him nodded his concurrence, while he chewed on his *Chicken a l'Orange.*

A woman at a third table was trying to remove some food from the front of her teeth with her tongue. Unaware or just uninterested in what she did, or indeed in anything about her, the man sitting with her continued to speak. "If the government in Pretoria won't do something about crime gangs and warlords," he told her, "then we, through the United Nations, should jolly well step in and do it for them."

At a fourth table, a woman loosened the blue ribbons around a shining white cardboard box. She drew from it a shining figurine: a lady and her bouquet in crimson porcelain. "Your husband is very good to you, Sorrell," said her friend, "The colour is so magical, the colours of a fairy tale."

Hollie turned towards Alec. "They really do talk like this in places like this."

"You make it sound boring."

She looked down at the glass on the table before her. "I don't only drink juices."

A waiter appeared at their table and offered Hollie a menu. He then gave one to Alec. "The chef's special today is venison with a sauce *à la Périgourdine,*" he told them, "a *Sauce Madere,* aromatised with truffles, served with vegetables. We also have coddled salmon with red wine sauce, dressed with spinach." The waiter paused, allowing his customers to contemplate what he'd told them before continuing. "May I get each of you something to drink?"

Alec looked at Hollie. "Would you like wine?"

She nodded, as if afraid to speak.

"We have a delicious Riesling," said the waiter, "with a delicate fresh nose, tart and juicy."

"Would you prefer burgundy," Alec asked Hollie, "a little like the colour of your dress today?"

Hollie nodded. The waiter gave Alec a wine list.

"Do you have any preference?" Alec asked Hollie.

She shook her head.

Alec sat back in his chair. "This one please," he told the waiter, pointing to the second wine under the heading "*Burgundy.*"

"The Pommard?"

Alec looked again at the list, again checking the price. "Thank you," he said. The waiter left.

"I feel inadequately dressed," said Hollie.

"People here never look at anyone else," said Alec, "not even the people sitting with them. The only person looking at you is me, and I think you look great."

Hollie again looked around, again drawing Alec to look. People at other tables sat unchanged from when they last looked around, making new rounds of old conversations.

Alec turned back to Hollie. "Will we talk first about you or about me?" he asked her.

"You," she said, turning back towards him. "I already know about me."

"What would you like to know?"

"Everything."

"We might have to come back tomorrow for another instalment."

Hollie laughed. "Tell me about your parents."

"They died when I was seven," said Alec, before answering the question he presumed she was reluctant to ask. "We were living in Etherley. My parents left me at home with a babysitter and came to Darlington to see a play, *Much Ado about Nothing*. Heading home afterwards, a truck driver thinking more about schedules than anyone's life tried to pass them, without making it.

"Sometime, I learnt to think more of other nights: days and nights beforehand, afterwards, and still to come. My great aunt Mimi brought me up. She always told me my parents still loved me and she loved me so much that I really had three loving parents. I didn't believe her, but it was nice of her to say it. She died when I was seventeen."

"I better not try to bring you up."

"She was old," lamented Alec, without further explanation. "I inherited enough money to make me the richest person I knew, although it meant less to me than to people around me. I studied, worked, travelled the world making deals for Northern Lights and me, and did everything I wanted. Now, I do more of the same, if I'm not careful."

The waiter set two wine glasses on the table in front of them. He showed Alec the label on the bottle. "That's the one," Alec told the waiter. He leant forward and whispered to Hollie, "I can't recall what I ordered."

She smiled, while Alec sat back and upright. The waiter removed the cork from the bottle and poured a small amount of wine into Alec's glass.

"I'm sure that will be fine," said Alec, without tasting it.

"Would madam like a small amount to taste?" the waiter asked Hollie.

She shook her head. The waiter filled her glass with wine and then Alec's glass before leaving the bottle and cork at the side of the table. He conspicuously noticed the two menus still open on the table and walked away.

"Tell me about your parents," said Alec to Hollie.

"My father was one of those formal and particular company executives, who wore starched shirts and ties held back with pins after other people stopped. He wouldn't so much as park a car where he wasn't supposed to. That was until I was fourteen and the day he was caught in a storm where the wind broke his umbrella. He slipped into a patisserie until the rain cleared, met a postgraduate university student with legs longer than her education, studying to be an actuary. Now they're managing a café in Cadiz."

"Wow," sighed Alec, reaching back in his chair.

"I'd rather have the truck." Alec was unsure what to say, while Hollie's voice softened. "My father let my mother have everything he left behind, and he left everything behind. She told me I'd caused him to leave, so I learnt to draw pictures of myself with the parents I wished I had. She spent years standing in patisseries through thunderstorms holding broken umbrellas. Now she just dresses in her most expensive clothes, hoping people notice her. She'd be scared to death if they did."

A waiter intruded upon her story. "Are you ready to order?" he asked.

Hollie leant forward towards Alec. "Should I really be here?" she asked him.

"Come on," he said, preparing to stand. "Let's find you a patisserie."

The cost of the orange juice and burgundy paid, a waiter brought Alec his jacket. Alec took his other jacket from Hollie's shopping bag and wrapped it around her shoulders. As they were about to leave, she grabbed the cork from the table and tried to press it into the neck of the unfinished bottle of wine. For her, Alec sealed the cork, tucked the bottle in her bag, and led them out.

4

WHORLTON

Saturday night, Alec accompanied Hollie to a comfortable semi-detached two-storey home along the Green in Piercebridge. Zane Entwist's thirty-fifth birthday was his excuse for a party, although Zane didn't need one, flaunting his relative youth before people who didn't consider themselves old. Puckering the muscles in his neck and shoulders, he walked with his head high in the grace to which he'd long aspired, carrying a flute Champagne glass while the music played loud. Seeing Hollie at the open door, he fondly kissed her cheek.

"This is Alec," she said, trying to talk above the music.

"Alec," Zane exclaimed, "superb, superb!" He thrust out his hand and exuberantly shook Alec's hand. "I've heard so much about you."

Alec looked at Hollie. "We only met this week," she told Zane.

"Oh," said Zane, scratching his head. "I must be thinking of someone else."

"Happy birthday," said Alec, offering their host a bottle of wine. "My birthday was this week, too."

Zane suddenly leant forward, staring into Alec's eyes. "Have you thought about what you want from your life?" he asked, before stepping back. "All I want is to smile."

"That doesn't sound like much."

"Oh, but it is. It's everything."

Zane took the bottle from Alec's hand. He fondly kissed the cheeks of all the women, shook the hands of all the men arriving, and waltzed around.

Stepping towards Hollie and Alec was one of the women with whom she'd sat in that lounge bar the night of Alec's birthday. No longer wearing her unconvincing business suit, at the party she dressed much as Hollie dressed. "Don't worry about Zane," she told Alec. "Nobody takes him seriously."

"Ingrid works with me at the council," Hollie told Alec. "She goes out with Zane."

"I amuse him," said Ingrid, taking another glass of wine, "while he does what he does or just is, collecting acquaintances he calls friends and friends he doesn't know. He's not good enough to live with, but too good to leave."

The second woman with whom Hollie had sat that night of Alec's birthday stood where the music wasn't so loud, nibbling from a plate of salmon sushi rolls. "Neve's an accounts manager at the council," said Hollie, introducing her to Alec.

"Do all your friends work at the council?" asked Alec.

Neve glanced down at Alec and Hollie's hands apart. In spite of the social shirt and trousers Alec wore that night, Neve asked Hollie, "Who would have imagined you with a suit?"

Alec interjected. "There are as many men saying stupid things in baggy, canvas jeans as say them in pinstriped suits," he responded.

Hollie took his hand. "You went out with that lawyer, of all people," she said to Neve.

Neve shrugged her shoulders. "He asked," she said.

Through the ensuing weeks and months, Alec and Hollie often shared long meals around restaurant tables and slow drinks in cafeterias and bars. They attended parties where people sometimes recognised each other's faces, but always pretended to remember everybody's name. With their divergent friends and the mutual strangers to whom they introduced them, Alec and Hollie listened and they talked, holding each other's hands under the tables when they didn't need their hands to eat.

Soon after Rupert Phipp met Hollie at their offices, he again stood with Alec one early evening in a bar. "I picture you with a corporative executive, young Alec," he told him, "in silk skirts and stiletto-heeled shoes."

"Hollie makes me forget about everything else."

Rupert stood silently. He drank more beer from his glass.

"She is very pretty," Alec added.

Rupert smiled. "She is at that," he said. "Drink up!"

Away from them, Hollie and Alec shared their observations of people they knew. "Rupert's very good with parties," said Alec, "but not with people."

"Zane's worse," said Hollie. "Ingrid could be beautiful, if she let herself." Knowing they were improper for saying what they said, they said it anyway.

When Hollie returned to the borough council offices from lunch with Alec, she noticed Neve gazing wistfully from her chair and desk, her head dipped to the side, resting on her shoulder. "You look like your heart's fluttering with romance," smiled Hollie.

Neve looked up at Hollie. "I love our new emblem," she said. Her long fingers with painted nails, which pounded the keyboard of her computer terminal or numbers on her telephone keypad, started softly stroking a small metal plaque standing in the centre of her desk. Presented to all borough council employees that morning to inspire them to work, the plaque displayed the recently redesigned council crest: two wide-open blue hands against a black and white chequered background. Every prior crest was obsolete.

Hollie's plaque sat at a far corner of her desk, behind the ceramic mug in which stood her pens and pencils. "I couldn't confer my love upon anything inanimate," she said, "however much I like it." The meaning of love for her was not the meaning it was for Neve. "I couldn't love anything but people."

"You mightn't feel that way if you met more people," responded Neve. "You don't have to deal with their complaints."

"We know people are important," agreed Ingrid, coming towards them. Her dealing with people of the borough required her to dress in business skirts and slacks at work. Embroidered to the pocket of her sparkling white business blouse, as it was embroidered to all her business blouses and her padded jacket, was the redesigned council crest. "That's why we have a human resources manager."

Less often than she'd previously done, Hollie and Alec sometimes retreated into the countryside on weekends. Roman forts and English castles were their histories only open on weekends. The last few fairs in country villages were places to buy jars of preserved fruits and jams. Some offered the words of aged storytellers sitting on tree stumps. The Mediaeval Fayre at Sedgefield became a little smaller each year.

One Sunday, they visited Whorlton on the River Tees, to walk down the hill and across the old suspension bridge. The inn wasn't serving lunch, so Alec and Hollie walked around.

The calm antiquated village was much like any other, except for the strange persisting sounds from across the green. Following them to the Church of St Mary's, its steeple obscured by trees, Alec slowly realised they were organ chords. While other churches had been deconsecrated and assigned to other functions, such as museum pieces for which people paid offertories for admission to inspect the art and stone, the noticeboard promised Holy Communion the second Sunday every month.

A one-armed gardener picked weeds from between the scattered gravestones in the grounds. The organ chords continued from the church while Alec and Hollie watched the gardener, toiling without obvious reward. He made Alec think of being old.

"I hope," said the gardener looking up at them, "somebody someday picks the weeds from my grave."

The church doors were open. Inside, the church was brighter than Alec would have imagined, revealing the stained-glass windows that had been dark outside; old churches were the last places English people saw images of Jesus. Resting on a table was a leaflet inviting mourners and other visitors to donate money for building maintenance.

At the front of the church, to the left of the altar, the aged organist stopped playing and looked around. His eyes squinted and his head continued moving about, his thick glass spectacles unable to seize upon the strangers standing near the door. Near him, was an old man wearing black robes, the vicar presumably, his shoulders hunched forward, polishing a candlestick.

"Hello," said Alec.

The vicar didn't respond. If the organist was almost blind, the silent vicar was almost deaf. The organist resumed playing.

English people christened babies in churches, when they still had babies. The last churches were places people went to die. Only the elderly attended church and old people passed away, while younger people rarely thought of anybody's death. Those vacant pews were funeral venues, where ministers of the cloth led prayers for the deceased's few surviving friends. Visitors arranged church funerals for their relatives and themselves.

Alec and Hollie walked along the aisle through the middle of the church, the rug muffling their steps, when the vicar turned and saw them. He smiled. Alec smiled, before the old man walked away, surely unaccustomed to being called upon by anyone not yet dying.

"People once married in places like this," remarked Alec, speaking over the organ chords.

"People once married," said Hollie.

At a whim amidst their lives in secularity, Alec stopped. "Shall we?" he asked her.

She stopped and faced him. "Get married?"

"It would be fun."

Hollie continued looking at him, while he slowly knelt down in front of her. His right knee resting through his trousers on the rug and his left knee upright supporting him, he looked up at her. She glanced around the church, before looking back down at him.

"Will you marry me?" he asked her.

"My mother wouldn't like it. She doesn't want to feel so old."

"We don't want to be too much like our parents," said Alec, standing up and placing his hands on her arms.

"Is this what your Aunt Mimi would've wanted?"

Alec edged a little away from her without releasing her arms from his hands. "Aunt Mimi didn't care when she was young but before she died, she wished she'd married."

"Should we marry because of what other people wish they'd done?"

"We're here now," said Alec, looking around at the white walls. "If we don't get married now, we'll go back to our sensible homes and jobs and might never do it. Then we'll be seventy years old, thinking marriage might be nice."

"We could get married when we're seventy years old."

"I want to see you in a beautiful white dress trailing behind you, while you can still walk with it. I want a priest to invite us to kiss, before I need a walking stick to stand."

"Aren't you worried about me being ugly?"

"We can be ugly together," said Alec.

"You think more about being old than anyone else I know, except Zane."

"I mightn't think about marriage again after we leave here, but we have whole lives to lead and whole lives being young and old. No one else considers being old, not even people already old."

Hollie continued studying Alec, staring expectantly back at her. "We don't need to marry to love each other," she said.

"If I don't marry you, then I won't marry anyone."

"I'm not marrying anyone else."

"That's something," smiled Alec. He released his hands from her arms as he again descended from her, until he was again kneeling before her. His bent right knee again pressed on the rug and his bent left knee supported him, looking up at her.

"I like my life the way it is," she explained, "my home."

"I want mine to get better."

Her voice became distant. "So do I."

Alec's head dipped to the floor. Hollie might've been telling him something of their relationship, but he wouldn't ask. She might've been trying to discourage him from thinking they could become too close, or been denying that they already were. Her soft-soled feet walked away, while the organ chords washed past them.

Alec driving, Hollie sitting in the passenger seat beside him, they both sat silently travelling east back to Darlington. His frustration felt no better expression than through his foot against the accelerator pedal, until a police car appeared behind them flashing its lights. Alec removed his foot from the pedal, glanced at the dashboard of his car, and realised he'd driven above the lawful limit. "I'm in trouble now," he said.

He slowed the car, pulled it the side of the road, and stopped. He remained in his driver's seat, his driver licence in his hand, while a Durham Constabulary policewoman stepped from the police car. She read the letters and numbers from Alec's registration plate, typed them into a small handset she carried, and waited. A moment or so later, she approached Alec's car. Alec lowered the window beside him. "Good afternoon," she said.

Hollie leant forward to look past Alec towards her. "Anna!" she said.

The officer leant down to see better the passenger's face. "Hollie?"

"How are you?" Their conversation was casual, as Alec couldn't conceive with a police officer detaining him.

"I'm really well."

"Anna Smythe, this is Alec Frewer," said Hollie. Alec didn't need her introduction. "Anna and I were at school together," Hollie told Alec, although Alec didn't care. "How are you and Lars?"

"We're too busy to see each other, between his shifts and mine. He's studying for his next promotion. I have my acting classes."

"You always were theatrical."

The police officer turned back to Alec. "Can I please see your driver's licence?"

"I told you his name," interrupted Hollie.

"I need to issue him with a ticket."

"You're my friend?" gasped Hollie.

"It's the law," she explained. The policewoman stared down Alec as she would've stared down any other speeding driver.

Alec handed her his driver licence. Hollie slumped back in her seat, her arms folded together.

The policewoman entered more details into her handset, until a small ream of paper rolled out she gave to Alec: the fine he was required to pay. He slipped it into his shirt pocket. "Have a nice day," she told Alec.

Hollie said nothing. She remained with her arms folded, looking forward.

Alec raised the window beside him and restarted the car engine. He watched the policewoman in his rear vision mirror return to her police car and drive away.

As he prepared to drive away too, Hollie unfolded her arms and opened the car door beside her. "No wonder people are so lonely," she said, "when friendships count so little."

Hollie stepped outside, leaving the car door open. Alec switched off the engine and followed her onto the grassy verge, while cars continued streaming past.

"She'd see more of Lars if she didn't prefer pretending."

Alec didn't understand. He didn't expect to understand.

"My father never had a speeding ticket," she said, for which Alec began to feel inadequate by comparison, "until Cadiz." He was suddenly not so sure. "No experience is a good reason to be alone. Some experiences are just good reasons to think carefully about the person you marry." Alec had no easy answer, not that he was willing to say. She turned towards him. "That was your marriage proposal today, wasn't it?"

He stepped towards her. "It's the only one I've ever made."

"I don't like waste."

"It was the second last one I ever will." He knelt down on the grass, damp against his trouser knee. "Will you marry me, Hollie?"

"You make me feel important," she told him. "No other person has."

"If you've a reason we not marry, then I beg you please to tell me."

She laughed. "If I told you, then I'd hope that you'd refute it." He smiled, while she shook her head. "I can't think of any reason.

Alec sprang from his feet, grabbed her with his hands, and

kissed her. He loved her and believed her. Surprised again, she kissed him.

A month and a half later, a Saturday, they were again in the Church of St Mary's, Whorlton. Standing before the vicar in their sense of an occasion, Hollie wore a thick white dress bought from a store. Alec wore his black-tie dinner suit and a top hat he had hired. The vicar shuffled through almost petrified pages of a book of uncommon prayer, until he found the procedure of marriage ceremony. The almost blind organist and one-armed gardener stood listlessly.

Without itinerant travellers that day, there was just one other guest. Sitting in the last row nearest the wall was Hollie's mother. Around Tabitha Mayfield's neck were several long necklaces of cultured pearls spreading like ripples down her chest. The white buttons of her white blouse were fastened high to her neck. At the front of her collar was a large oval brooch with the porcelain figure of a classical Greek woman kneeling with a vase. She sat silently, conspicuously unmoved by the attention her daughter had drawn upon herself that day.

"Wilt thou have this Woman to thy wedded wife?" the vicar solemnly asked Alec, struggling to enunciate the words he read. "Wilt thou love her, comfort her, honour, and keep her in sickness and in health; and keep thee only unto her, so long as ye both shall live?" He then studied Alec's lips for any movement.

"I will," said Alec.

The vicar looked at Hollie. "Wilt thou have this Man to thy wedded husband? Wilt thou love him, comfort him, honour, and keep him in sickness and in health; and keep thee only unto him, so long as ye both shall live?" He studied her lips.

"I will," she said.

"I now pronounce you husband and wife."

Alec and Hollie faced each other. He held her precious smiling face in his hands, her cheeks soft against his gentle palms. His outstretched fingers brushed back her hair to expose more of her lucent face, before he wrapped his arms around her and spun her around. His arms held her leaning low and backwards, looking up at him. He leant forward and kissed her.

The surprise of strangers had ceased amusing Alec; those strangers needed something to surprise them. Few things surprised anyone anymore.

When Alec and Hollie finished kissing, Alec pulled her upright. Adjusting themselves in their clothes again, Hollie turned back towards her mother. Alec's eyes followed.

Hers was a different kind of silence. The older woman sat rigid, with water in her eyes and a vestige of a sad smile in her lips.

5

HOME LIVES

Alec and Hollie chose a two-storey home on Ettersgill Drive in Hummersknott, the westernmost part of the West End, where all the red-brick houses were more like large cottages than houses detached. Front timber doors, eaves, and window panes were white as if they'd been freshly painted, including those for the big bay windows every house seemed to enjoy. Most of the garage doors were also white, but with a smattering of blue or red for no obvious reason; even the double-car garage doors were less obtrusive than they should have been.

The smell of greenery was more pervasive in the suburbs than parks and pavement trees made it in the markets part of town. Hedges more so than ivy remained trimmed, although some shrubbery flourished so full it threatened to overwhelm the red brick walls and fewer fences. Rear gardens were never so well presented, except among people who enjoyed hobby gardening in the soil of private spaces or who paid gardeners to seem to enjoy it.

Alec mowed their little lawns and sometimes swept their little paths, but remained as uninterested as Hollie in wasting time manicuring something natural into something unnatural. Plants and shrubs grew as they dared. His nose and cheeks increasingly enjoyed the golden freckles that sun gave men who shouldn't be out too long.

On the small patio behind their home, Hollie sat barefooted in their low, canvas chairs, with Alec in his shoes and their visiting friends. He drank beer from burly mugs. She more often drank camomile tea from pottery mugs, sometimes burning a round candle on a wooden stool nearby. Hollie bought packages of frozen meals for nights they allocated cooking dinner to her. Alec took them to restaurants or brought home cooked food for nights they allocated the task to him.

Meanwhile, everybody aged. Elderly Englishmen and women became more and more preponderant.

Few young people in London and other cities no longer English worked, or paid taxes when they did, compelling the government in Westminster to wield the law and raise the ages at which old people received retirement pensions. It printed more currency and used inflation to make those pensions almost meaningless. It taxed private pension funds it said were still too large. Their savings waning in value, English people who'd planned to retire from their careers couldn't do so without surrendering the trappings of their wealth they weren't willing to forgo.

Too tired to do too much, the oldest Englishmen and women laboured less often and less well; technologies didn't ask too much of them. For fear of being poor and in order to keep shopping, they continued working until they nearly died, expending their accumulated wealth every day they stayed alive. They all had something left to do, for as long as they had workplaces, stores, and homes to redecorate. Industry continued unconcerned by life beyond the company accounts at pending balance dates.

Gerald continued reporting to Niles Stafford at the Stafford Joinery. Sample picture rails, architraves, and photographs of him with them surrounded Gerald in his office. Few things surprised him. Nothing unsettled him, not even the disparity between the joys that he believed life could be and the frustrations he suffered. Whenever his achievements warranted a prize or the strains of a bad day or two threatened to disappoint him, he bought himself a body massage in smooth oil.

Through weekend leisure times, South Park often drew Gerald wandering from his home. On the lake swam silent swans, with feathers as white as had been Vanessa's pure comforting complexion.

With every year Niles Stafford sustained the long peak in his career, Gerald seemed more ordinary in his abilities. What once invigorated only subdued him, although he always wore a smile expecting other people to smile too. That career he once strove to keep without allowing relationships to intervene was just a room in bricks. Concentrating upon his duties, he'd felt too little for too long.

From Gerald's desk, he sometimes watched his secretary at hers. Elsa was around about his age, her fulsome dyed-brown hair bouncing from her colourfully dressed shoulders every time she moved. If he thought she noticed him watching her, he quickly mentioned work. "Have we sent that varnish contract to Mister Stafford?" he might ask. "Did he reply?"

"Yes, Mister Keaton. Not yet, Mister Keaton."

Only when they both sat at the table in the office kitchen, eating their independent lunches without other people near them, did Gerald ask: "Have you thought of having dinner?"

She finished swallowing the food in her mouth before replying. "I eat dinner every night."

Gerald took and ate another mouthful of his lunch, not good at social mores. "Have you thought of eating dinner *with me*?"

"I don't like socialising with work people, Mister Keaton, unless we're all there."

He nodded, engaged in unfamiliar conversation. "Are you in a relationship, Elsa?"

"You and I shouldn't talk about our lives away from work, Mister Keaton."

The only people Gerald preferred to friends were women who could be more. "We've been colleagues for a long time now."

Elsa looked back at her meal she was far from finishing. "You'll find someone, I know."

Increasingly for lunch, Gerald ate at his desk, turning pages of books and memoranda without reading what he saw. He could not compose the words to convince Elsa that a love relationship need not disturb her. He didn't think words could.

When time allowed, Gerald wandered from his office to exercise his legs and breathe the open air. He browsed at the storefront displays of merchandise in gross abundance, without buying anything. Sometimes he studied passing women's faces for Vanessa's face among them, without knowing what he'd say if it was. So long since last he saw her, she might've changed her style of hair. He thought of going to Newton Aycliffe or Heighington just to walk, but if she saw him she'd think he'd gone there to observe her.

Once, on a day he'd wandered so far as to reach High Row, he thought he saw her. The woman's height and build, her certain gait walking along, were Vanessa's, as was her face's shape around her sunglasses.

He slowed to study her, watching her accept from an old man a dark blue helium-filled balloon, advertising aerobics classes at a gymnasium. Wearing her heels too tall for her small feet, she stumbled on the paving stones and fell, dropping her handbag and small computer case. The balloon slipped from her hand and rose into the sky.

Gerald started to walk towards her, while the old man continued handing out balloons. Only a few yards away from her, a thin man collecting money for the victims of a cyclone in Nauru watched her on the ground. Other men and women walked around her, dropped notes and coins in the collector's tray, and continued walking. Men and women sitting on the benches watched the woman's balloon twirling in the air as it quickly rose away.

The woman composed herself, collected her bag and case, and clumsily stood up again. She brushed down her dress and stockings. She took five pounds from her purse to give to the collector.

"Thank you," he smiled. "Love everyone."

Not Vanessa, she strode past Gerald, leaving him standing alone. Her balloon became a shrinking dot against the sky, until Gerald couldn't see it anymore.

With his patchwork clothes, face unshaven, and water flask on his belt, the thin man collecting money was the only person on High Row that Gerald recognised. "When was the cyclone in Nauru?" Gerald asked him.

The collector stared at Gerald, as if no one else had asked. "Last week," he replied, "Saturday, I suppose."

"How do you get the money to Nauru?" asked Gerald.

The collector looked around. No other person passed. "Charities have offices," he said.

"Where?"

"You trying to annoy me?"

"I'm curious."

"You donating?"

Gerald could afford to be polite. He took a pound coin from his wallet and placed it in the tray, concluding their banter. The collector curtly turned away.

Soon after six o'clock a few evenings later, when his car was being serviced so he was headed home by bus, Gerald finished a long meeting with Mister Stafford. He packed some papers and a computer disc, which he was taking home to work upon, into his briefcase and left his offices. Dusk was settling overhead and fluorescent lights from tall poles illuminated the streets and paths.

The thin man with the tray hanging from his neck was again standing in High Row, accosting people walking past. Gerald slowed his gait, watching him. "Love everyone," said the collector. To the people who dutifully dropped notes and coins into the tray around his neck, as almost everybody did, he said, "Thank you."

With nothing more than curiosity and no one else to see, Gerald sat on a bench. His briefcase resting on his lap, Gerald watched him.

Walking along High Row was Alec. "I already gave," he told the collector as he passed.

Gerald watched the collector for twenty minutes, while the last of the working people walked under light. The Row became relatively quiet before people would set out again for dinner or a show. The collector removed the notes and coins from the tray around his neck and stuffed them into his pockets. He removed the flask from his belt and drank the last of the water in it, before walking away. Gerald stood up from the bench and, carrying his briefcase, followed him along Bondgate.

Entering Skinnergate with the empty tray and sign still around his neck, the collector stepped across the path of a lone woman walking towards him. "Love everyone," he smiled at her.

Gerald also stopped walking. The woman found some coins in her purse and placed them in the tray.

"Love and peace be upon you," said the collector, before resuming his journey. He took the coins from the tray as he walked and placed them in his pocket.

Gerald continued walking twenty or so yards behind him, along well-illuminated pavements and across well-illuminated streets. The day was too late for any charity offices to be open, so Gerald could draw no inferences from the collector not going to them. If he went to a bar or restaurant, then Gerald would watch what he bought and try to speak with him.

The collector walked past another man with a sign inviting charity for the victims of cold weather in Turkmenistan. The two said nothing to each other.

Approaching a two-storey building on Stanhope Road, the collector removed the tray from his neck and carried it under his arms. He climbed the steps up from the pavement and stepped the short way to the door he unlocked.

Before the collector could enter the building, Gerald hurried up the steps and to the door. "Good evening," smiled Gerald, holding the door open for the collector to walk through.

He looked at Gerald, without obviously recognising him from their short conversation a few days earlier. He then stepped into the building.

Gerald followed him into an entrance hall, from which there were several flats, as Gerald couldn't otherwise have done without a key. "I'm Gerald," he smiled, as the door closed behind them, "nice to meet you."

The collector proceeded up a flight of stairs while Gerald walked behind him. On the upstairs landing, the collector stopped outside a numbered door. He found a key in his pocket and opened it.

Gerald slowed and stopped beside him. "Is this your home?" asked Gerald.

"I'm busy."

"People interest me," said Gerald, trying to make conversation to a man without conversations.

"You're odd."

"Is someone inside?" asked Gerald, turning his head to look through the open door. Inside the flat, through a second open door, he saw a single chair standing at a table, on which lay a small computer and a short pile of paper bags. Near it was a television set.

"Push off!" the collector told him, as he stepped across Gerald's vision. He closed the door against Gerald's face.

From the hallway, Gerald heard from the flat recorded songs of abstract love. He imagined the collector memorising words and tunes he never sung, while he sat at that table counting the money he'd collected. He might deduct enough pounds to cover his living expenses beyond amounts the government and borough council gave him. Of a morning, he might deliver the balance in a crumpled paper bag to a charity, which wouldn't ask him anything. Each night and rainy day, he'd scour the news services for crises to alleviate. Only he knew his name, to use in conversations in his head. He wouldn't think again about the man who'd interrupted.

Carrying his briefcase, Gerald stepped back downstairs, thinking about the collector because he thought about himself. He returned to the pavement, where the music's lilt reached him through an open window above. Also headed home to another night alone, Gerald knew what he could easily become, if he was not already.

Marlborough Drive was often quiet of an evening, but for the sounds of birds in warmer months and sometimes dogs as pets. Passing cars briefly masked the quiet but the quiet remained, waiting to resume.

At the building in which he lived, he couldn't help but pause, waiting for the glass-panelled door to close. Bright and beautiful Vanessa had moved on. Six years since that night, only he remained.

Without brothers or sisters, Gerald's old mother and even his old father telephoned him more often than he telephoned them. He visited them each Christmas Day, when he sat with them saying little, before ambling back to Marlborough Drive.

On a table in his lounge room, where only he could see them, were gifts he'd bought himself. Medieval images of women spilling themselves on drunken farmers adorned a porcelain beer stein, but no beer had ever wet it. A decanter gleamed, but never interposed wine from a bottle to a glass in his hand. The polished cedar trinket box was empty.

Decorating the walls of his apartment were picture and poster impressions of places he'd never been. Only when visitors stood close to them could they see the pictures were prints, but few people visited. Among them was a single white lighthouse on the distant Jersey Shore, beyond the wide Atlantic Ocean he'd never crossed. He'd never been to America. He'd never been anywhere, but for business.

His was just another small-box apartment, from which beamed arrays of reading lights and electric screens. Differences between people's homes were few, when all Gerald saw were small snippets of their furnishings only visible at night.

What might've been a second bedroom in Gerald's home remained a place to concentrate upon a matter from his work or other meditation. Standing on the floor was a white exercise bicycle mounted on a frame. Dressed out of his business clothes into a tracksuit emblazoned with the name of a gymnasium he'd never entered, Gerald mounted the bicycle most evenings.

His legs pedalled slowly at first, riding flexed his muscles. His blood that most of his working life left stagnant flowed freely through his veins. A meter mounted on the handlebars reported how fast he would've ridden and how far he would've travelled if he were riding on a road, although the bicycle never left that room. He rarely rode full paced unless his thoughts were something to anger or to stress him, before the riding tired him and he slowed. Physical exhaustion helped him sleep each night.

Gerald rode hard and far that night. The motion of his legs, grips in his arms, and pulsing of his heart and lungs increased as the pace of his riding quickened, his blood a bursting torrent. He finished riding exhausted and unsatisfied, while the pedals slowed beneath him. He dipped his head, to where there wasn't much to see but the floor and his desk drawers. In the middle drawer were several keepsakes.

He alighted from the bicycle, opened that drawer, and shuffled through those keepsakes. Finally, he found a dusty envelope addressed to him at work. He removed the envelope from the drawer and slowly pulled from it a photograph. It was the man that he once was, or once had dreamed of being, with Vanessa in High Row, the last day he saw her.

Gerald's thumb softly touched her face in photograph, a semblance of companionship in lieu of any better. She was vivacity, although Gerald cared too much to think anything else. He gazed into her eyes, and thought of all they could've been.

He'd been certain of such truths that final night, but he'd been wrong. They'd each tried hard to keep something that never had been theirs. His efforts might've encouraged her to part more than encouraged her to stay. She'd tried her best to bring him into her life, as best as she could do, without telling him she loved him. Perhaps she did; Gerald couldn't know. She might've known more than she said to him before she left.

He'd thought he knew most matters of their lives and where his life was going, but he'd not known. He'd learned to doubt so many things he once knew to be true, without everybody telling him the things he should believe. No longer did he believe in anything that anyone had said. Perhaps he never had, although he no less doubted his long ignorance. His once perfect life hadn't been so perfect.

His mind had turned enough to want a close relationship and to want that close relationship with her. The feelings they could've made together were feelings he was learning to understand, after so many years apart. He could've lost nothing more by loving her, although he didn't know when he started to believe it. Sometime through it all, he'd become a little like her, except she held captive one bright and sad small corner of his heart. He had no right to hold captive any part of hers.

Nervously to be doing so, Gerald took his oldest diary from the drawer, with the numbers of her life he used to know. Words of conversation rehearsed inside his head. "This is Gerald Keaton," he would start to say, and wait to hear if she recalled his name. She might be embarrassed to hear from him, or be angry with him, but he had few things left to lose. He would speak with her only once, if that was all she wanted. If she didn't answer, then he would leave a message he had called.

He telephoned the number of what had been her home in Heighington. The line was not connected.

He dialled the number of what had been her mobile telephone. It too was not connected.

In spite of it being evening, he dialled the number of the offices at which she'd worked, her family company, in Newton Aycliffe. The line was not connected.

Accessing the computer network, the public telephone directory did not include her name, although several subscribers excluded their names from public access. Her family company had closed.

Gerald sent her electronic mail, asking her how she was keeping and hoping she was well. The network didn't recognise her old address.

To emphasise her life as she wanted it to be, for any reason at all, she might've gone away. A thousand people might've been with her, not wanting Gerald to be among them. She might've loved another man, somewhere unknown to him. She might've gone alone or a wife to America, to that cottage outside Newport. Gerald preferred to hope she loved another man and kept that love a secret from him, than to think she'd become what he'd been that final night. She might've never found another man, and woken wearily every morning as he woke.

Gerald slumped back in his chair at his melancholy desk inside his lonely home, trying to understand what happened to his life. More alone than just one parting should've made him, his memories meant nothing very clear.

Photographs, like pictures on the wall, were images of

something else; Vanessa in her photograph stared past Gerald to the ceiling. They'd too rarely held each other in their arms and had no more opportunities. She might've surrendered everything to keep him forever in her life, if she knew she could. Their time had ended without him saying enough. She'd been a chance to love he never understood.

He would not give life away for anything less than anyone he loved, without knowing anyone alive to love him back. Instead of searching for Vanessa among the faces that he passed, he'd dwell upon those faces for anyone to love. He could love and lose a dozen times, and fare better than never having tried. If he loved without losing only once, then the futility of all else he did would hardly matter. Never could he know the lives that might've been, without loving someone new.

Gerald hoped, without a reason for his hope, that somebody would someday come to love him. He might once have called love a travesty, a constraint on his career and life, but his love for Vanessa did not constrain him. He merely wished it had. He shouldn't think so much about her: his fool's omission. He wished he'd gone with her.

6

PAUCITY

Gerald frequented the shops along Grange Road, where an old man wearing a black Palermo hat he'd bought last season often argued with the old man selling magazines about something that one of them had read. They only knew each other to argue. The wooden shutters on the flower vendors' ornamental carts were down.

Walking her white poodles on long leashes was a woman with decorated hair, dyed to the colour nature made it decades earlier. An aged man stood hooked over his shortened walking stick. An old woman wearing a bulky cardigan stood complaining about the cold, with only Gerald listening.

Riding along an almost empty pavement was a man on a motorised wheelchair, weaving around people no longer there. Seeing the wheelchair come towards him, an older man walking with a cane stopped. Briefly standing aloft on his two weak legs, he struck his cane at the passing wheelchair, laughing at the more helpless passer-by.

Returning to Marlborough Drive, Gerald heard a dog yelping. Bounding towards him, the dog was small, with a lively coat of long brown hair. It ran until it stood before him, panting excitedly. Gerald started to walk around it, but the dog moved back into his way.

Around its neck was a collar and identification tag. "Where are your owners?" asked Gerald, looking around.

The dog panted too much to answer. The only other pedestrian in the street wasn't paying attention.

Gerald checked the name on the dog's collar. "You don't look to me like a Khan."

The dog yelped in recognition.

"I don't suppose you can tell me where I can find someone?"

The dog was silent.

Gerald laughed a little at himself, before stepping over the dog towards the front door of the building in which he lived. The small dog barked loudly but he ignored it, until he saw its reflection in the glass, watching him. He turned. "I can't keep you," said Gerald. "I don't have the space."

The dog stood still, staring up at him.

Gerald sighed. "Come on, Khan," he said, knowing he was a fool. "I'll call the dog warden." The dog bounded towards him and inside, where their single-person conversation continued. "Someone has to look after you."

The borough council dog warden told Gerald he couldn't find Khan's owner. He sent abandoned dogs to a centre in Langley Moor to try to find them new homes.

Gerald deliberated before telling him: "I'll look after it."

From a store along Grange Road, Gerald bought round tin cans of dog food. Labels declared the contents of the cans, but didn't advise how much to feed a dog each day. Gerald took a can, opened it, and took it outside. He shook the tin tube of meat and jelly until it fell onto the ground, where Khan gorged on it.

Gerald expected Khan to yelp in appreciation, or at least acknowledgement, of what he'd done. It didn't. It finished eating and looked expectantly up at him. All it ever wanted was the food.

Each early evening, standing upright in the centre of Gerald's car parking bay with its head pointed to the street, Khan waited to welcome Gerald home. His sense of its attention was of anyone glad to see him. "Hello," said Gerald, crouching down beside it and warmly patting its side and neck. "How are you?"

The dog cantered beside him where he walked, brushing his legs. They led each other up to their apartment, where it stood and sat close to wherever he stood and sat.

One day, after several weeks of such welcomes, Gerald's voice dipped. "This is stupid," he said, and wondered why he'd spoken aloud. He'd become older than his years, more staid and unproductive than anybody noticed. He would be forever doing things he didn't understand.

"I still have trouble thinking of you as being Khan." Names of products grew from teams, adopted by committees, but Gerald was alone, without customers to whom to sell. Khan remained the name for Gerald to talk to it, call to it, and identify it in his thoughts.

The most commonplace surgeries in hospitals were tucking skin and pruning fat. Cosmetic delusions made aging people seem younger to those unwilling to consider them. Hiding in their clothes of brash extravagance and false shades of human hair, they sat idly in public places. More tragic than they realised, they denied their age and lives, without anybody bothering to look. Still, the middle-aged became old and the old became sick with the afflictions from which medicine couldn't defend them. The age that could've brought them wisdom brought only death.

"Can I please speak to Jason Smith?" asked a woman telephoning the Stafford Joinery offices.

"He doesn't work here anymore," replied Elsa, working as the telephone receptionist amongst her other duties. Most people didn't describe anyone they knew as having died.

"Do you know where I can find him?"

"I'm not at liberty to give you that information."

Older people didn't understand they were getting old until they were too far gone. Sometime before their final breaths, they felt their age upon them. The things they'd done were once glorious to them, vital to their causes few of them paused to contemplate. They'd chased wealth to buy everything they wanted and spent more money in each dawdling year than their grandparents earned throughout their lives, none of which meant anything in the moments of their deaths.

They'd bought what they'd called life, their luxuries and adventures, but would die destitute among their silver accolades and crystal chandeliers. University certificates boasted what the smartest and most studious had thought to be achievements, but the wise old fools had nothing left to show for all they'd learned. The genius of their brains would soon be rotting in the soil. The moments of their lives that seemed important the days and nights they first were lived became inconsequential in retrospect. People focussed on the little things they never did were dying or dead.

They might've died with thoughts of family or died with some regrets, but nobody was there to hear them say. The night fell across their eyes, and the slow narcissistic death creeping up on them seized them in one last instant of the dark. They were buried or cremated, while younger people drank wine and tea.

The music in bars and cafeterias became softer. Most patrons could no longer stand too late, reminiscing about what other people did. "Did I tell you about the night my friend drank a yard of ale?" Tarpin Hobbs asked a stranger, with whom he often drank his wine. "Wonderful stuff, never seen anything like it; fifteen litres, you know." The number of litres increased every time he told the story. "No one ever conquered it again." If Tarpin thought about longevity, he expected to live for scores more years before dying peacefully at night.

Ten years after Alec and Hollie met each other, over her coffee he'd spilled, they commemorated Alec's fortieth birthday in their comfortably clean home. Serene images of mountains and other scenery hung in frames from the lounge room walls, while lying in a table drawer were certificates of courses they'd undertaken for their vocations or their interests: Hollie's school prize for academic merit; Alec's university degrees; Hollie's creative arts award.

Their friend Zane had repainted the walls and ceilings of his home in Piercebridge with various shades of marigold, in preparation for the party celebrating his forty-fifth birthday. He'd tinted his hair to remain as it had always been and walked around his home wearing a smoking jacket and carrying an empty cigarette holder as if they exuded sophistication, although he never smoked anything for fear of the damage it would inflict on his appearance. Exuberantly, he greeted the same people who attended all his parties, kissing Hollie's cheek and shaking Alec's hand at the front door of his home.

"Happy birthday," said Alec, offering their host a bottle of wine. "My birthday was last Wednesday."

Zane became serious, leaning slightly forward and staring into Alec's eyes. "Have you thought about what you want from your life?" he asked. "I want to smile." Zane took the bottle from Alec's hand and walked away.

Ingrid continued to live apart from Zane, resigned to her conundrum. When she thought nobody was watching her, she scratched the tip of her shoe against a low part of a freshly painted wall, leaving a blemish from which she quickly stepped away. Upon seeing Alec and Hollie watching her, she approached them, her flute glass of Champagne in her hand. "How are you with your art inventory, Hollie?"

It was the first question Hollie's friends ever seemed to ask her. "Fine," she said. Printed copies of the inventory she compiled and constantly developed circulated from one crowded council desk to another. She was making lists and compiling descriptions to furnish council records that nobody would read.

"I was thinking of you," said Ingrid, stepping to a coffee table and picking up a glossy Hinds jewellery catalogue. She handed it to Hollie, who thumbed through the elegantly presented pages.

Alec looked past her shoulder at the craftwork and imagination he initially admired, but each new page of something clever became numbing in its abundance, their profusion diminishing their value in his eyes. Hollie closed the catalogue before reaching the final page. On the rear cover was a photograph of well-cut diamonds: jewellery not yet made. "Too much," said Alec.

"Too little," said Ingrid. "It's my *raison d'être*, my reason for being," she told Alec. "What's yours?"

He shook his head; her phrase was one he hadn't heard for a long time. "My great aunt Mimi, my maiden aunt, said it was me."

"I'd rather have diamonds," said Ingrid.

Hollie reached up and kissed Alec's cheek. "I'd rather have Alec."

Ingrid looked across the room at Zane. "I'd like to have both."

Late that night, Alec and Hollie lay together in their bed in Hummersknott. "Don't we already have enough diamonds in the world?" asked Alec.

"We have enough of most things."

Alec sat up in their bed and looked at her face lying against her pillow, lit only by the moonlight through their windows. "What doesn't the world have too much of, these days?" he asked her.

"Us," she smiled. She put her arms around him and dragged him onto her.

They soon lay beside each other. "The world could do with millions of you," Alec muttered.

After a short silence, she asked, a little hesitantly, "What if it had two of me, or you?"

Alec didn't move. Without them talking about it, he knew she'd taken measures not to fall pregnant. He stared into the night.

Hollie collected herself, climbed from their bed, and switched on the bedroom light. Standing by the door in her long silk nightdress, she stared a little quizzically at him. "What if the world had three of us?"

Alec sat up in their bed. "Is that what you want?" he asked.

She sat beside him on their bed. "Are we still the people we thought we were, when we married with romance as much as reason?"

Alec's words and sentiments several years earlier slowly returned to mind, without him inferring anything from them. "We happened to be in a church."

"We happen to be in bed! We could've married when I'm seventy years old but I can't become a mother then, or a long time beforehand." She too was forty years of age.

"Maybe we can't have children even now," said Alec, wanting to be sensible.

"Then we don't have to worry about a decision."

"Aren't you happy now?"

"I'm happy!" she said exasperated. "We live in a street of family homes in a neighbourhood of family homes, but the children are growing up. They're the family homes that used to be: of families who live apart." She rose again and left the room.

Alec dressed into the gown he rarely wore, but the night so late was cool. The lights shining in their home were the only lights shining so late at night from any houses in the neighbourhood. He walked slowly from their bedroom into the silent hallway leading into the lounge room.

She sat on the woollen sofa, with her legs pulled up close to her so her bare feet were on the seat and her face pressed into her knees. She hadn't sat like that for years.

Alec poured himself a glass of cold water from the kitchen tap. He sat beside her.

"Are we thinking too much about it?" she asked, without facing him.

He whispered, "What should we feel?"

She threw her arms into the air, almost losing her balance before he caught her in his arms. "I don't know what I want!" she cried out, falling more into his hold until her face looked up at him.

He looked no less at her. "We know so little."

"We have more than enough of everything else," said Hollie.

Alec smiled. "I can't get enough of us."

During a morning tea conversation in the council staff canteen, Hollie told her friends what she and Alec were considering, as their friends spoke coolly of plans for holidays or items of kitchenware they wondered whether to buy. Whatever Ingrid already owned didn't deter her from wanting more.

"I'm much too selfish to have a baby," said Neve. "When I think of babies, all I imagine is crying and mess."

"Isn't that like seeing adults only in terms of the worst moments of our lives?" asked Hollie. "Abusing the driver of another car? Pushing past someone on the stairs?"

"I don't want adults near me either."

"Have you ever seen a baby?"

"I know what they're like."

"I disagree, Neve," said Ingrid, chewing on a cream chocolate éclair. "I think having a baby is selfish." She made those words insulting, before turning to Hollie. "Don't expect any of us to make allowances for you."

"Has Zane talked about children?" asked Hollie.

"I don't want *anything* compelling me to stay with Zane."

"Did your parents stay together because of you?"

Ingrid stopped eating, holding her éclair near her mouth. It was a rare moment of intimacy between them.

"I'm sorry," said Hollie.

A small piece of whipped cream fell from Ingrid's éclair onto her skirt. She picked the cream from her clothes before looking up again. She blinked several times before asking, "What were we talking about?"

Alec's colleagues were no more supportive. To recognise the end of another accounting year, they dined together at a bright restaurant table in the Houndgate Townhouse. After eating too much of the charcuterie, they gorged on hot fish and meats with sauces from square white plates, supplemented with round white bowls of salad and steamed vegetables the waitress repeatedly replenished. Interspersed between them stood several bottles of red and white wines, through various stages of being drunk; glasses slowly emptied before being hurriedly refilled.

Meals were times to talk. "This is not a world into which anyone should bring children," insisted Tarpin, studying the food before him on his plate. "We have pollution, poverty, and pestilence," he explained, before chewing on his thickly cut steak in a supple Béarnaise sauce. "I read an article about them, just yesterday."

"Our child might alleviate them," said Alec, "wherever they are."

"Nobody changes anything," scoffed Tarpin through his mouthful of food.

"Everybody changes something," said Alec.

Tarpin used his fork to push another cut portion of his steak through the sauce. He lifted it to his mouth.

"Some people," Alec added, "change things more than others."

Rupert ordinarily punched out his words. So far that conversation, he sat quietly.

"I don't object to children," said Valda, cutting her fillet of sea bass, "but not near me."

"We were babies once, children, boys and girls," Alec reminded them. Worse than forgetting what they were, they might've remembered. "If you don't like children, you don't like yourselves."

"I like myself," sneered Valda. She drove a car larger than most cars, and wore suits with shoulders squarer than most men dared wear.

"I quite like children," interjected Rupert, before tilting his head towards Valda for Alec to see. "Adults I can't tolerate."

The diners finished their meals, or as much as they would eat, before the waitress removed their plates. Some of them ate desserts: Tarpin a cherry-glazed gateau. Others picked away at the cheeses. They drank hot tea, coffee, or chocolate. Alec and some of his colleagues changed seats around the table to talk more easily with more people.

The waitress set before them small trays on which lay rows of thin mint chocolates in shining black wrappers. Rupert picked up one, tore it open, and ate it. Valda took another and slipped it into her handbag.

After asking the waitress to bring them a bottle of Sambuca, Tarpin rested back in his chair, still sipping his cappuccino. He turned to Alec. "Have we talked you out of baby-making?"

Alec pressed his lower lip against his upper teeth while he considered his response. All they'd really done was convince him not to mention it. Alec shook his head.

"You've become something of the revolutionary."

"Counter-revolutionary."

7

A CHILD AMONG SURROGATE CHILDREN

Outside Alec's office, the photographs affixed to the partition around Harriet Simpkin's desk were of her two pedigree Bichon Frise dogs, whose names Alec could never quite recall. A few years older than Alec, Harriet only wore white fabrics, concealing from everyone but her and Alec the silky white hairs of her small dogs. If her dogs stained her clothes, she discarded her clothes but not her dogs.

A dresser dyed, cut, and styled Harriet's thick dark hair on the first Thursday every month. A pet salon groomed her dogs' white hair every Saturday, in addition to the grooming Harriet lovingly afforded them each day. The dogs remained in her home while she worked each weekday, never setting paw outside without their matron. (In fear they might harm plants or other animals, council officers caught stray cats and dogs for someone else to take.)

The evening of her forty-third birthday, Harriet placed her shopping bags on the step outside her front door, removed her keys from her handbag, and unlocked the door. Her bags again in her hands, she slowly pushed open the door. "Darlings," she called out, stepping forward onto the white carpet and closing the door behind her with her shoe, "Mummy's home."

Her dogs jumped up from her white-upholstered furniture in

59

the lounge room or their dedicated white cushions on the floor and bundled along the hallway towards her. A huge smile rushed through her face as she knelt down, letting the bags slip from her hands to the floor. She spread out her arms ready to hug them. "Did you miss Mummy?" she asked them, as they rushed. "You did!" she said reassured. "You did miss Mummy!"

She laughed as they frolicked, finally settling into her embrace. Her eyes closed as their warm hair caressed her cheeks, her arms holding them with her. "Mummy bought more presents for you!"

She sat with them on the floor. "Look, Terrance," said Harriet, as she pulled a yellow plastic rattle from a shopping bag.

Terrance yelped, raising his paws. He knocked the rattle from her hand.

Harriet laughed, while both dogs grabbed for the rattle. "No, Howard," she said, calling him back. "Mummy has a present for you, too!"

The dogs continued bobbing for the yellow rattle, while Harriet produced a blue plastic rattle. She rolled it along the floor towards them, crawling after it. "You love Mummy, don't you?" she said. "You love Mummy?"

The dogs frolicked with their rattles, while Harriet began preparing a hot lamb casserole for dinner. "Mummy had to arrange a conference today," she told them.

Harriet served the casserole on a china plate and two matching china bowls. The dogs watched her laying two bowls on the floor, and barrelled through their meals without waiting. Harriet sat with her plate and a fork at her dining table, a dark polished timber piece, near them. "I am thinking of trying some paprika next time I make a casserole," she said, thoughtfully examining the portion of food on her fork. "Do you think I should try some paprika?" The dogs continued eating their meals, while she placed the food from her fork in her mouth, chewed it, and swallowed it. "We could try paprika."

She believed her dogs loved her. They never said or did anything to disagree.

Her weekday evenings were all much like that, until one when only Terrance met her at the door. "Howard?" Harriet called out, "Howard, darling?"

Panic gripped her, and she ran along the hallway into the lounge room, where Howard lay on a white cushion breathing deeply. "What's wrong, my darling?" she started to cry. "Please, please tell Mummy."

Howard didn't respond. "Why, why won't you tell Mummy what's wrong?" she pleaded.

Harriet rushed him to a veterinary hospital. Pacing back and forth outside the examination room, she feared the worst for him and for her without him, while Terrance playfully patted his front paws against the colours on a soft-drink vending machine. A door suddenly opened, and Harriet turned to see the veterinarian holding his hands together. "I am sorry, Ms Simpkin."

"My baby!" she wailed, as she threw her arms against the wall. She slumped down to the floor, crying desperately. "My baby, my baby, my beautiful, sweet baby!"

Howard was cremated at a small private ceremony in an animal crematorium. Wearing a long black dress she'd bought for the funeral, Harriet stood weeping before the little wooden coffin. Standing sombrely in a black suit, a crematorium official conducted a service helping her grieve, while Terrance at the end of his leash jumped about.

Afterwards, Harriet struggled to compose herself back into the person that other people saw. She and Terrance went to a pet shop, from which she chose a new pedigree Bichon Frise puppy. "My baby," smiled Harriet, cradling the puppy in her hands and gazing with all her love upon it, "my beautiful, sweet baby." Soon hanging by her desk were photographs of Terrance and Gordon, playing with their toys.

More than a year after Hollie ceased the measures preventing her from falling pregnant, when autumn leaves were golden brown and the sun glistened in the damp, she suspected she was carrying within her the first traces of a child. Thus she sat before her mother's physician Doctor Perry, who for as long as Hollie knew him had worn a succession of clean white coats over his clothes and hung a succession of black rubber and steel ended stethoscopes around his neck; Hollie was a rare patient not there for being unwell. Testing Hollie in his office, he nodded.

His confirmation afforded her twinges of a strange new uncertainty. At the corner of the doctor's desk, beyond the pad of paper on which he wrote prescriptions for his patients, was a photograph of his wife in her doctor's coat. All Hollie knew of her was that she'd never born a child.

The doctor began writing on a piece of paper. "This is someone you can see," he told her.

"See?"

"How old are you?"

"Forty-one."

"There are risks."

Doctor Perry's euphemism became clear. "I don't want a termination."

The doctor checked his computer. "You better have some counselling."

"I don't want counselling."

Doctor Perry resumed looking at her, before turning back to his computer. Unusually, he didn't wait for her to leave before typing, as doctors did, short details of her condition in his computer. It afforded them more time together for them to think, through which she presumed he was trying to decide what his oaths and duties required of him when his powers were inadequate. When he finished, his printer produced a sheet of paper he gave Hollie. "This is a list of a dozen psychologists and social workers," he told her. "I always recommend counselling."

From the doctor's surgery, Hollie visited Alec at his office. She placed the doctor's list of names on Alec's desk. "Should I talk to someone?" she asked him.

"It's your decision."

"I know the politics, Alec! You and I, we're a couple."

Alec pushed the paper aside. "I'll keep being your counsellor," he told her. "You keep being mine."

She sighed. "I should tell my mother."

"Shall I come with you?"

"You've done enough already."

At the appointed time for Hollie to visit her mother in her

home in Blackwell, Tabitha Mayfield was again wearing a white blouse fastened high to her neck. Around her neck were several cultured pearl necklaces. The large oval brooch with the porcelain figure of a classical Greek woman kneeling with a vase was again attached to the front of her collar. Sitting in a slightly smaller antique armchair facing her, Hollie knew there wasn't any point procrastinating. "I'm pregnant," she said.

Her mother pulled away, her face grimacing. "Do what you need to do, no need to involve me."

"Alec and I decided to have a baby."

"It's not up to Alec," gasped Tabitha. "Do I want a daughter who's bare foot and pregnant?"

"I wear stockings."

"You don't want to be *just* a mother."

"I don't want to be *just* a cataloguist."

"You dreamt of playing the flute?"

"I never wanted to play the flute."

"You did, when you were young."

"I never wanted to play the flute."

"Oh," said Tabitha, her voice dipping as she turned away.

"I wanted to paint."

"There!" exclaimed Tabitha, turning back to her daughter. "I knew you wanted to do more than compile catalogues."

"I can paint and have a baby," said Hollie. "I don't want to paint anymore."

"Do you know how to change nappies?"

"We'll learn, and the baby won't always be in nappies."

"There are things worse than nappies."

Hollie sighed. "You make it sound like being a mother was the worst thing you ever did."

"I'm not saying that," insisted Tabitha, "but it did complicate matters when your father entered that patisserie."

Hollie dipped her head, vowing not to let her child feel what her mother let her feel. "Alec doesn't like pastries."

"Neither did your father." Her mother watched her. "I won't be able to help you."

Hollie muttered, "You never have."

"Now can we please talk about something else, your painting?"

In the care of old doctors and nurses learning old medicines, Hollie's belly swelled as women's bellies around her didn't. The rest of her remained thin, while fat people were fat all over: their stomachs, limbs, and faces. (People who might've otherwise been fat burnt their excess food in sweated sessions of musical aerobic classes.) Men and women stared at the curiosity in their midst.

Finally, twelve days after her baby was due to be born and after too long a labour, in the Darlington Memorial Hospital, Hollie gave birth to a son. His eyes were blue most like his father's. His blond hair was even gentler than his mother's. His locks reminded Alec of the locks he once wore, before his hair was cut short and groomed. While his weary wife lay in her hospital bed and a nurse cleaned the boy, he kissed her.

They named the boy Brandon, conferring upon him a name his mother chose because she particularly liked that little village near Durham City, along with his father's family name, Frewer. Their son's age they counted in hours and minutes, while the people around them seemed suddenly to age.

No shops in Darlington catered to baby human beings that customers no longer bore, but Alec and Hollie checked catalogues for London children. They bought imported colourful small clothes and shoes, none of which lasted very long. Computer research and libraries educated them enough to tutor doctors and nurses in vaccinations the boy required. They took time away from their jobs and Hollie increasingly undertook hers from home, while their colleagues worked their same long hours and complained they were too busy to go home.

Among the necessities and luxuries sold from the ubiquitous pet supply stores were perambulators, in which pet owners rested their small charges while they pushed them along. The stores did not offend people by saying prams could also carry human beings.

Public restaurants politely advised Alec and Hollie they couldn't cater to the requirements of children, delicately dissuading them from bringing their baby son into the premises.

Cinemas didn't want a disturbance if the baby made a sound. Hollie shielded her child's ears and eyes from the people increasingly incomprehensible to her.

She and Alec pushed their pram into a park from which no person was excluded. Men and women enjoyed the warm spring day by jogging, walking, or sitting on benches in the shade. The faces of people playing chess on black and white chessboards might've been irritably familiar to each other.

People with time to pause from their business and leisure didn't notice people past whom they walked, but noticed prams. Without looking at the people pushing them, they looked into the prams and at the small dogs for which they smiled. When they were close enough to Alec and Hollie's pram to see it contained a baby English boy, some paused, staring incredulously. Some older people smiled. Some stared sorrowfully, in response to which Alec and Hollie smiled sympathetically at them.

Some passers-by looked at the baby several times. "What breed is that?" asked one. "Is it a monkey?"

"No more than I am," replied Hollie.

"Is it real?" asked a woman of about Hollie's age. "Is it a doll or a new robotic toy?"

"He's a small-scaled person," replied Alec.

"Is it yours?" asked a man.

"He's all of ours," replied Hollie.

Most people were polite enough to hide their stares; the rules of etiquette hadn't prepared them to meet babies and their parents. People who smiled at photographs of distant babies the beneficiaries of their charity declined to smile at a baby among their kind.

Alec and Hollie entered High Row around about the time for lunch, among the men and women congregated before buskers. The baby seemed to gaze impressed at the water falling down the steps; the feature Alec had often passed without noticing was suddenly attractive.

The thin and lanky man with a tray around his neck was collecting money to build a school in Ethiopia. "Love everyone," he said. Hollie dropped a two-pound coin in his tray, while he looked into the pram. He knelt down and poked the baby's little cheeks as if to see if he was alive. Without addressing the person too young to donate, he stood upright to confront Alec and Hollie. "Did you do this?"

"No one else," replied Alec.

"That's so irresponsible of you," he told them, waving his arms in the air in wild disgust and almost spilling his tray. "Do you know what resources he's consuming?"

"Not as much as you."

"Why didn't you have an abortion?"

"Why didn't your parents?"

"I'm helping people."

Hollie reached out and recovered from the tray the coin she'd put there. "I'd rather love people I know," she told him, "than pretend I love people I don't."

The man strutted away. He continued strutting, and strutted on out of the Row.

Passing him, as they walked back towards their offices from a seminar to which Alec had declined his invitation, were Tarpin and Valda. Wearing their business suits and carrying portfolios of papers, they slowed and stopped in front of Alec, Hollie, and their pram. "Aren't you worried about not realising your full potential," Tarpin asked Alec. Tarpin had recently been appointed the new Northern Lights Company chief executive.

Alec picked up his infant child and rested him on his shoulders. "This is my full potential," he told Tarpin, before lifting his son from his shoulders, throwing him up into the air and catching him with both his hands. His son laughed a little as he laughed. Alec again rested the boy in the pram.

Valda wore another of her jackets with padded shoulders and long skirts of red and blue, much like successful women portrayed on television. From her handbag, she removed a shining gold-plated business card holder embossed with the name of the bank conducting the seminar they'd attended. She held before Hollie her business card, on which only the company logo superseded her name and title in large font: "*Valda Walton, Finance Director*." Valda declared: "*This* is power!"

Hollie, wearing her loose-fitting pale cream blouse, flowery cotton skirt, and flat-soled leather shoes, crouched down beside her son. Putting her arms around him, she lifted him up until his face was higher than Valda's business card. Hollie replied: "*This is power.*"

She sat on a bench, resting her son on her lap. She pulled her blouse from her waist, tucked her baby's face beneath it, and fed him from her concealed breast.

"Don't you feel exploited?" asked Valda.

"Don't you?"

Tarpin simply stared, as Alec knew he wouldn't have stared so blatantly at breasts on a beach. "There was a time, Tarpin," said Alec, "when I was drinking a yard of beer and you were hoping no one would ask you to drink one too, that all you wanted was to enjoy yourself."

"There are times for enjoying yourself," replied Tarpin, "and times for concentrating on something else."

"You and I could never agree on which times were which." Tarpin and Valda hurried back to work.

Sitting on another bench was Gerald, watching the strangers with their baby. He wasn't thinking about them so much as about himself, the choices he'd made, and the choices he hadn't realised he was making. No longer searching for Vanessa in every woman's face, he searched for himself in Alec's face.

Alec noticed him gawking at them. He spread his arms out wide, calling out: "There are no other babies!"

Gerald stood up and looked around. He slowly turned, studying all the other adults, seeing them for the first time, before looking again at Alec. "I once knew a woman," he called back to Alec, leading Hollie to look up. "I think what she treasured most of all was her family."

Alec looked at Hollie. "Was it you?" She shook her head.

Gerald's voice tapered away. "She wanted children to have lunch with her some Sundays," he told them. Too rarely had Gerald contemplated fatherhood, but he romanced a dream that love might've made him father Vanessa's child. He turned and walked away, muttering: "We could've had such lovely lunches."

8

ENDANGERED SPECIES

Sitting quietly beside him in his apartment, Gerald cared about his dog and looked after it, whether or not it cared about him and would look after him. He felt a little less lonely for it being with him, but it wasn't a human being. He could talk but not talk with it, and the expressions that it made were small relationship aside relationships with other people. It couldn't communicate with all the nuances and traits of a human mind and soul. His only company was better than having none, but only a human being could be his friend. They were alone together.

The dog was a distraction, until the day Gerald returned home to Marlborough Drive and couldn't see it. "Khan!" he called out, wandering around. "Khan?" He didn't see the dog again.

Cocktail parties were becoming smaller, catering to fewer people with fewer canapés. Customers became fewer in the stores, but fewer staff remained to serve them when they came. Fewer people wanted services and fewer people provided them, but the system staggered onwards while everybody worked and spent. Governments had measured their economies of material goods and services in total so not to worry about what was happening per capita. They began to measure them per capita so not to worry about the reducing number of their capita. Gerald noticed, and not only because it affected the special projects that he managed for Mister Stafford.

Gerald's body became fuller. He wouldn't ride his exercise bicycle in working clothes, and he came home too tired most nights to dress out of them before going to bed. Besides, riding his bicycle was time to think without learning anything. His movements became slower, with his once strong gait slowly surrendering to a less certain, ambling pace. His once thick brown tufts of hair were thinning, among subtle strands of grey. Nobody in his life cared enough for him to think of dyeing them. They weren't important. Quietly one day, without telling anybody and without anybody telling him, he'd become middle-aged.

His life and work had been the same event, without anything to show for them but door frames and window sashes that customers soon forgot. Nobody disturbed his style of work and friends when he preferred to live alone than live without the little trappings of his life; nothing superseded his seemingly important job. He'd been busy succeeding at his work, but didn't know why he had. They were reasons in which he no longer could believe. His labours couldn't satisfy him anymore and, in his most pained and doubting moments, he wondered if they ever had. The career that once promised him so much was promising him much less, much less than he'd been offered the night Vanessa went away.

Some businesses struggled with too few people to sustain them. Replacing appliances that no longer functioned became easier than finding someone to repair them; machines were more important than people still alive. Everything was less in the pond becoming smaller.

The shrinking economy in a dwindling population made major businesses into minor ones. It discarded what had been minor ones, leaving behind empty offices and vacant window fronts. Some stores closed when their last shopkeepers became infirm. The surviving storekeepers around them pillaged the last of the old stock.

People shuffled into surviving businesses, replacing people

they'd never met. New colleagues became their new companions.

Customers wanting financial advice and package holidays in air-conditioned buses walked along the street until they found what they wanted. Men wanting warmth and a sea breeze reclined in canvas deck chairs, where they hid under shade before the sun became too high. Women who'd been voluptuous in trim swimwear on a beach still sauntered on the sand.

Whole industries folded, but the system fed itself with cycles of just enough activity. People were the cogs in everybody's wheels, but the cogs were breaking without being replaced.

"Hello," spoke a recorded voice on radio and television sets. "Did you know that almost one in ten species of birds around the world is now threatened with extinction, including the Colombian yellow-eared parrot?"

The advertisements moved listeners and viewers to think and talk about the parrot and its predicament with the authority the recorded voice had given them, and to write long letters of protest to the Colombian president in Bogotá. They keenly transferred wads of money to buy a woodland roosting site for the parrot in Colombia, so far away from home. Gerald made his small donation when Elsa organised a morning tea in the Stafford Joinery offices.

Gerald couldn't recall when anyone last pressed the button from Marlborough Drive or knocked upon his apartment door, aside from tradesmen and occasionally his parents. His friends were people with whom he worked, sharing time away from offices in public eateries and drinking houses. Niles Stafford invited him to his club, before they each returned alone to their old homes. The people with whom Gerald ate lunch on Sundays didn't mean too much to him. He didn't mean too much to them.

The only resident of the building in which he lived with whom Gerald spoke was elderly Doris Poedecker. Dressed in cashmere cardigans and pleated skirts, she often stood at the board in the building entrance hallway, affixing carefully prepared notices to residents and visitors. She also affixed a colourful poster picturing the predominantly green plumage of a Colombian yellow-eared parrot, petitioning people to save it.

Accompanying Doris wherever she went was her small brown cat, at which other residents looked when they spoke with her. Doris' voice was slow and methodical, catching in the back of her throat each time she spoke. "I hope you're not one of those young people who make a lot of noise," she said to Gerald.

He thought she was talking to someone else, but forty-five years of age had become young. "No, no," he said.

"That is a relief," she said, turning away from him.

By the building doors were mail delivery boxes for each of the apartments, marked with apartment numbers and residents' names. When residents died, Doris calmly removed their labels; just half the boxes remained labelled. She placed invitations to the meetings of building residents to administer their homes in each of the named delivery boxes, although Gerald never went. Curtains covered the windows of unoccupied apartments.

Curious to know, and to do something different one evening than he had done the last, Gerald attended a meeting of the residents of the building in which he lived. It convened in the lounge room of the building chairman's apartment, so the chairman didn't need to walk too far to reach it. Gerald knew him only as the man who wore thick-rimmed glasses and nervously hummed to himself whenever Gerald saw him; silence might've enticed Gerald to engage him in conversation. Gerald presumed he did much the same with everyone, except Doris and at meetings of the residents.

At the meeting, the chairman's large chair and a small officiating table faced three men and three women sitting in armchairs and sofas spread around the room. Gerald was far and away the youngest among them. Wearing warm clothes, each of the older residents had lived in the building for half a century or more; they could've been born to their apartments. Hanging from the walls around them were wooden tribal masks the chairman collected from his youthful travels to Africa.

Doris poured cups of boiling tea, placing the first cup on the table before the chairman. A man wearing tortoise shell spectacles placed his spectacles on the side of the saucer before taking it from her. A woman, with her arduously styled and rinsed hair set high upon her head, sat knitting a grey scarf. The second last cup Doris offered to Gerald.

"Thank you," he said, before sitting back in his chair.

She also served dry biscuits, before pouring a last cup of tea for herself. To one side of the chairman's table she sat in a chair much smaller than the chairman's chair, with a small notebook computer into which she recorded minutes of the meeting. Her cat becoming a little overweight lay on the floor beside her feet.

Doris had distributed to all the residents copies of a twenty-page printed document. "I feel it is opportune," explained the chairman in his deepest, most formal voice, "to take this opportunity to improve the building rules."

Gerald glanced through the one hundred and seventeen rules for the dozen or so residents and guests that never came. Around him, the aged residents concentrated closely on the documents in silence, but for the soft chewing of their biscuits, drinking of their tea, and relatively loud replacing of their cups on crockery saucers. They were the few in a building that could've accommodated ten times their number; those who hadn't always been alone had come to be alone.

"The current prohibitions of the building only prohibit the sounds of babies crying and children sounding from a flat," the chairman told them. "The new prohibitions prohibit them from the building altogether."

"Where are these babies?" asked Gerald.

"No speaker is to speak," said the chairman, "until the Chair permits the speaker."

Gerald looked around him for an empty chair, before again looking at the chairman. "Do you mean *you* grant a person permission to speak?"

"The Chair," said the chairman.

All the elderly people bar one glared at Gerald. The woman knitting remained focussed on her craft.

Gerald raised his hand. "Excuse me," he said.

"I am the Chair."

"Excuse me, Chair."

The chairman checked the list of residents Doris had laid before him on his table. "Mister Keaton."

"Where are these babies? Where are these children?"

"That is hardly the point, Mister Keaton. I don't want sounds in communal hallways."

"Adults make sounds," said Gerald.

"Are you rudely trying to be rude, Mister Keaton?"

Gerald struggled to find what to say. He thought of saying something about animals, but dared not further alienate the people in the room.

"You are being disruptive."

Without looking away from the scarf she was knitting, that woman spoke up. "Children are unruly, undisciplined, and loud."

"So are some adults," said Gerald, "but not here."

"We can't exclude adults," she said as she knitted.

"Please, Mister Keaton," said the chairman. "We must retain decorum."

The woman knitting her scarf muttered, "Children make me uncomfortable."

"You make me uncomfortable," said Gerald.

She looked up from her knitting.

"I have to live with it."

She looked back to her knitting.

"I don't like children," said the chairman.

"Then you don't like people," replied Gerald.

"I like some people."

"Which people?"

"Nobody you know, Mister Keaton."

"If you ban children, you ban the future," pleaded Gerald, speaking on behalf of people not there and a long lost feature of people who were.

"Do you know any children, Mister Keaton?" asked the chairman. "Are you a parent?"

Gerald hesitated. "I could've been."

"Why do you care, Mister Keaton?"

"We have an aging population."

"No one is aging," laughed the chairman, moving the other elderly people to smile.

"You don't realise you're old because you don't remember being young."

"You're ridiculously being ridiculous."

The old women in the room were too old to be mothers and old men might've been unable to be fathers. "Don't any of you care?" Gerald implored them, standing up and pleading into the well of morbidity around him. "Have your hearts petrified?"

"We don't need that sort of ruckus here, Mister Keaton. I must ask you to sit down."

"Mi-i-ster Chair-man," quivered the elderly man again wearing his tortoise shell spectacles. He might have been the oldest person in the room.

Everybody in the room turned to face him. Gerald sat slowly back in his chair.

"I have-have always felt," continued the elderly man, his wavering voice aloof, with tones of education more affected than real, "that if you-you scratch a litt-le someone who talks ab-about an a-aging pop-ulation the wa-ay this man does, you-you quickly fi-find discrimination."

"We're dying out!" said Gerald.

"'We' Mi-i-ster Keaton?" the old man retorted, nodding confidently and looking around for other residents to see his point affirmed.

Reaching forward in his chair and with his clenched fists holding the air because they couldn't hold the people around him, Gerald strove to engage his small audience. "You wouldn't let the government of Brazil pass a law against Brazilian children like one you're passing here," he told them.

The old man waved the back of his shaking hand in Gerald's direction.

"You'd be in a frenzy trying to stop it!"

The chairman waited until Gerald finished before responding. "You will find this rule at Montagu Court and other blocks of flats, Mister Keaton."

"Then we'll all be damned."

"If you use that sort of language again, Mister Keaton, then I will evict you from this meeting."

The other residents turned away from Gerald, as he slumped back in his chair. The room was silent, before the woman knitting her long scarf spoke aloud. "We only want peace."

"Don't you also want life?" pleaded Gerald, trying to understand them as much as trying to persuade them. Their sense of things being well, in their small shade of a big planet, sorely condemned them.

"Stupid boy," the knitting woman muttered. Being called a boy wasn't so derisory in Gerald's mind as it seemed to be in everybody else's.

The meeting resolved to amend the rules as the chairman suggested; Gerald's was the only opposing vote. Doris began preparing another pot of tea.

"You may go now, Mister Keaton," said the chairman.

Gerald stood up from his chair, placed his saucer and almost full teacup on a table, and stepped up to the chairman at his table. Leaning down and forward, Gerald spoke so that only the chairman could hear his words. "You don't like people, do you?"

"Not all the time."

Turning around, Gerald faced the other residents. There they sat before him, sitting without speaking, staring blindly back at him, testament that something must be wrong. Theirs was a deep resolve to keep complete their fatal comfort zones, in which they'd pass away. He could've laughed at them, but they made him much too sad. Their idle opulence was more arrogance they were as great as they could be, feeding each other's arrogance with ignorance. He'd tried but failed to save the people growing old.

The facts Gerald once knew well enough never to contemplate, the intrinsic permanence of what they were and did, had gone. Those things he once presumed to last forever mightn't last too long at all. They the people were not eternal, but depended on themselves more than he yet understood. Seeing their failings was much easier than seeing what he could do to save them. Words alone might not have changed his choices. "Good night, everyone," he said.

An hour or so later, Gerald watched Doris at the board in the building entrance hallway. Shining over her was the temporary electric light that anybody entering the hallway in darkness activated, while she affixed a notice prohibiting children from the building. In her hand was a document reporting apartment building rules in Brazil.

His culpability convicted him, no less responsible than they'd been for their problem by what he'd done and never did; he believed his prophecy only when he could no longer act upon it. His realisation so late in time was of little use to him; it might've only added to his tragedy. He couldn't change his life behind him, sentencing them to die.

The light eventually expired. The blissful stupidity in which he'd lived might've been a better place to perish.

9

BARREN PEOPLE

Standing his son in bare feet beside his bedroom doorway every birthday, Alec marked Brandon's growing height with a pencil on the wall. He and Hollie followed every change in their son, and would follow every change in the man he would become. Outside their home and in the parks, they kicked a football towards each other. They cheered impressed at everything each other did.

Hollie maintained her styles of floppy hats and long dresses, although her dresses came to have more flowers in their patterns, at least through warmer months each year. Alec's casual shirts away from work became brighter shades of red and blue, like those his son wore. More importantly, they wore the hairs and faces that age and nature accorded them. Their blonde hairs dulled, without dyes to lie. Their skin creased but remained healthy, without medical procedure.

For the most part, their home in Hummersknott remained unchanged, save only for the seasons of the year, while the population through north-east England continued to subside. Governments and English people left the populations swelling in some parts of England to themselves, without knowing what they did. Those populations had no reason to brave the cold.

Hollie's mother underwent her most exhaustive cosmetic

surgery and finally followed her father to Cadiz. Sometime thereafter, her problematic parents passed away, or probably passed away. She knew too little of them to regret.

Through County Durham, once cherished houses, flats, and apartments fell dark and empty when their residents died, without anybody new to occupy them. Rats and mice removed any last traces of food, before proceeding to the next soon empty home. Paint peeled from walls and windowpanes. No one brushed away the dust and spiderwebs.

The lawns once neatly mown became longer in the rain. Gardens once manicured became unruly. Weeds choked the grass and grass choked paths and driveways once cleaned too often. They could've all been primitive beneath accumulated leaves. The well-worn gardening gloves and old shoes abandoned in the sheds became small homes for bugs and insects.

Without heirs to the inheritances or social sanctions left to care, strangers occupied ancient families' stately homes and recent rich's modern mansions. Reclining in finely crafted furniture, the newly landed squatters bandied about heirlooms that lords and ladies had rarely risked damage by touching, while they too aged and died.

Cars and bicycles became fewer on the roads, although the slower driving people left alive still filled lanes of traffic and parking spaces. They took the best cars from the dying and recent dead; cars were more numerous than people. The rest lay dormant at the kerbs, on driveways, or sealed alone in private garages; homes of people who had died remained home to their old cars. Cars abandoned outside empty premises became dirty with the dust, between falls of heavy rain. Their undercarriages sheltered resting birds and animals.

No child after Brandon was born into Hummersknott. With declining numbers of births beforehand, the Hummersknott Academy closed.

With so few English children born in Darlington, the last handful came together at their last convenient school: Polam Hall. The youngest class of four once typical small boys and three once typical small girls sat without anyone to follow them.

Only they and the few children ahead of them, along with their teachers and other staff becoming older, occupied the grounds that half a century earlier had catered to hundreds of playful children. If the aged adults those playful children had become weren't sitting fast alone inside their homes, then they'd travelled far away.

The hollow halls and empty classrooms echoed with the few sounds of little feet. The last children sat in lessons only with each other, where their teachers taught them dated variants of knowledge without mentioning that anything had changed. They learnt enough mathematics for computers to make the calculations they'd need to know. They soon forgot the brief history they'd learned to write.

Another dwindling final year of students graduated each start of summer, and the caretaker cleaned the room in which the youngest class had sat. He emptied the wastepaper basket, closed the windows, and locked the doors for the last time. Adults wanting rooms for their cake-decorating classes didn't want to use the rooms for children. They sat in comfortable large chairs in long-vacated schools, where no senses of any children still remained.

Office bureaucrats reformed syllabuses that nobody would learn, before proceeding into new responsibilities for adult education. Teesside University academics wrote erudite treatises to read among themselves, conducting evening lectures for mature-aged students feeling clever in the twilight of their lives.

Among Brandon's teachers when he was nine years old was Mister Wheeler, a largish man with an unnecessary beard embedding his frown. "There are too many people on earth," he told them, showing images of a shanty town in Mozambique, with needy children dressed in rags around mud rivers. Young Europeans who could've saved their homelands had taken up their missions in faraway places, digging wells and building huts for the hordes in impoverished villages until they were too old to work.

The children stared disbelieving at the images. Alien to them was more than the poverty of a dirt village. It was the wealth of children playing.

The poor young people in distant lands weren't dying as they were dying in rich old England. Outside the windows of their classroom, the clean school and streets of Darlington were becoming emptier, without any thought of play. Lewis raised his hand, asking to speak.

"Yes, Lewis," said Mister Wheeler.

"The world is not all like that. *We* aren't overpopulating."

"Are you conducting this class or am I, Lewis?"

The class of pupils glared at Lewis. He didn't speak in class again. Some weeks later, Mister Wheeler fell sick and died alone.

A Sunday morning with his family in their lounge room in Hummersknott, nestled among lush trees and grass, the images from Mozambique were again in Brandon's mind. "Why are you so different?" he asked his parents.

His father replied. "Apart from the fact we're a family, son?"

His mother tilted her head towards the window. "Why are our neighbours so different?"

"Why aren't there children, mummy?"

"Sweetheart, some people are frightened of anything they can't control as easily as they control...," she quickly looked around, "buttons on the remote control."

His father glanced at the coffee table on which lay an electronic handset, which operated the television set. He rose from his chair, went to his son, and with all his strength raised him in the air. "There are only good reasons for having children," he told him, looking into the boy's eyes, "and few good ones for not having them."

"What are the good reasons for not having children?"

His father slowly ventured a reply. "Some people are very sick, and their children can be sick."

"Alec!" rebuked his mother.

His father slowly lowered the boy to the floor.

"Some people," she resumed, "are waiting for perfect parents for their unborn children. They fear learning that none of us is perfect." His father's face fell. "They miss the people that could've been good for them."

His father stepped towards his mother and kissed her. He kissed her long. With his parents so well distracted, Brandon walked away. Reaching up to the front door handle no higher than his eyes above the floor, he opened the door and stepped outside. Quietly closing the door after him, he walked along the front path from his home to the pavement, and on to the house adjoining theirs.

Living in that house was a big man, with several walloping chins and cheeks above his wide imposing belly. Brandon had only ever seen him as he boarded or alighted from taxis outside his home, wearing a dark pinstriped suit and waistcoat from which hung a gold fob watch. Always he held his head back so that his eyes looked sternly down upon everyone, including people taller than him. If the man had noticed the small boy then he never acknowledged him.

Brandon reached up his hand. Loud enough for anyone to hear but not so loud as to seem rude, he knocked on the man's front door.

The door soon opened. Standing there, wearing a dark pinstriped suit and waistcoat from which hung a gold fob watch and with his head held back, was the multiple-chinned man. Slowly, his head straightened and then bowed forward, until his eyes stared down at the young boy gazing up at him.

"Why don't you have any children?" asked Brandon.

The fat man's brows and eyes rose slowly as he drew a long breath. "The impertinence," he sneered, and swung closed the door.

Brandon proceeded to the next house along the street, where he again reached up and knocked on the door. There was no answer.

He continued to the next house, where the door moved away as he knocked. He pushed it further open.

The sunlight coming through the open door fell upon a woman of about his mother's age, which few people living near him were, sitting with her eyes closed before him on the floor. Wearing a lightly fitting long white dress and no shoes, she sat with her legs tightly crossed. Her hands rested on her knees, with her palms upright, fingers relaxed, and thumbs pressed

SIMON LENNON

lightly against her index fingers. On the floor beside her was a small clock. The red hand of the clock alarm was set for six o'clock that evening, more than seven hours away.

"Why don't you have any children?" asked Brandon.

Her eyes blinked, her concentration broken. Her eyes slowly opened, honing in upon the little person watching her.

"Why don't you have any children?" he asked again.

The woman raised her eyebrows, pursed her lips, and dipped her head to the side. "I need to know that it's what I want."

"Why?"

She playfully shrugged her shoulders, before composing herself back into her pose, allowing her eyes to close. With nothing more to say, Brandon slowly pulled shut the door, again shading the sunlight from her face.

Occupying the next house along the street were a man and woman several years older than his parents. The woman opened the door.

"Why don't you have any children?" asked Brandon.

From a room inside the house, the man called out: "Who is it?"

"The neighbourhood boy," she called back.

"What does he want?"

"He wants to know why we don't have children."

"Tell him to mind his own business."

The woman stepped out of her home and pulled the door behind her until it was almost closed. With Brandon, her voice was soft. "I have a very important job," she explained. "I'm a doctor, at the hospital."

"Having children won't take much time."

"Mister Cheevers and I want our time to be for us."

"I understand," said Brandon, courteous enough not to admit he didn't. "Goodbye."

"Goodbye."

Brandon walked back to the street, where he noticed her still watching him. She continued watching him walk along the pavement to the next house.

Brandon continued walking along the winding roads and around corners, knocking on doors as often as not without reply.

At one house, people were already laughing on the far side of the front door when Brandon reached up his hand and knocked. "Ssh," said a woman. "There's someone outside."

The door suddenly opened, held there by a man with one hand on the handle and his other hand holding a giggling woman in a tightly fitting red dress. She quickly pulled herself away from him, patting down her dress. "Yes?" said the man.

"Why don't you have any children?"

"What?"

"Why don't you have any children?"

The man looked at the woman, slapped her bottom, and grinned. "I don't want her any less beautiful than she is now," he laughed.

"Ooh," she said. Playfully, she pushed her hand against his chest, reprimanding him.

"Don't you think my mother is beautiful?" asked Brandon.

The man looked at the woman, she looked at him, and he swung the door closed. Brandon heard them laughing and giggling beyond the closed door. "Has he gone?" she asked the man.

"Forget him," he told her, slapping her bottom again. She laughed aloud, while Brandon walked away.

Nobody answered the following three doors on which Brandon knocked. As he walked back to the street from the third house, a thin athletic woman jogged towards him. She wore tiny short trousers and a brief white shirt trickling with perspiration, the sports-clothing manufacturer's logo conspicuously placed over her heart and chest. A cord from two tiny headphones attached to her ears hung to a small plastic object clipped to a strap around her waist, although her body swung only in the rhythm of her running. Her arms and legs slowed as she neared the small boy standing outside her home. She removed her headphones as she stopped. "What's up?" she asked Brandon, shaking her short, sweated hair before running her fingernails through it.

"Why don't you have any children?"

She scoffed. "I don't train like this every day to do *that* to my body," she said, walking past him to her home.

Through the rest of the morning and into the afternoon, Brandon walked along the pavements around his home, knocking on the doors of houses he'd never before visited. Most houses were empty, although he sometimes caught sight of someone watching him from a window without opening the door or a shadow moving across a peephole.

An aging woman with blonde-dyed hair and wearing white powder, red lipstick, and blue eyeliner held a small round silver mirror in one hand. She smoked a cigarette in the other.

"Why don't you have any children?" asked Brandon.

The woman dropped back her head and rolled her eyes. "When you are fifteen years older perhaps, darling!" she told him. With a sweep of her wrist, she flicked closed the door.

The front door to one home opened to a particularly elderly lady, older than other people he'd encountered. "How are you today, young man?" she smiled, her eyes bright and warm.

"Why don't you have any children?"

"We do have a child."

"You do!" said Brandon excitedly. "Can I please see him?"

"I'm afraid that Gerald doesn't live with us anymore, although we keep his bedroom just as he left it. He lives in a very nice apartment in the West End."

"Does he have any children?"

"I'm sorry, young man, no, he doesn't. He works very hard."

"Oh," said Brandon. "Goodbye."

Walking towards him on one pavement were a man and woman much older than his parents, who Brandon had often seen walking. The man wore a bright pink shirt and deep blue denim jeans like the clothes of younger men. She wore a small yellow top closely hugging her skin and exposing her thin waist. Her short black leather skirt exposed much of her pale thighs. The heels and soles of the man's large brown leather shoes and woman's long black leather boots clipped the path as they walked. Brandon stopped and waited for them to reach him. "Good day to you," the man greeted him.

"Hello," said Brandon, looking up at them. "I'm asking everyone why they don't have any children."

The man laughed. She smiled. "You're asking us," he said, as he and the woman walked around Brandon. "We're much too young to be parents."

Turning his head to watch the man and woman walking past, Brandon noticed a woman watching him from the front window of a house across the street. In her hand was a large glass of red wine. Quickly she drew closed the curtain, hiding from his view. Brandon didn't go to her house.

Opening another door was a woman almost as pretty as his mother. Coming from a kitchen somewhere behind her was a spicy aroma Brandon didn't recognise.

"Why don't you have any children?"

The woman tilted her head to point back behind her in the house. "What, with him?"

Still another door opened to a home furnished much like the home in which Brandon lived. The man and woman standing there looked at each other. "Money," the man told Brandon. "We can't afford to raise children."

"Poor people in poor places have children," said Brandon.

"I couldn't live being poor," said the man. "I'd rather be dead."

"I'd rather be poor."

Brandon continued knocking on the doors of strange houses along the avenues, drives, and closes much the same, becoming lost as he walked. One softly spoken woman, very much like his mother, kindly knelt down in front of him. She knelt where she could talk to him with their eyes at almost the same level. "We'd like to have children," she told him, "lots of children, but we can't."

"Why can't you?"

"Sometimes it happens," she told him, trying to smile. She alone seemed to understand the importance of his question to him. "I'm so very sorry."

She remained there patiently, not sending him away. "I wish you could have children," said Brandon.

"Thank you, my friend," she smiled again. "I wish so, too."

The small boy turned around and walked away. From the end of her front path, he turned back towards her home. The woman, still kneeling, again smiled.

Sometime mid-afternoon, knowing little more from his exercise, Brandon walked back upon his home. He'd not noticed his father quietly following a distance behind him, watching over him, as he'd done since Brandon walked from their home that morning. Alec deliberated upon a treatise he was unqualified to begin; he and Hollie couldn't tell their son what they didn't know. Like the church bells that had ceased ringing could have rung, Englishmen and women tolled with a plethora of explanations why they were childless and kept each other so.

10

THE HOUSE OF BROKEN GLASS

Brandon grew to become taller than his parents, with blond hair thick and sprightly, while the woman jogging past his home began to walk. People who'd walked rested in chairs and sofas watching her.

"Why don't I have any brothers or sisters?" Brandon asked his father.

"We didn't realise what was happening."

"What is happening? What will we do?"

"Mummy and I will always be here."

Brandon walked away. His father hadn't understood.

At Polam Hall, Brandon often stared at the tarnished silver trophies on glass shelves in a glass cabinet, which kept them from being receptacles for dust. The most recent trophy was thirty-two years old. At the back of the cabinet were old photographs of football teams who'd won competitions. There'd been many teams back then, but Brandon's class of seven final boys and girls weren't enough to be a team. They played no school-life competitions.

The faces in photographs had become adults, some old enough to die. Brandon's face reflected in the glass could've been any one of them, not knowing what to say. His life was close to failing, not for anything he did.

Staring with him through the glass stood other young boys to men and girls to women, denied their futures. "I can't help but thinking," said Algernon, "that the most important issue of our time is our low birth rate."

Turning from the glass, they gazed uneasily among themselves. "Are you suggesting we devote our lives to making babies, raising children, the way people *used* to do?" asked Isabelle, holding Lewis' hand.

An answer to her question resonated through Brandon's head, an answer for men and women they'd learnt well not to say. He struggled to find words of his sincerity that he was strong enough to say to peers he'd known since he was small.

Isabelle released her hand from Lewis'. He tried to take her hand again but she refused him. "We're teenagers," she said,

The last careers counsellor spoke to children persevering at the school much as he'd spoken to young men and women for more than thirty years, but without the options for further study once available. Without anyone to teach them and without the chance to learn, Brandon's class of aspirants could not be doctors, architects, or lawyers. Most of what the counsellor had to talk about were menial roles, but still he called them all careers. The aged people who persevered in work would teach their last apprentices the little that they knew, fumbling through their dead-end stock-in-trade.

The tallest girl in Brandon's class was Trudie Blanquist, who began modelling clothes for television advertisements and shop posters. Models at European fashion shows remained young, while the audiences opining, marvelling, and condemning from the long rows of chairs beneath the catwalks aged in the dark.

Trudie's face was particularly pale, even more so since a dentist removed her rear teeth to heighten her cheekbones and tighten her skin. A surgeon adjusted the positions of her eyes, according to the directions of her agent. Other surgery ensured her chest stayed flat, when it would otherwise have bloomed. The worms she placed in her stomach helped her minimise her weight when she erroneously ate too much and couldn't vomit it away. None of that was obvious when long dresses waved from her legs and sleek stiletto heels. Parading before spectators, for whom nothing should distract them from the merchandise, she posed without expression.

While cameras flashed, lights blazed, and music played, Brandon and his parents stood with Trudie's agent at the back of the Dolphin Centre, watching Trudie strut along the catwalk. Knitting needles seemed to puncture her nose and metal clasps spread apart her lips and mouth into a rigid orifice. Her gaunt white face stared coldly beyond the repeat audience not watching her. That day, her eyes half-closed were conscientiously morose, the soulless figurine not detracting from the mesh of rusted iron sheets weaved through white woollen shawls she wore.

Spectators cheered the aged designer when he stepped onto the stage. They called his show a triumph.

Brandon studied the people cheering, who'd seen only colours, styles, and patterns hanging in procession. The flesh mannequins were canvases drawn from much of Europe, forgotten when the artists painted over them. He would've called Trudie a clotheshorse, but people were too fond of horses.

"Son," said his father, standing beside him. "Do you recall asking what we thought was different about us from other people? We look at people and think about those breathing human beings."

His mother turned to Trudie's agent. "She used to look so pretty."

"Fashion is art, not beauty," the agent explained.

"What does that make Trudie?"

"Rich," her bleached teeth smiled.

If Trudie returned to school, then it would be because she would not allow one career to spoil another. In Brandon she confided that, at the home she bought her parents in Brancepeth with a heart-shaped waterbed, she slumped exhausted on the silk.

The homes around Brandon's home in Hummersknott were much alike, but one particularly impressive house always drew his eye. That day when he was nine that he knocked on so many doors, he'd entered Halnaby Avenue, along the edge of the countryside and Baydale Beck. At the top of the widest and longest driveway he'd seen, on a property that seemed twice the size of any other, were two open garage doors. Inside the garage, were two lavish motor cars in pristine mint condition.

The most interesting vehicle was a massive vintage car from the early years of the twentieth century, unlike every other car he'd seen. Imposing round headlamps hung from each side of the striped steel radiator shell. Wipers hung from the top of the windscreen.

Crouched beside the older car, the man of the house held a yellow cloth. Careful never to let his hands touch the car, he painstakingly polished afresh the already shining deep blue chassis, silver work, and rolling black metal fenders above the wheels, apparently without noticing Brandon staring at him. Brandon didn't interrupt.

Across a smooth green lawn was the house, facing sideways from the street. Through the bay window of the lounge room, Brandon saw the lady of the house stand painting a canvas on an easel.

Too short to reach the iron knocker, his knuckles knocked on the front door. He knocked twice, without reply. She surely heard him, but continued mixing colours on a palette.

Through the ensuing years, Brandon rarely had cause to enter Halnaby Avenue, but he never saw the vintage car driving along Ettersgill Drive or any other street. Nothing much about that cottage seemed to change, not even the flowerpots brimming with bright flowers. The white woodwork was repainted before time could tarnish the previous coat of paint, while Brandon became a little older each year of his short childhood.

That was until six years later. A web of cracks had appeared in that bay window from the lounge room. A bird had most likely crashed into the glass, but the cracks became more and more incongruous each day Brandon returned to check the house and no one repaired the window. The grass had already become longer than careful maintenance had kept it, for a home otherwise so well presented.

Brandon, fifteen years old and becoming certain in his stride, went back up the long, wide driveway and back along the shorter path to the front door. Taller and stronger than he'd been when last he stood there, he struck the iron knocker hard. Again, no one replied.

He struck it several times, before peering through the window. Standing in the centre of the lounge room was still the easel on which a canvas rested, but no one painting. Aside from the broken window, the room was neat and ordered, with paintings hanging squarely from the walls.

Brandon turned the front door knob, but the door was locked shut, as Brandon expected it to be. "Is anybody there?" he called out.

With only a weak excuse for intruding upon the property, he wandered around the cottage. The garage door was locked.

Behind the cottage were another lengthening lawn and gardens, without anyone enjoying them. In a surfeit of brown clay pots were coloured-petal flowers, their aromas sweet and fresh since Brandon came to smell them.

Along the rear of the cottage were several closed windows and doors, including those to a large garden room. Brandon turned the door handles, but couldn't push them open.

Stepping backwards to survey, his heel struck a small rock. Brandon imagined somebody, not him, using it to break a window.

Reaching his arms above him, the longest fingers of his right hand ran along the trimming above the utility room door where his parents hid a key to their home, not expecting to find anything. Instead, he found a key.

"Is anybody home?" he called out for good measure, as he unlocked and opened the door. Passing through the utility room into the kitchen, the air was still, as it was never so still in Brandon's home. The people who'd lived in so neat a cottage had kept it clean, or paid somebody to keep it clean. He might never again be in that house he shouldn't have entered, although the sounds of someone or a car arriving ought to allow him time to flee before anybody saw him.

Cautiously, Brandon stepped through the hallway and dining room into the lounge room, amidst exorbitant oak furniture made in the quality of antiques before their time. Several liquor bottles stood on a polished bar cabinet, where the fifteen-year-old boy in a house not for children poured himself a glass of sherry. Sipping alcohol for the first time, he coughed it from his mouth. Before the little liquid on the floor stained the carpet, Brandon hurried to the kitchen, found a tea towel he wet with water from the tap, and soaked it up.

The unfinished painting on the easel was of an English cottage beneath a wide blue open sky. It might've been becoming the cottage around him, but for its setting in country meadows. Lying on a thin shelf on the easel were several brushes, cloths, and a row of little cups and glass bottles of paint through which shone their tones of colour. The dry brushes had been cleaned well since last anybody used them.

Treating the home of people who weren't there like a gallery that wouldn't open, Brandon examined without touching the finished paintings on the walls, always listening for a sound. The romantic images of country houses in the green with softly smoking chimneys were like the cottage through which he wandered, but never quite the same. One hand painted all of them, signed with a name like Charion Morton.

Standing on the mantelpiece above the fireplace were two matching gold-leafed frames. In one was a photograph of a smiling barefoot Asian girl dressed proudly in a white blouse and blue dress. The only blemish in the picture-perfect room was the dirt on which she stood.

In the second frame was a seven-year-old letter from a last surviving charity, to which Egbert and Charion Morton sent a hundred pounds every month to help Sokhorn. The girl had been eight years of age, making her by then fifteen years of age, as young and old as Brandon. She lived in a tin house in the Kampong Speu province of Cambodia with her mother, two brothers, and sister. She spoke Khmer, was Buddhist, and had access to clean water but no health facilities.

The Mortons could lose their house and still have more material possessions than Sokhorn. She wouldn't care about things she never knew. Brandon would struggle without the only things he'd known.

Also on the mantelpiece lay a black leather wallet of keys, including car keys. One key unlocked the garage door, which

Brandon pulled open. One car space was empty, but beside it, forever young, was the vintage car he'd seen there seven years earlier.

Never before had Brandon stood so close to such a vehicle. Reaching out his hand to touch it, he noticed a small dark mark, like a mole on human skin, tarnishing one strip of the radiator shell. Brandon scratched the mark with the soft edge of his fingernail. The car was clean again.

Daylight reflected in the chassis as Brandon carefully examined it. The upholstery roof that covered the long rear leather seat didn't cover the two front seats. Those seats so soft and smooth seemed never to have suffered cruel sun, sodding rain, or the weight of human beings, although several tin cans of petrol stood on the floor behind the car. It was a different mix of petrol to that which modern cars employed.

Brandon turned a bulky silver handle and opened the driver's heavy door. The man he'd seen polishing that car seven years earlier would be furious to know what he was doing, but the man wasn't there to see him. After checking that the soles of his shoes were clean, Brandon stepped onto the running board. He climbed into the driver's seat. The upholstered seat was strangely lumpy, although the steering wheel was lush to hold.

Knowing only what he'd observed his parents doing, Brandon took up the stance of somebody about to drive away, but the technology before him wasn't what he recognised from the cars his parents drove. The dashboard gauges were rotating pointers on round dials. The gear stick and handbrake were long unwieldy levers reaching down through the floor beside his feet. The car controls became no less complicated the more he studied them. He might never learn to drive that car. He wasn't setting forth.

If their other car appeared before him bringing home the Mortons, then Brandon had no excuse for being there. He quickly pulled his hands from the steering wheel, alighted from the car, and closed the door. He closed and locked the garage door and returned the keys to the mantelpiece exactly where he'd found them.

He stopped. The photograph of Sokhorn was the only picture

of a person in the house. No paintings portrayed people. The void made Brandon wonder who, if anyone, the Mortons loved. The artist might've planned to put a face in the painting on the easel, but that was not for him to know. She might've died without finishing the work.

Painting her pictures without people, driving his car without a mark, theirs was a comfortable family home without a family. Monthly debiting a bank account was their easy way to raise a child: a levy for a colour photograph and letter to place prominently where visitors would notice. Distant children wouldn't spoil their art or cars.

Within sight of an oval dining table with six red-cushioned chairs, Brandon imagined Egbert and Charion Morton eating imported seafood and tender steak with peppercorn, talking about their pauper pretend-daughter. They might've considered her the child they'd been unable to bear, or the child they'd declined to bear. They might've loved her.

Without knowing what she did, Sokhorn had indulged them their delusions: love, purpose, family. Those gifts were more than the meagre money they'd given her and someone spent on her behalf. She might've helped them think they had a future. They had none.

Their lies distracted them from facts. The Mortons might've meant well, but good intentions never kept anyone alive. Aimless hobbies to take away their time and dead charity to strangers had obscured their lonely lives, but left them poor alone. When Brandon quarantined from his thoughts the Mortons' failures, he was proud of them for wanting to be good, but they should've cared more for Brandon than photographs of people they didn't know. Their people would not be aging to their deaths had they born the children they had funded. The Mortons should've cared more for themselves.

People who Europeans thought required their help fared better than Europeans did. The dirt poor were prospering. Brandon's once rich brethren were perishing.

Sokhorn had already done enough for them. Her first heart and works were for her people with her, without regard for benefactors dying. Brandon might've envied her, for she would lose only charity while his world crumbled away. She had no need to fear losing her donors' patronage. All money had bought Brandon were food, clothes, and shelter to keep him until the day he couldn't spend it anymore. The best times of her life were ahead of her. The best times of his might not be.

Perhaps one day, if time proved him to be the last Englishman alive, he would try to find her and ask her if she could take him in. He didn't think she would.

Brandon presumed many things about a girl he'd never met, living in a country he'd never seen, but Sokhorn need never be alone. She had no need for the Mortons' photograph, even if they'd sent her one. Her mother had no need for Brandon's photograph or letters from an agency about him. Sokhorn had a family. The Mortons didn't. Hers made Brandon's seem so small. She surely had friends, as the Mortons might not have had, and as Brandon had too few.

He hoped that nothing would keep her from being happy, feeling all around her. She would cope better in her company than he would cope alone. More sensible about being alive than had been the Mortons, more people would mourn her passing in a village than would mourn the passing of all the sponsor couples in empty handsome homes.

If Egbert and Charion Morton were dead, then nobody was coming to that cottage. Their faces had faded from the view. Their only names were on a letter a trespasser had seen, and hers on paintings no one wanted. The room kept so beautifully was in a broken glass of home.

Brandon stood again before the easel in the centre of the room, with its partly finished painting of a pretty English cottage. The paint in the small cups was dry, but the paint in little bottles under seal was usable. Placing the back of his hand against the row of little bottles, he found the shades of white and pink most like the colour of his skin, Egbert and Charion Morton's hands, and all the people once living in Hummersknott.

No artist, he removed the bottle lids, dipped the end of a brush into the paints, and mixed them on the palette. Brandon raised the brush towards the canvas, where he painted a young man's face and ears against the green. He took another brush, dipped it in another small paint bottle, and gave the figure thick blond hair. He gave him blue eyes and a serious straight-line red mouth. He gave him clothes like the clothes that Brandon wore.

The painting was better, but not as good as it could be. Beside that boy, Brandon painted a girl's face. He gave her blonde hair, not like any particular English girl. He painted her in a dress for playing, not like the clothes that Trudie wore. Her dress was less important than her being so close to him.

Brandon did not believe in anything but people he could see: his parents, school children, and neighbours. He didn't want a shining car if no one sat beside him. He didn't want paintings of empty houses if his house was also empty. He didn't worry for the world, but only people that he knew.

He continued painting boys and girls until they covered every space of green across the canvas. He then stepped back from his creation.

Paintings were poor surrogates for people, and Brandon remained in childhood solitude inside an empty house. His images in oil were dreams of what a life could be, no less fakery than Sokhorn's photograph atop the mantelpiece.

The couple living in the cottage might presume the vandal at the canvas had broken the lounge room window, but their home was broken long before Brandon entered. He'd given it a moment of a purpose before the art and cottage rotted, the car in the garage rusted. If the Mortons walked upon him then he'd tell them what he'd done.

They never came. Later, Brandon learnt the car crash on a motorway that killed Egbert confined Charion to a coma, before she died without heirs or heiresses. An elderly English couple in Luton sponsoring a child in the Philippines also sponsored Sokhorn, who didn't notice that anything had changed.

11

THE COLLAPSE OF ALL CAREERS

Fresh catastrophes might've unfolded without technicians tending to the machinery they left behind, so the last of the English factories were carefully wound down. Moving parts fell still, as they would always be. Toxins that might've leaked into the air, soil, and water were sealed forever. Drug manufacturers endured longer than other plants, producing pills and potions for people dying. The businesses of food, medicine, and warmth would persevere a little longer, but the economy in County Durham was falling down.

Companies ceased trading with the sale of their last stocks to sell. The afternoon the Stafford Joinery closed, its last skirting board sold, was no easier to bear for having headed towards them through recent days, months, and even years. Perhaps Gerald never quite believed it would occur, at least not within his lifetime.

Taking refuge in the presence of the only mentor he recalled, Gerald drifted into Niles Stafford's office. Stafford sat shattered at his desk, staring into air. A partly full Beefeater gin bottle and partly drunk glass in his hand stood before him, where liquor had never before stood.

Gerald slumped into the chair facing him, without reason in their work for either one of them to be there. The corporate presidency to which Gerald had striven for so long would never become his, but worse than ambition unfilled was the sense that fulfilment would not have left him feeling better. Were Stafford's office his, Stafford's title and life his, then Gerald would still have felt so listless. Without the long careers in which they'd resided, they were similarly alone. "I'm sorry, sir," said Gerald, with as much apology as regret.

Stafford's eyes slowly turned towards Gerald. His voice slower than it had ever before been, Stafford asked, "How long have you been here, Keaton?"

"Thirty-two years, sir."

"Thirty-two years."

The workplace remained their human interaction, where they'd previously only talked about timber moulding never to be made. Gerald might've been the only person Stafford knew to listen to him, to whom he could confide his mourning. Without the company to which his grandfather gave their family name, the austerity that once defined him left him too little of anything to do.

"Thirty-two years might seem like a long time to you Keaton, it would have seemed a long time to me when I was your age, but I started working here when I was nineteen years old." The man who'd been frugal with conversation suddenly could do nothing more than talk. "Do you know how old I am now, Keaton?"

"No, sir," lied Gerald.

"I am seventy-eight years old. I've been working for this company, my company, for fifty-nine years. Fifty-nine years, Keaton. Fifty-nine years."

That was also Gerald's age. Stafford wouldn't have known.

"I built Stafford Joinery from something very small into a name that people admired, revered, pre-eminent in its field. It's the greatest single entity of my life and I was so proud of it, so damned proud. Do you understand pride, Keaton? Do you know what pride is?"

Gerald didn't know if Stafford expected him to answer. When he realised that he did, he didn't know what to say.

"What was it, what was it, for which I was so proud?" asked Stafford. "Don't you ever think from what you see around you that our lives were not so good. Our lives were magnificent, the greatest lives on earth. We made what we made with precision, skill, and pride." Those words, their memory, seemed to slow his pace of thinking. His hand started raising his glass but stopped, replacing it on his desk. "Stay there," he said, struggling to stand up from his chair before stepping from his office.

Stafford soon returned with another glass, which he stood on his desk in front of Gerald. Never before had he poured Gerald a glass of liquor but that strange day, without the roles they understood, he filled Gerald's glass. If it wasn't for Gerald to drink, it was to keep him there to listen. "Thank you, sir."

"Sir," laughed Stafford.

Gerald took the glass in his hand without drinking. Stafford poured more gin into his glass and sat back in his chair. The differences between them were less important than their sudden similarities, without Gerald knowing if his nineteen extra years to be alive were a consolation or a curse. When Stafford brought his glass to his lips, Gerald raised his glass and sipped a small amount.

"There was a time, Keaton, not long ago, that I knew what I was doing and where I was going, but I wasn't going anywhere."

The words could as easily have been Gerald's. Unable to imagine being anywhere else, Gerald let the older man speak for both of them.

"I've known people retire or lose their jobs with no idea of what to do." He and Gerald had become the people that he knew. "I don't like playing cards, and I don't like pruning flowers, but that might be all there is."

Gerald wanted to refute him but could not. Their empty homes convicted them of isolation Gerald could not yet understand. Their inability to work convicted them of age he did not yet believe.

Stafford swilled the gin in his glass. "I better call you 'Gerald'."

In her mimicry of work, Elsa sat at her computer terminal typing words that she deleted, until the electricity ceased. She then fidgeted at her desk, only leaving it to loiter in the kitchen or stationery room, until darkness drove her from the docile premises at sunset. "I am sorry for leaving so early, Mister Keaton," she said, their words of parting for a day and not forever.

Gerald thought of saying the same to Niles Stafford, still at his desk. Instead he said, as he said any other night, "Good night, sir." Stafford didn't answer.

The next morning, in a pattern he needed to sustain a short time longer, Gerald dressed into his business clothes. He returned to the silent gloomy offices and factory as if it were a normal working day, although they'd become much harder to enter and get around without electric lights. Without business to perform, he could walk all day between empty rooms in which only he was there.

Elsa was already at her desk, trying her best to read a colourful company brochure from three years earlier she put down when she saw him. "Good morning, Mister Keaton," she beamed.

Stumbling from the pretence, Gerald wanted to say something about them being there, in a dark commercial building becoming cold, but they knew too little about each other for him to know what he could say. He wanted to give her work to do for which she would not be paid, but couldn't think of anything. "Good morning, Elsa," he said.

Niles Stafford was in his office, standing by a sunlit window, examining a design of dado rail that would never be manufactured. Gerald did not disturb him.

Gerald entered his adjoining office, returning to his squalid desk. Lying there were old memoranda and other papers he'd read too many times, along with timber samples: the treasures of his life. He picked up the largest and most beautiful sample among them, a ceiling piece to surround a light fitting in which patterned scrolls of golden leaves lay over regal blue, and examined it. If Gerald had achieved anything in his working life then it had been timber pieces that other people crafted, in emptying homes and offices. They'd been his life within the confines of his career.

He couldn't hold anything in his hands that he had made or point to anything he'd built, not really. He couldn't touch any invention or item of manufacture resulting from his thought or labour.

His failure bound him to his pointless vantage, the inconsequence of all he'd done. His life at work had been futile, in the oblivion to which they all had fallen. For what had he been toiling at his desk and other people's meetings simply to go away and die? His computer calculations and notes of passing conversations had not helped anyone, least of all himself. The labours of his life had failed to save them. His knowledge and reasoning meant nothing, if he couldn't resuscitate the dying outside his office. He hadn't kept himself.

The only accomplishments of people's lives surviving were the offspring they left behind. Gerald's parents' trivial achievement was their son, but it surpassed the lying glories of men and women dying without descendants. Gerald could pinch his arm, touch his hand, and ascribe them to his parents. He could not ascribe anything to himself.

Gerald carefully placed the ceiling piece in a wastepaper basket, which no one would empty. It could lie there forever and nobody would care. The empires in a grain of sand were never more than petty fiefdoms for the damned.

His head hung slumped, held up by his hardy hands against his bony forehead, staring through the space into the walls. He'd tried his best to be the best he could be, worked hard for too long a time doing all he could do, but his career had been working towards short ends unto himself. Nothing seemed to be important. He couldn't think of anything meaningful he'd done.

"Elsa," he called out, as he normally summoned her.

She hurriedly stood up and dashed to his open office door. "Yes, Mister Keaton?"

"What do you like to do?"

She looked back at him.

"We can't stay here."

"What would you have me do?"

His work was finished but his life, however close to its conclusion, was not yet finished. "We must move on."

"Where?"

"Anywhere." Doing anything was better than pretending to do something.

She remained standing, until Niles Stafford appeared behind her, carrying his set of keys. Gerald pulled himself upright. Elsa turned around to face him.

"It is time," Stafford told her. "I'm sorry."

Again she remained standing, before walking slowly back to her desk. Gerald rose and followed her as far as his office door, standing beside Stafford. They both watched her pause to study photographs of an office party at the corner of her desk, before slowly collecting her crammed handbag.

"Elsa," said Gerald.

She quickly turned around, smiling.

"We could have that dinner, tonight."

The smile waned from her face. "I need to find a job." Leaving behind the personal possessions she left behind each day and the men she barely knew, she left.

Only Gerald and Stafford remained at the offices and factory. Unable to say anything he'd not already said, Gerald watched Stafford sweep and then mop the kitchen floor and wipe the table as cleaners once had done, not wanting to interrupt or deny him. He watched him carry a bag of soiled cups, broken wrappers, and discarded parts of food from the kitchen to the garbage bin outside the building. Stafford cleaned the common areas, desks, and offices, returning that timber piece from Gerald's wastepaper basket to his desk. When he'd cleaned all that Gerald knew could be cleaned and then some more, Stafford stood still in a corridor.

"Goodbye, sir," said Gerald.

"Good luck, Keaton."

"You too, sir."

Gerald took from his lowermost desk drawer the dusty box containing his leather-bound diaries, embossed with his initials and the date of every year passed: the thin records of his career. From his desktop, he took his dairy of things to do for the year under way. Not knowing what else to do with them, he stowed them in his apartment, in his lowermost desk drawer.

Two weeks later, as he wandered along a pavement near his

defunct place of former work, Gerald recognised the old man in a business suit, meticulously sweeping the streets of leaves. He stopped before him. "Good day, sir."

Without interrupting his work, the old man glanced at him. "Good day, Keaton."

Gerald considered asking him if he was well, dressed and groomed as he had been at the Stafford Joinery. Niles Stafford continued sweeping as if Gerald wasn't there.

Gone from their roles and perceived responsibilities, the lives of lawyers and window cleaners, artists and prostitutes, dissipated into chores. Exiled from their acclamation lost, company chief executives were indistinguishable from itinerants selling flowers to restaurant patrons who didn't want to buy them. Without their most eminent posturing, they were as rich as were the poor, as much successful as having failed, as much admirable as contemptible. Whatever skills they'd once perfected were often meaningless, their lives gone past without consequence in their new lives and deaths.

Willing to wipe dust from dirty windows and repair broken rooves with very little, if any, remuneration, they soon exchanged their labours. They dared not work without an audience but needed people back again to be what they had been, in the aftermath of their careers. The work of people no longer there was unimportant.

The day the Northern Lights Company resolved the last of its affairs, its last investment gone, Alec collected from his desk the few personal effects of importance to him. His colleagues wandered lethargically about their offices, like mourners at their wake. Work alone had given them something upon which to concentrate.

Valda Walton had led the dwindling company in recent weeks, while Tarpin Hobbs had been holed up in his home feeling sick. She was sitting in her office chair, grappling with the company's last financial statements finalised that morning, when Alec stood at her open door. "Will you be all right, Valda?"

She pulled the papers to her chest. "My work is my legacy," she told him, starting to laugh. "My work is my legacy," she said again, as she started to cry. Alec began walking towards her, but she threw the papers towards him. Her arm was weak and the papers sprayed into the air. Trying to rise from her chair, she screamed, "My work is my legacy!" She slumped back in her chair and wept.

Harriet Simpkin collected the photographs of her two Bichon Frise dogs, William and Oswald, from the partition around her desk. Secure within her house, Harriet sat in her lounge room sofa with them resting on their cushions. "Mummy lost her job today," she told them, holding back the first small tear from her right eye, "but I don't want you to worry about it. We will always have each other." Staring at them while her body weakened, her head fell slowly against the armrest. "We will, won't we?"

Every day, Harriet sat talking wistfully to those two dogs about the work that she once did, her head slipping deeper into the sofa. "Mummy was very important at the company," she told them. "Mummy collated the reports." She paused to think about that aspect of her work. "I wonder what became of them."

Her words often drifted away from work to her new life in her confinement. Lying on her side along the sofa, with her bare feet against one armrest and her head flat against the other, she gazed down upon her dogs mulling together on the floor. Determined more to feed them than she bothered to feed herself, she kept them with her while stray animals scrounged outside for meagre morsels. Her domesticated dogs would struggle to survive in arid streets of a toughened town, without their human guardian and captor: their human servant.

"You won't leave Mummy, will you William, will you Oswald?" she begged of them, tears moistening in her eyes. Their eyes were partly open and partly sleeping, while her stares into the room around her became more vague and abstract every day she was alone.

The once perennial electric lights, which people rarely noticed in the ceilings and the walls, no longer shone from bleak abandoned offices. Easy lifts carried people to the highest viewing platforms, from which aged men and women looked down on shorter buildings and the streets. They were their last delusion that nothing anywhere had changed, until each lift used too often failed to function. Buildings that had been palaces became too difficult to mount; few people cared to climb the overwhelming steps. Warrens once of office workers stood sealed but not yet buried, like upright mausoleums without bodies. They would never again open.

The streets were bland without flocks of people in colourful attire; what had been the most mundane became magnificent in retrospect. The working wear of people no longer working hung in bedroom cupboards, to nourish moths and butterflies. Left lying below them, impractical business shoes became stiff. Gerald yearned to see the population dressed for life again more than he'd once thought to value life.

The prices of frivolities collapsed, however much people thought they needed them. A glut of silverware and trinkets filled idle stores along the high streets, faded into night in day. Cabinets of once expensive wares remained available to people strong enough to break them, in darkness they could breach with the light of a cheap torch and aging batteries. The merchandise was theirs to take without constraint, but wasn't worth having when they could have it all so easily. People who could loot anything they wanted were too old to bother doing so. They mustered just the exercise to replace what fell and broke.

Those frivolities might've never been worth having. Men and women couldn't do more with them than they'd already done; luxuries could not amuse them.

London traders brought manufactured foods, beverages, and medicines to the last of the north-east England stores, much more expensive than they'd been. They brought the petrol for people no longer able to drive their cars on whims.

Remnant farmers brought salted hand-cut strips of meat to butcher shops. They brought untreated milk from cows to corner stores. The last cartons of long-life milk preserved old milk with which Gerald was more comfortable, but that milk would soon exhaust. He baulked before the chicken eggs of many colours: browning shells darker than the indifferent shades of white he'd taken from supermarket shelves.

Growers brought their fruit and dirt-encrusted vegetables to greengroceries; foods that had no seasons when supermarkets imported them became vulnerable to ice, rain, and wind. No longer immaculate and neat, the new produce was ugly, with twisted shapes and rough coarse skins. Their imperfections made them less appealing, less natural, although they were in truth too natural. The fruit and vegetables tasted to Gerald much like those in cans.

Aged chefs remained in command of the last of the dining venues, concocting sauces however subtle from ingredients customers had given them and garnishes available. The meals listed on old chef-set menus were unavailable. Far from the expert cuisine that patrons once ate without regard, there were only simple dishes without style: pork and other chops with creamed pumpkin and cracked pepper. Wines progressed past their best maturity, without more recent vintages. Machines that percolated coffee from imported beans stood idle, by open cans of instant coffee granules.

Gerald had taken the finer meals he ate for granted, expecting always to have them. He wished he'd paused to enjoy them a little more.

Extravagancies no longer beckoned Gerald so much as the dates printed on plastic packets, tin cans, and cardboard boxes, before which their preserved contents should be eaten. Stewed-fruit cans and dried-fruit packets would last for several years, but still deteriorate. They filled the cupboards and pantries of his small kitchen where few of them once stood, along with spare can and bottle openers for fear that one might break. No longer the great pleasure it once was, food became mere sustenance to be consumed.

Market gardens arose behind some houses, providing a few more vegetables for people living there: laborious beetroots and tomatoes without variety. Their circumstances brought Alec and Hollie closer to the food they ate than they'd ever before been, but vegetables grown without fertiliser and tillage were bland, woody, and fibrous. Hollie cooked cabbages and potatoes with salt in boiling water and served them with whatever she could find. Alec ate raw radishes and lettuce.

Trees that had been decorative, feeding only birds and squirrels, gave way to fresh fruit providers. People too old to nurture seedlings thought they could plant pear and apple seeds and promptly pick their food. They were quickly disappointed. People who'd lauded impatience as a virtue needed to learn patience; impatience was a legacy of times they had other things to do.

Soon, there were market gardens in public parks around County Durham, from which gypsies stole food they hadn't cultivated. Industrious men and women still saw nobility in working without reward to satisfy the wants of lazy, roaming thieves. The industrious went hungry.

12

DARLINGTON MEMORIAL HOSPITAL

The final efforts of British government bureaucracy were increasingly devoted to providing gas, electricity, communications, and water. It sequestered the last reserves of old term assets, stripping vaults of gold and silver. It sold whatever islands and other land anyone would buy to fund the last gasps of English lifestyles. Galleries and museums became potted repositories for the bits and pieces of a past nobody bought.

Wearing identification badges on their shirt and dress lapels, the last of the volunteers maintained the forts, castles, and other buildings of old England they'd long safeguarded, but couldn't restore the antique people dying around them. They sealed with imposing locks and chains the jaded buildings within their custody, preserving them for tourists no longer coming. Gilt-patterned doorways, medieval tapestries, and repeatedly restored wallpapers languished in the dark. The volunteers died, and their treasures died with them.

Public libraries remained open in County Durham, for unpaid librarians to sit where they were comfortable. People who'd walked past them when they had somewhere else to go bravely went inside. They even borrowed books with crisp, neat pages previously unread; what computer records had made redundant were again useful, not just for people wanting to touch the words they read. A little literature helped them think, when they hadn't thought enough or thought too much. They helped them dream, when they needed desperately to dream.

The last thespians read old sonnets in the daylight of Market Square in Darlington. They performed short plays for the small audiences surviving.

Depleting council finances required the closure of several services. Having lost her job, Neve remained at her desk, whimsically playing with her borough council plaque in her hand.

"What will you do?" Hollie asked her. They were the only people there.

Neve turned around, slowly shaking her head. Her eyes trained on Hollie. "What can I do?"

"You don't *have* to do anything."

Neve continued staring, before turning her head away. "I could grow petunias, I suppose," she said. "I always liked petunias."

"You can have my job," Hollie told her, unconcerned whether she had the right to give it. "I've more to do than lose my time in work or leisure."

Neve perked up. "We need to preserve our art!"

"We need to preserve ourselves."

Hollie walked away, without bothering to take her last possessions from her desk. She rode her bicycle along Feethams, headed home with thoughts she should be doing more to help people around her, when she came behind a black-and-yellow ambulance. Its pace was casual, without a siren sounding. She began to follow it, circumspect in what she thought, until it reached the Darlington Memorial Hospital. She'd not been there since she gave birth to Brandon.

The only buildings still drawing crowds in County Durham were hospitals. They'd become hospices and sanatoriums for people waiting to die, where free men and women mooched about with walking sticks and frames. The once powerful and powerless, the brave and timid, were equal among the dying and dead. Filling the kerbs and car park were the cars of people who'd driven themselves there, without driving away again.

Hollie stopped her bicycle where it would not obstruct anyone. Stepping from the ambulance were two men not quite old, one a little taller than the other, both at least a dozen years older than she was. The hospital orderlies wore matching uniforms of orange shirts and trousers atop white rubber shoes. Opening the ambulance rear, they helped a frail, much older man into a black wheelchair.

The old man's arms and body trembled. His crooked, outstretched fingers shook, wanting to hold something without anything to hold. Dumped into his wheelchair, his hands and fingers remained stretched outward, gripping fast to nothingness.

The taller orderly looked to Hollie beside her bicycle. "Few patients get visitors," he said to her. "Are you preparing for when the rest of us aren't here?"

"I'm trying to help."

Leaving her bicycle, Hollie walked behind them pushing the old man in the wheelchair. The orderlies' only qualifications were their relative youth and health aside the people they brought. Their reward might've been feeling useful or the promises of hospital beds when they were difficult to get. Carrying the dying to their deathbeds was the best work left available through the last days of their people, better than taking bodies from beds to bury.

The doors across the hospital's main entranceway remained closed. The wheelchair stopped, an orderly pushed one door open. The space beyond the door was dark, lit only by the light of day coming through the door and windows. "Don't you have electricity?" asked Hollie.

"We don't want to attract more people," the taller orderly replied.

Inside was an odour that any breeze behind her couldn't blow away. The reception area was crammed with old men and women sitting in different sizes and shapes of chairs, save only for an aisle between them wide enough for a single wheelchair. Beyond the aisle were two wide doors, without handles. Frosted covers along the ceiling were all that remained in memory of the bright fluorescent lights that once lit everything. Dust soiled the grooves of the inactive air-conditioning vents.

Uninterested in the men in orange uniforms or another anonymous cripple in a wheelchair, the pond of docile, lonely faces stared at the younger woman. Paused from reading to look up at the distraction, some people near the windows sat with thick books of text printed in large type; torn and yellowed pages for people with poor eyesight. Others were forever gazing towards the open door and daylight. Their frightened, weary eyes affirmed where they had come and to where they all were heading.

In that den of morbid looming death, Hollie had never before felt so young. She had never before felt so old.

"They come here every day," the taller orderly told Hollie, as if they couldn't hear him. "Fearing the first symptoms of diseases they don't understand, they're too frail to trust what they sense about their bodies. Their beds at home keep them warm, but nobody brings them food to eat, so they shuffle their last motions to be here. They bring their chairs or use the chairs that other people left, passing books around the room. If they're too tired to go home, they sleep here overnight." The television monitors that once dulled time for waiting patients were dark. "If we played them movies, then more of them would come." The speakers high on the walls were silent. "If we played them music, they'd only cry."

None of the old men and women spoke. They might've been too tired to talk, or might've had nothing left to say. People didn't need to speak when they were all thinking the same thoughts, although that hadn't deterred them when their thoughts were not so bleak. They mightn't have bothered imparting their thoughts or cared about the thoughts that others made.

"Some wait for the next available bed," the orderly explained, "although being here doesn't move their names up any list. Some want people around them, until they're feeling better or become so sick they die where somebody will find them."

"How do you save them from pain?"

The orderly shook his head. "We don't send them away."

At the far end of the aisle between them, one of the two wide doors squeaked open. Coming through was an old woman in a bland grey dress, carrying a basket. She offered slices of bread to people bedded in their chairs.

"Thank you, dear," said some of them. Others took bread without speaking.

Without looking up, the woman offered bread to the old man in the wheelchair he didn't take. Unconcerned about ingratitude, people without vocations tended to the sick and weak they too would soon become.

Nobody needed to tell Hollie that the scene before her was being played every day, in the last hospitals still open in towns and cities that had aged. The scene would only end when the last of them to die was in their final resting beds. She alone among the people there would see that day and every sullen day thereafter.

"Come along," the taller orderly told Hollie.

The shorter orderly slowly pushed the wheelchair carrying the old man along the aisle reserved for them. The taller orderly walked behind them, while Hollie followed him. The eyes of the old men and women tracked Hollie moving past, their heads slowly turning as she walked. The guiding light from the windows behind her abated, as she walked further into the dusk the ceiling cast.

Theirs were the shadows against the double doors, which the wheelchair slowly pushed open. The wheelchair rolled into the night of a wide corridor, broken by weak light from doors kept open along the faded walls. Following it was each orderly and finally Hollie holding the door open, until she let it swing closed behind them. From somewhere, perhaps everywhere, soft sobbing came. The floors of speckled vinyl reflected the last trickles of small light from windows that Hollie couldn't see, around open doors and corners of the corridor.

The orderlies and Hollie followed the old man in his rolling chair, a short procession the orderlies led along the corridor and through an open doorway. In the light of clear glass windows was a ward of six hospital steel beds, with thick white pillows and sheets not quite so white.

"Seventeen plus twenty-seven," muttered to himself one old man in a bed, holding his spectacles in his hands. He paused before deciding, "Forty-four." Pleased with himself, he continued. "Forty-four plus twenty-seven." He remained silent.

Seeing him struggle to calculate what once he must have calculated easily, Hollie thought of telling him the answer, but doing so would only sadden him. Too softly for anyone else to hear, he whispered his best guess.

In another bed, an old man held a gold fob watch in his hands, running his fingers around the edges. Hanging from a metal rod above his head was a plastic bag of saline fluid, which dripped through a long tube into a bandage on his wrist.

Among the few professions to survive the end of economics were medical: aged doctors and nurses, along with people trying to be them. They administered morphine and other anaesthetics to shield the dead from any sense that they were dying. Their legacy would end when their last patients died.

Another old man sat on his bed, staring at the framed photograph on the bedside table: a young man with long brown hair and firm square jaw. The old man's hair was white and face was falling from its bones.

One bed in the ward was unoccupied, but with open sheets and a blanket awaiting the next man to die among them. The shorter orderly parked the wheelchair beside the bed. "I can help," said Hollie.

"You can't," the taller orderly told her.

She held the old man's elbows anyway, as the orderlies wrapped their arms around him. His shaking was more pronounced than ever as they grappled lifting him, while he struggled to escape. The old man was heavier than his frailty implied: the dead weight of the nearly dead. Finally, they pushed him into bed. Safe within the sheets, the shorter orderly drew the blanket over him.

Hanging from the foot of the bed was a clipboard with an ink pen, held by a piece of string. Several names and dates of admission and death were listed on a sheet of paper, with lines crossed through all the names. The last man to lie there died that morning; the sheets and pillowcase seemed suddenly unclean. The taller orderly picked up the clipboard and wrote the date of the admission next in the list, although Hollie wondered why. "What was his name again?" he asked the shorter orderly.

"Stafford, Niles Orton Stafford."

"You have a better memory than I do."

"I'll forget it before the next one."

The orderly replaced the clipboard at the foot of the bed. The shorter orderly pushed the empty wheelchair from the room. Hollie followed them, back into and along the dark corridor to another ward lit by windows from the day outside. Five old women lay in the five visible beds: more aged cripples in their burial cloths. A plastic white curtain surrounded the sixth bed in the ward.

In one bed, a woman cradled in her arms a large black frame in which was a certificate. Her name was embossed in gold scrolled lettering.

A woman in another bed held up her limpid wrist. She gaped into the twists of light reflected from her diamond bracelet, as if it could too easily fall if she stopped concentrating hard upon it.

Another woman sat still and high against her upright pillow, not spoiling her strawberry blonde brushed hair. Thick wads of white powder covered her face and neck. Dull lipstick coated her lips. Bright pink polish adorned her fingernails conspicuously resting atop the sheets in front of her. Masquerading as a woman younger than she ever was, she watched Hollie watching her.

Hollie glanced at the small table beside her bed, hosting an array of paints and perfumes, among hairbrushes with tattered bristles and combs with broken teeth. The round silver hand mirror she recognised. The woman had lived near Hollie's home, but her hair dye no longer convinced. The powder and lipstick were no longer so well applied.

The taller orderly dragged aside the plastic curtain around the last bed in the room, revealing an old woman lying motionless. Hollie gasped. No one else did.

The dead woman's separated eyes hung almost closed. Her speckled skin draped against her reconstructed facial bones. Every twist of cosmetic surgery that once made her aging face look young, only made her aged face look older: grotesque vindictive swipes at what she once believed. Along the inside of her arms were needle marks.

Beside the body on the sheet lay a little watch, its rear battery compartment open and empty. The dead woman's fists clenched close to her.

"No mortal man or woman can help her now," the taller orderly told Hollie. The shorter orderly pushed the empty wheelchair beside the bed.

"How did she die?" asked Hollie.

He stared at Hollie and her ignorance. "Old people die."

The shorter orderly took hold of the woman's nearest hand. He prized open the dead woman's fingers, revealing in her hand a small silver coin. "Head or tails?" he asked the other orderly, preparing to toss the coin into the air.

"You have it."

The shorter orderly examined the coin, before leaving it by the watch. He didn't bother opening the dead woman's other hand.

The orderlies lifted the dead woman's body into the wheelchair. The shorter one pushed it away, with the other and Hollie following him. "Our mission," the taller orderly told Hollie as they walked, "is trying to make transition into death as simple as we can, trying not to leave a mess behind."

They returned to the dark corridor, where the orderlies turned away from the reception area and stopped. "You don't want to come any further," the taller orderly told her.

Hollie stopped. She stepped back a little.

"Would you be doing anything more important than we're doing? Please clean up after us when we've gone."

The two orderlies turned and pushed the corpse away. The orderlies would likely die before Hollie became a patient there, and her son would not allow his parents to die in such a place. With a family with whom to be, Hollie turned and walked back along the corridor, towards the two wide doors.

Pushing open a door back to the reception area of dying eyes watching her again, she turned her face towards the floor. Her low-heeled shoes flapped on the vinyl with each slow step she made. Looking downwards, she saw her feet and legs easing embarrassed along the aisle, threading through the crowded melee of trouser legs and surgical stockings along her vision edge.

Close to the door outside, her downward eyes were attracted to a small blue crystal lying on the floor. She stopped to study it, and bent down to pick it up. The crystal in her fingers was a sapphire. Suddenly, from the pool of chairs around her, an old man's rough skin and bones grabbed her arm.

Squeezing Hollie's arm with his last force exerted in that grip, her arm trembled with his hand. She saw the old man's face, her eyes met his, burrowed from their hollows pleading fiercely with her. The air breathed freely through Hollie's lungs and her heart beat surely, but they breathed and beat weakly inside him. If death frightened the old man, the death of everything frightened him still more. His mind beyond those anguished eyes begged her, as did scores of other men and woman in the room, but only God could make the chance they wanted.

Holding her arm fast in his hands might've helped his flesh and soul feel something of a youth, a sense of future and of hope. Hollie's hands almost sixty years of age were tender soft, like those of someone else's baby, for the old man dying so soon before her. Any virtues he took did not deplete in her.

"I know," whispered Hollie. "I know." Anything she could do for him she had already done. All else she could do was vow not to live as they had lived, but she'd vowed that long ago.

Hollie thought of apologising she could do nothing more, but her regret would not alleviate the moments of his passing. He might've wanted her to save him and must've known that she could not. He might've wanted her to ferry him back through time to ages past where only fantasies could take him, to do things he hadn't done. Hollie would've changed their lives if she could do so, making all of them parents of the children to keep England alive, but the past wasn't hers to change. She would've done so for her family as well as doing so for them.

The old man continued staring at her eyes, grasping her pale arm. Hollie wanted to leave, without languishing in the pain they'd brought upon them all, but wouldn't wrestle herself free from the old man's touch.

His eyes slowly relaxed. He nodded, as he released his grip on Hollie's arm. A timid, uneasy acknowledgement broke from his brittle lips.

Hollie pulled away her arm. She placed her hand in the old man's open hand, touching him a final time, before walking away. Lying in the old man's palm was the sapphire she'd picked up from the floor.

13

SURROGATE DEATH

Gerald stood beside his aged mother at his father's funeral, comforting her in her distress, as did their last surviving friends. He'd rarely thought enough of death in his short long life, but all the people his parents once knew were dead or soon would die. Most of what he knew about his parents lay in the fact that he was ever born. They were different to other people by reason alone of being his parents, and were different to most other people by being parents at all. They'd been kind enough to bear a child when few English people did, but if they told him things about themselves then he had not been listening.

His mother's friends also passed away. Only Gerald stood mourning at her funeral.

He returned alone to his parents' empty home on Bedburn Drive, Hummersknott, where the last car his mother drove stood parked inside the garage. Her aromatic garden remained neat between houses with gardens becoming overgrown because Gerald had tended to it, in her final months of life.

Gerald opened the windows to allow fresh air and light of day to cleanse the rooms a final time. Washing powders, an umbrella, some books from a shelf, might be useful to him. He stowed them in his car. Few foods were in the refrigerator trays and kitchen pantry shelves, but he took what he could eat and drink. Portions of perishable food that rats might want he left in a corner of the garden. He made the telephone calls to disconnect the utilities from the house, before he switched off every electric power point and checked each tap was tightly fastened.

On a shelf in the lounge room stood two silver trophies. The larger one his parents received playing bridge in local tournaments. The inscription on the plaque at the base of the smaller trophy recorded that it was awarded to a member of a champion schoolboy rugby team: "*Gerald Keaton.*" He wondered what became of him.

The bedrooms were upstairs. If Gerald could give away the clothes his parents kept in their bedroom wardrobe then he would, but other empty homes already housed too much to wear. Some of his father's clothes and hats fitting his head Gerald took. He tidied his parents' bed.

On his mother's dressing table lay a white photograph album, without the dust of elsewhere. Any sense saved in photographs was his companionship: his past returned.

Standing in the silence but for the turns of heavy pages, faces frozen in photograph from before his birth let Gerald contemplate his parents being young. His mother had been elegant, his father brash. The faces smiled and stared, exuding them and time together. They never seemed to age, but people age.

A photograph was of a baby Gerald didn't recognise. Playing on the grass in another photograph was a small boy he couldn't quite recall. His photographic face had become artificial through adolescence into manhood, boasting happiness for everyone to see. They bound him to an age much younger than the man had come to be. His parents were again the parents of his youth and he was the child of theirs: that family of faces in which each of them belonged. His life was sweet for being his, much too short to end.

His journey was to history when he had no future left. Photographs were poor substitutes for people.

Gerald had no call to rush back to Marlborough Drive, where the street was grey and his apartment dull. No longer had he the life and leisure that once distracted him: working in his office, drinking in a bar afterwards, and eating dinner in a restaurant. There'd been a time he was content to seem to be setting forward, presuming without reason he was doing more than his parents ever did.

Their great society would soon expire, but his childhood home was a place to be when too few of them remained. Standing at the conservatory, where the air was warm but the trees and garden so immediate through the glass surrounds, wasn't quite as tranquil as it had been when he was young, but was still more peaceful than anything else he knew.

Gerald explored the house for clues about his parents and about him, searching for the story of a life when he had nothing else to do. Understanding some small aspects of his parents might help him learn a little of the place from which he'd come, if not the place to which he headed. He, the orphan son, inspected the house more thoroughly than he, the parented child, ever had.

Gerald's childhood bedroom was alien to adult him, but remained familiar to something long forgotten lost inside him. It had been his room, in a time he played, and laughed, and knew someone.

His mother said she set sheets and blankets neatly on his bed for guests to use, but no guests had ever come. The last of his young man's clothes hung in the wardrobe. Hanging from the wall was the last picture from his youth: a small boy gazing sheepishly. Gerald recognised in his reflection the children that all of them once were. "What do you know?" he asked. "What can you teach me?"

The top panel of his old oak desk contained pens and paper for letters that nobody would write; his parents hadn't thrown much away. Nearer the floor were two small doors to several shelves storing cardboard boxes. Struggling to keep his balance reaching low with his clumsy arms and legs, Gerald eased down to the carpet. Strangely childlike sitting there, his thick legs could not cross easily. He left them stretched across the floor, while he opened the first box.

It contained papers from his adolescent life unseen by Gerald since he was young: school reports, notes of sports he'd played and activities he'd tried. He saw again a little boy no worse than the aging man became. His thick, rough fingers couldn't have drawn and painted the pictures in his hands: wild and foolish strokes not obviously anything. Birthday cards from his parents commemorated ages much too small to have been his.

His parents might've kept them to contemplate but never did, or might've looked at them each day. They'd valued them enough to keep them safe, while Gerald wasn't there.

Another box contained exercise books that Gerald used at school: reckless words of a small boy he hadn't known for years. The aging adult was no longer reckless. The small boy's handwriting had been frail, as Gerald's would again become.

Browsing through the books, Gerald recovered poetry he'd written; he hadn't so much as read a poem since leaving school. If adult lives were ever time to make believe then he'd surely reached that time, but the boy's imagination had become incomprehensible to him. The man who'd written poems as a schoolboy couldn't write them anymore. He couldn't compose another if it was his chance to save the world and people in it. In a sense, it might've been.

That room remained so much as it had been, convicting Gerald that his parents thought about him far more often and profoundly than he'd ever thought of them. He was an interest for them getting old; that might've been all they needed him to be. He was also the guest for whom they kept his room.

Gerald would remove the relics before a burglar took them, but no burglar was coming. Gerald returned the boxes to where he'd found them, the place his parents kept them, and closed the two desk doors. The boxes weren't merely his to keep.

Thoughts of standing up from the floor daunted him in his maturity. Gerald remained sitting where he sat when he was young.

He'd shared so much his childhood days and nights with his parents, but shared too little more. He longed to know how great or deep had been their affection for him, but he alone could not determine it. If he sat with them again, then he would try to glean their feelings from anything they said and did.

His eyes became cloudy, as they should at funerals. Gerald realised why he'd come.

His parents' feelings for their son, like their feelings for each other, remained elusive. They might've loved, been loved, least of all by him. They might've loved more or less than they were loved. They may not have called their feelings for him love. Their feelings might've mattered only to them and might no longer matter, aside from being the family unknown to him before that day. Gerald wondered whether to wish he'd told his parents more about his life and him, but there was no purpose in what dead men and women knew. If his parents hadn't loved him, no one had.

Thoughts turned to dreams and back again. Imaginings might've been revelation of a truth, in another place in which he sat alone. They might've been just him, groping for solutions and a love, and been more than his parents' identity with him and kindness warranted. His parents might've felt less sadness for the brevity of time he spent with them than was the sore regret he'd come to feel, sitting in their old and empty home. His feelings needed to be important only to him, but they were so hard to find. His life was the only life he knew.

Turning himself to his side, his hands pressed against the floor helped Gerald clamour up again. Finally, he stood, a little wearily, back on his feet. He closed the top panel to the desk; the key to it was missing. He closed every window and checked every door was locked, to seal that home secure. He drew closed the curtains across the windows, leaving the records of his past to lie alone.

A headstone to recall them and somewhere for him to go, his parents' pretty house memorial was still just a memorial. A memorial needed memories and Gerald might've been the only person to remember them. The most colourful of the small flowers in the garden he'd kept were yellow. Respectfully, he laid a posy outside the door. Flowers, like funerals, weren't for the dead, but for the mourners.

Gerald drove slowly back past homes becoming empty to the apartment in which he'd lived since arriving there a young man. All but two residents had left or passed away.

Doris Poedecker continued writing notices that only Gerald read: the lift had ceased operating and couldn't be repaired; the borough council's intermittent garbage collections had stopped and residents should leave their garbage where it would not entice stray animals. She could've placed her notices outside the door to Gerald's apartment or knocked on his door, but she continued addressing notices to all the residents and affixing them to the board in the building entrance hall.

When he hadn't seen another notice for too many weeks on end, he wondered if she was too sick to leave her home. He thought of taking food to her, until he saw another notice. However sick she was, no medical officer could force her from her home and her brown cat, forever rubbing its fur against the stockings on her legs.

Electric street lighting became rationed, but no notice to residents appeared. Several months had passed since Gerald last saw Doris. A month had passed since her most recent notice, about the cessation of the last bus services. Like her other notices, it mentioned below her name the number of her apartment, in the top storey of the building.

A little weary after climbing so many flights of stairs, Gerald pressed the button beside the door of her apartment. The bell that once rung inside her home no longer functioned; he didn't know if his still did. He knocked on the door, then watched the tiny round glass peephole beneath his eye level for any far-side shadows. None appeared. Gerald placed his ears to the door and listened. He couldn't hear a thing.

After going back down every stair and outside, Gerald stood on Marlborough Drive and looked up at the top storey of the building. Doris' apartment windows were closed, except the spare bedroom window ever so slightly open, as the old woman might've kept it for her cat. The curtains were all open except those thick curtains to the main bedroom, as a woman sleeping through the day would close them. (The floorplan of Doris' home would have been the same as Gerald's.)

Becoming wearier, Gerald again trudged up every stair; walking up and down so many stairs might've killed her. In his free hand not on the banister, he carried an iron crowbar from the boot of his car, uncertain how to use it to open a locked apartment door. For good measure, he again knocked on Doris' door. If she answered then he would smile. "I'm checking you're safe," he would explain.

"Thank you," she might smile, although she'd never before said so much to him. "I've been unwell." She might then add, "I was about to come down and put a notice on the board." Its subject might be residents carrying crowbars in the corridors.

Gerald became uneasy that he would find somebody dead. Human beings were dying, but he'd been spared the sight of death; his mother's doctor found her passed away in bed. Dead people left bodies, and Doris might've been a corpse on a musty kitchen floor. Faces of the dead he'd known, however slightly, were more frightening than all the faces of the dead he'd never known alive.

He should've left, if he ever should've come. Instead, he placed his hand on the doorknob and slowly turned it. Expecting the door to be locked, the handle turned full circle. Only people fearing death above them left their doors unlocked. Fearing that he would find her dead beyond the door, Gerald tentatively pushed it forward. A latch behind the door might've held it almost closed. The door opened as he pushed.

The air was old. Doris could easily be lying there, dead or just alive; Gerald didn't know what smell dead people made. He would need people's help to move her. Perhaps he should have already called. Leaving the crowbar on the carpet outside her door, he stepped inside.

A short hallway opened into a lounge room like the one in his apartment, but with décor much older and darker than in his. Doris wasn't there.

The cushions on the chairs and their upholstery were savagely torn. Knocked over on a table, amidst ruffled white lace, were at least a dozen little resin badgers. More replica midget badgers lay on the floor. He half-imagined Doris' cat leaping maniacally from a corner, its claws poised to kill him.

The layout of the rooms was the same as his apartment, however foreboding was her fashion. Gerald opened the windows for clean air to seep into the room.

Across the closed kitchen cupboard doors and around the handles were superficial scratches. Gerald opened the most scratched door, revealing in abundance on the shelves tall tin cans of cat food. That meat and jelly had been a feast for pets, but was not for human consumption. He closed the door again.

In the bathroom hung two long-sleeved blouses and pleated skirts. They all were dry.

Stepping closer to the bedrooms, the air quickly became pungent. A sickly stench almost overpowered him, before he pinched his nose to thwart the smell. The smell of something rotten might've been food through several weeks. The odour might also have been a body dead.

On the floor of the lesser bedroom was a cradle. In it were several small torn cushions and strewn sheets. Gerald opened the window wider, pushing away the worst of the aroma. Only the main bedroom remained.

More cautiously, he approached the open doorway into that darkened room. The stench of stagnant death swamped the air. Too many patients suffered allergies for doctors and nurses to allow pets near hospital beds, and Doris might've preferred to die with her cat in her apartment than live anywhere without it. Again, Gerald pressed his fingers against his nose. He closed his mouth.

Stepping into the shaded room, he saw the end of a large dishevelled bed. He hurried past the bed to the thick curtains he threw apart. Quickly, Gerald opened the windows, admitting clean air.

The light and outside air alleviated everything as Gerald again breathed freely. Slowly, he turned around. Across the chaotic queen-sized bed were strewn white sheets, in the midst of which lay Doris' unrecognisable cat. It had torn its mistress' sheets and blankets, grappling for food or terror-struck, before dying ragged, alone in its captivity.

The screams of a beleaguered cat desperate for sustenance and mercy hadn't reached Gerald in his downstairs apartment; the apartments had been built for peace and quiet. It kept the sounds, not just of people, far apart. They might've permeated the adjoining empty premises or reached the empty street outside, where passing cats and dogs had no regard to help another dying animal. Men and women wandering wearily couldn't have known from where the screams were coming, or they might have become too deaf to hear.

The month since Doris' last notice was time enough for the cat to starve. She might've gone to a hospital, entrusting her cat's care to somebody who died.

Its wretched corpse remained, but Gerald couldn't bury every dead animal he found. He would take it far away, as Doris would've wanted him to do in her next notice.

Warily touching the bedclothes but not the body, Gerald couldn't help but smell it close to him. Holding his head away and holding his breath did not keep out the stink. The cat was warm, not long dead, as he wrapped up that little death, from which oozed the fluid of its dying. He bundled up the soiled sheets and blankets, leaving the mattress almost clean.

Nothing leaked from the mortuary cloths, as Gerald, holding it away from him, carried the swaddled cat through Doris' apartment to the building corridor and down the stairs. Still wondering what do with it, he carried it from the building.

South Park had once been respite from traffic, when surrounding streets had been too loud, but no longer was there noise from which to take relief. What had been silent became a sound, with only Gerald there to hear. Lapping its banks as it had always lapped them was the rippling River Skerne, its waters dark, devoid of human presence, much as the county was becoming.

From the middle of the bridge, Gerald held above the flowing waterway the rolled bedclothes. Human laws forbid him dropping a dead cat body in that once public place, but human laws weren't important anymore. Always careful to keep the touch of death away from him, he loosened the sheets and blankets, until the cat fell out. The water splashed, and the lowly body bobbed up and down before settling on the surface, drifting away. Gerald dropped the bedclothes into the river for them to rot.

The water might usurp the body of the cat or carry it downstream. The birds might peck at it, if it washed onto a shore. Fish might eat it in the water. Its journey over, the cat would disappear.

The deaths of shrivelled pets in homes and endurance of livestock in the pastures might have been ironic. Farmers had bred cows, sheep, and pigs for human beings to eat, but few farmers remained to kill them and deliver meats to market.

A blanket in which the cat's body had been wrapped became caught in a small nook on the riverbank. Nothing mattered by it being there while it rotted, or until a wave of running waters dislodged it; only something someone saw could be unsightly.

Death's aroma emanated from Gerald's hands. Leaving the bridge, he washed his hands in the river until they were almost clean.

Gerald returned to what had been Doris' home, from which he saw South Park as he couldn't see it from his apartment. Parks once quaint sojourns from modern pressures had become equally sullen spaces.

Doris' kitchen contained preserved food and beverage for human beings, which Gerald would eat and drink before they wasted. The bottle of milk in the lukewarm refrigerator was sour. What had been meat, fruit, and vegetables were difficult to recognise, smelling as putrid as the cat. Carrying the refuse with him in the shopping bag Doris had used to bring them there, Gerald closed the windows, drew closed the curtains, and closed the doors.

On the grass of Marlborough Drive, Gerald turned her shopping bag upside down and strewed the rotting foodstuffs. He poured the sour milk onto the ground, through which it seeped. Discarded containers he dropped in a low gutter by the street, where birds and animals could lick more little sustenance. He stuffed the empty bag into a rubbish bin, not for any reason.

Rain threatened to fall as Gerald stepped back into his aged apartment building. Alone in that brick matrix that once had been so many homes, with its noticeboard crammed thick with papers, he'd become the final resident.

14

SMALL PORTALS TO OTHER WORLDS

Hanging by its last adhesive from a dusty storefront window, a notice invited people to send old spectacles to Africa. Gerald's eyes would fade and he would need eyeglasses, but Africans weren't sending redundant spectacles to Europe. People left behind would have to help themselves, but Gerald couldn't grind the late optometrist's leftover lenses or fit them into frames.

The families of North Lodge Terrace and the like kept to themselves, provided English people and police didn't infringe upon their area. When Darlington Borough Council and other services waned, they moved to cities with more of their own.

Too few people remained to conduct elections in County Durham and fewer bothered to vote, but if anyone wanted to sustain the process, then he or she could become a Darlington borough councillor; council wards were immaterial. Committees folded leaving just the council, which brought its meetings in the town hall chamber forward to the middle of the day, so they could return home before dark. The worshipful the mayor adjourned the meeting if rain was falling or the day too hot or cold.

An old woman wrote the minutes of every meeting with a pencil in a notebook, to file later with other rotting records. The minutes recorded a councillor's absence, without mention of a reason.

Gerald was the only observer in the gallery when three councillors discussed means of bringing more chicken eggs to town, without reaching a conclusion. They agreed only to discuss the matter when next they met.

Without debate but with three long speeches favouring the motion, the three councillors condemned new laws in Suriname, violence in Paramaribo, and the Surinamese government's imposition of a curfew. Councillors passed resolutions sympathising with the plight of Surinamese, demanding peace and negotiation, and granting refuge to rioters fleeing police and to police fleeing rioters. Councillors supported economic and political liberalisation in Suriname, without needing to know the status of its economy or politics. Deprived of official means of conveying the council's resolution, since the last British Honorary Consul left Paramaribo, the mayor would send it by electronic mail.

Among the pretty pictures Gerald had collected through his life, hanging from the walls around his home, one more than any other dragged his gaze upon it: the white lighthouse at Sandy Hook, New Jersey. Few ships and aircraft still breached the wide Atlantic Ocean, and Gerald would never see the sands of the Jersey Shore. He would never cast his eyes upon reality behind that meek impression. It ridiculed a man without a reason to look closely at the journeys he never took, to places he'd never see. He'd earned enough to do most things he never did.

Holidays were obsolete for people with too little work from which to rest and no reason to go anywhere they could not remain forever. African, Asian, and ocean paradises found they didn't need the handsome travellers; the travellers no longer came and they were no longer handsome. Chair lifts and gondolas stood idle in West European snowfields, while the last people near them pursued milder weather in the lowlands. Few waiters still served cocktails on the sand and pebble beaches.

His large cream-coloured sofa had dulled becoming worn, but was still Gerald's most comfortable place to rest. Oblivious to everything outside the windows of the last drab homes still occupied, the last British radio station broadcast familiar melodies. Music that evolved when Gerald was a boy no longer did.

The Darlington Arena closed, the last British television station broadcast sporting contests from distant stadiums. Instead of clubs, those distant people chanted for their countries.

Most prolifically, the station broadcast old movies and television series, diverting the eyes and ears of people left alone from feeling lonely in their homes. Watching young actors and actresses kiss to harpsichord descants were old men and women who'd never kissed so well. Gerald smiled and cried vicariously according to the orchestral overlay, seeing actors and actresses who'd long died of their old age. Immortality in celluloid wasn't immortality at all.

For as long as he watched and listened, Gerald believed the world remained unchanged. What had been distraction from something became distraction from everything, throughout his waking hours. He shared his home with imagery.

The last public utilities became increasingly unreliable. Telephone exchanges failed, without people to repair them. Power plants and grids stumbled without regular raw materials, leaving more and more blackouts. Without electricity to power pumps and valves, water couldn't come through taps and natural gas couldn't come through pipes. The people left became too few and knew too little to manage the machinery upon which they depended. Engineering that conquered ground and sky had stalled.

Computer terminals and television sets succumbed to their involuntary slumber. Gerald stared simply at the cold dead projection glass, waiting for lights to shine and sounds to stir. Seeing only his small portion, he could no longer see the world.

The homes in which men and women had walked a thousand times in electric light without a thought became alien to them. Only the uneasy lights of torches from their hands and expiring batteries guided them through the dark. They were lowly days with nothing left to see or do and all day in which to see and do it.

Gerald took battery-powered games from stores without storekeepers, paying for them by leaving money he didn't need on the counters. At home, he played the contests in transistors and on small screens in his hands: aliens at war and animals catching fruit.

From his lounge room window, Gerald stared across Marlborough Drive, hoping that people he didn't touch would entertain. An older man sitting at an open window also stared outwards, his head and eyes moving until they met Gerald's. The two men stared at each other, without acknowledging the other. Gerald thought of waving, but if the old man also waved, he wouldn't know what to do. They couldn't talk across the open street.

If Gerald saw him when he walked outside then he might speak with him, although he wouldn't know what to say. They'd known enough in olden days to talk of work, of plays and restaurants, but couldn't talk about them anymore.

The two men continued staring at each other, until a bird flying between them allowed their eyes to follow it away. When next Gerald noticed that window across the street, a curtain was closed across it. They'd let their land die choosing to live alone, and couldn't easily change their choices because England was nearly dead.

Each time the electricity supply restarted, Gerald's appliances revived. His television set once more played illuminated dots. He reset his kitchen clock to the correct time, resumed watching television, and never needed to recall the blackout had occurred. The setting was much like it had always been.

The men and women dying hadn't lived their lives, but merely watched or heard the ones who did. They still weren't participating, wasting their wasteful time.

Gerald's life alone was worse than just being without the good things he once knew, for he'd lost more than merely means of work and leisure time. Recorded faces and voices left behind were weak substitutes for love and life; songs sounded sadder every time he heard them. None of it meant much without society.

Embedded in the silence, his dream of a long memory searched for companionship that present senses couldn't give him. Long-ago Vanessa became vivid in his brain. The evaporation of his life that could've kept her from him only revealed more of her to him. That sweet woman exuded life in population and prosperity, seemingly enduring and content, too many short years earlier. She'd left him sitting alone too late each night. Every means to leisure was merely killing time without a woman with him there.

Not for any reason except to know he'd tried, Gerald drove six miles from Darlington to Heighington, where the air was damper than at home and shrubbery obscured much that had been visible when last he visited. One among another row of two-storey terraced houses, he stood before Vanessa's home.

No longer was he so strong as to grapple over the gate, but the gate once locked no longer was. Cautiously pushing it open, the rusting hinges squeaked. Swollen wood scraped against the path, sweeping back rotten fallen leaves.

Approaching the white front door, seeing again the colourful plants in pots, her words and mood, her sense and sensitivity, when last he saw her recurred inside his mind. The white silk curtains were drawn closed beyond her lounge room window. If her home was still furnished as it had been, with sleek white walls and carpet, he couldn't see.

The knocks Gerald's hand could make against the grooved door were much softer since last he'd knocked there. His imagination pictured her opening the door before him, wrapping her arms around him, and kissing him more passionately than she'd ever before kissed him.

The liar's reason that once quelled his feelings for her no longer could. "You were so right," he'd tell her unconstrained, laughing with the freedom of his release from beliefs he once demanded. "I love you."

"I love you, Gerry, with all I am."

Gripped in their joy and passion, they'd kiss again. She'd not mention the gravity of his past error, but he'd mock himself for everything he'd said when they were young. He'd learned to love her. He'd loved her more than he'd confessed before she went. She'd be content to love him no less for it, to let him cuddle her inside their home.

Nobody answered. She might've been staying with friends or been away on holidays; she'd closed the curtains before leaving. When Gerald knew her, she'd not kept pets that required her there or other accommodation while she travelled. He would travel anywhere to find her, but did not know where to go. If he waited long enough, then she might come to see him.

The longer Gerald stood remembering, the more he saw the changes time imposed. Moss was in the flowerpots, rust reddened the door hinges. Bugs had excreted small blotches of white and grey on the window. Gerald placed his hand on the doorknob and tried to turn it. The door was locked.

A small space between the curtains and window frame allowed him to peer through the glass onto the lounge room floor. Sunlight through the silk left supple shadows on the carpet, on which lay a broken vase.

Gerald wasn't brave or cruel enough to break through her front door into her parlour; it mightn't still have been her home. He knew just enough to contemplate, waiting hopelessly for her.

Sitting at his desk each day in Darlington before his small computer screen, Gerald watched the passing people becoming old as he would be, or might have already been. News reports said little of the agedness, but cameras broadcast images from public places around the world.

England's story was that of much of modern Europe, Australasia, and Northernmost America, in different rates of ascending gross decline. Estranged colonials in other continents made the mistakes Europeans made at home, faring no better than the other. Continents were dying in their hometowns.

Americans had been so proud to forge their nation, but too few of them remained to defend the Rio Grande. They were whittling far away, wanting cups of middling coffee before they died. European peoples were never more alike than in the manner of their passing; the traits that might've made them each unique were vanishing with them.

The magnitude of what was happening became more vivid with every vacant street and square of encroaching rigor mortis. Gerald stared at the pictures from his sanctuary in solitude. Thoroughfares that once thrived with pedestrians and vehicles were increasingly moribund. The surrealism of one city became more like a nightmare every time his crazy mind saw the vacancy repeated. Places in which people once streamed nonchalantly through their lives were becoming litanies of emptiness, leaving no evidence of the affliction that befell them.

Those images became fewer. Vandals and new authorities killed the cameras.

Climatic change hadn't brought Europe to her knees, whatever people did. Any usual disaster would've slain Gerald in his home; he'd not have come to be alone.

The combat they'd euphemistically called with terrorism might've been more wars Europe lost, but the wars that weakened Gerald's forebears along their journeys hadn't brought Europeans down. There'd been no peals of thunder in the skies, no cataclysm destroying buildings with a bang. There'd been no lightning flashes splitting cities, no huge hailstones crushing countries. No cloud of their calamity was their undoing, no gases poisoning the air. No bodies of the dead and few bodies of the dying, no reasons for the looming end, endured.

The dangers that destroyed them lay not in their vicinity but in themselves. No pestilence could've ravaged human flesh across so much earth as did the death Europe inflicted on herself. The warnings of catastrophe never contemplated Europeans fading to the few. Great man, the civilised races who once conquered the world, was simply growing old. The end of aged populations that could've been more gradual came more suddenly than improper forecasts predicted; forecasts of most things had been inaccurate. What might've happened over generations happened in barely one or two. The West frittered far away.

A camera image revealed to Gerald at his computer screen the clouded waterfront in Newport, Rhode Island. A solitary figure walked slowly away, his or her face hidden from Gerald's view.

The figure moved carefully but gracefully, as Englishwomen moved when they were middle-aged. Gerald checked the image date and time to assure himself the image was contemporary. Behind his screen in a small home, Gerald watched her walk inside a camera lens.

He stared mesmerised at her movements, becoming weary as she walked. He adjusted his computer settings trying to make her image larger, but could not discern the person in the pixels. His face close to the screen tried to see around her hair and coat, but the captivating stranger continued walking away.

She could've been anyone; Gerald assumed from her build and gait she was a woman. She might've been the only person left in Newport, or been among thousands but the only one then walking along the waterfront. She might've done all the things Gerald did in the city of her solitude or none of them. She at least was still alive. Perhaps he was, too.

Gerald's hand touched the screen. His fingertip gently caressed the image of a coat across her shoulders. He wanted her to stop and turn to face him, but she couldn't hear his will. If he could shout and draw her back to him then he would do so, but nobody could hear him in his home. If he could press a keyboard button to power a microphone to call her then he would do so. She walked away from camera shot.

She did not walk back again. No other person came. Gerald listened, but could not hear Americans anymore.

In her quiet little home, the woman he'd observed might have seen Gerald's image broadcast from a publicly positioned camera in Darlington, before the last camera stopped, but she and he would never meet. The Newport broadcast ceased. The *Newport Daily News* had stopped reporting news.

While the last lonely Europeans sat in suicidal cities, towns, and villages, other races strode where Europeans didn't. Turks hustled late on bustling streets, not just in Istanbul. Chinese crowded more than Lan Kwai Fong, unconcerned by Europe's quick demise. Through cameras there, Gerald watched activity and youth no longer his.

Their governments granted refuge only to their kind and the handful of others rich enough to pay their way, with more than worthless Western currencies. Unable to reach the Dardanelles, trains to cart refugees from Europe carted them back again.

"*Is the rest of the world waiting for the last of us to pass away,*" typed Gerald, "*or won't it wait?*" He dared not fear invasion, least of all from other parts of England. "*Does it care?*" He received no reply.

Scouring the computer world for company, Gerald felt least lonely exchanging messages with other fractious names. He wrote about recorded music to which he barely listened and movies he hardly watched, but the computer sites were increasingly inactive. The thoughts of hope that life might rescue him faded each time Gerald saw less than he'd last seen. Any technical or electrical corruption could've explained a failure to transmit, but every message reporting a signal's non-receipt connoted technology crumbling down. They were bricks in cyber space and the edifice abating.

The last journalist from the *Northern Echo* newspaper occasionally offered little snippets of the news. In one report, Gerald recognised the name of Niles Stafford's cousin Jaclyn.

Half a century earlier in Leeds, she'd adopted baby Dofi from Ghana. Jaclyn gave her everything she thought a mother gave her child and took from her everything she thought a child gave her mother, but Jaclyn's conviction couldn't make Dofi her daughter. When Dofi was old enough to do so, she beat Jaclyn with a stick and took jewellery that Jaclyn's mother had bequeathed her. Dofi fled back to her family in Birmingham.

While Jaclyn worked and aged, charwomen cleaned her home and gardeners kept her flowers: the people charged with household chores to make everything endure. When Jaclyn became old, caregivers pushed her in her wheelchair, washed her wrinkled body, and cleaned her sheets and bedpans for a fee. "Why would we help her without being paid?" Rizwan asked his wife, providing for their children.

The hosts and hostesses, the aged strangers indulged for being idle, became too few and weak to matter. By the time Jaclyn was eighty-two years old, her dopey eyes fluttered in the haze. Young masseurs pampered her to feel important for having them so near. The only skill they needed was pretending that they cared about her withering skin and bones.

Without friends to hear the words she spoke, she presumed servants to be her friends. She paid Rizwan a little extra to let her finger bones crawl along his soft brown back. Her wavering eyes wallowed in dreams of love, while he surveyed items in her home deciding what he wanted. She asked nothing more of him than to be allowed to touch him, and she gave him a new possession each time he did. Money was all she had and no one else to whom to give it.

From the comfort of his private accommodation, Rizwan laughed at her. When he tired of gifts, they made him angry. "We're harlots," he told his family, "letting her think she loves us."

His wife put her arms around him and stroked his hair. She eased his anger while he was with her, but he loved her too much to accept what he was doing.

Comforting him was the knowledge he was less pathetic than his hostess. Other customers said later that Jaclyn meant only to be kind, that she needed pretence of her youth.

One night while she was lying in her bed, Rizwan took a spare towel from a table. He strangled her small neck.

In Darlington, the man who'd collected so much money around to alleviate other people's problems didn't recognise his own. Carrying an empty tray since the last charity offices had closed, he strode across the streets, confronting a woman carrying a bag of vegetables. "We can't afford the waste," he told her. "Love everyone!"

She started to walk around him but he lunged at her, pushing her to the pavement. Her bag fell from her hands and her vegetables spilled. She gasped for breath, but he began kicking her chest. Passers-by began to shout as loudly as their frail lungs allowed them, while he vengefully kicked the woman on the ground, breaking her brittle bones. She tried to scream and protect her chest with her hands.

"We have responsibilities!" he told her, more virulently kicking her head. "Love everyone!"

Blood rushed from her mouth. She held her hand against her

wounds and lost her grip each time his ferocious foot crashed into her. The red blood she'd spilled swelled into a growing puddle.

Finally exhausted from his rage, he looked around at the crying people frightened of what he'd do to them. His menacing stare demanded they not do what the dead woman had done, although they weren't sure what she'd done. Back home in his solitary cold and dark, he died of his starvation, before police could learn his name.

15

FLYING ON THE GROUND

As their populations withered, able-bodied Englishmen and women collected their best possessions and fled their aging towns. They could've revived their people, but instead went anywhere to find people where they could live alone. From other aging places came other lonely people.

Another clock tower above a Victorian brick building marked the Bank Top railway station, which for many generations had linked Darlington with the rest of England, Scotland, and Wales. Travellers somewhere hurried one way toward the trains or the other way towards taxis, buses, or their cars without anyone to wish them well or welcome them back home; people they called friends were somewhere else. Old soldiers alighted from arriving trains and dawdled to the homes they'd much too rarely seen. The station was their last place to leave and first place to come to Darlington.

Most people at one time or another walked upon the Bank Top railway station. Gerald would've gone there for a train to take him anywhere to go or to welcome anybody coming home to do anything but die, but he found that final thoroughfare empty. Personal luggage trolleys remained neglected by a wall.

Treading through the lifeless concourse, the place for crowds and noise echoed with every single rhythmic step Gerald took.

The stalls and shops were closed, the ticket office unoccupied. Ubiquitous colour posters of the Colombian yellow-eared parrot beckoned attention from people no longer passing by. Two leaves blown in from town lay on the breezeless floor.

Electronic boards once listing times of trains arriving and stations through which they'd come were dark. Departure board displays no longer listed times of trains departing and stations through which they'd go. The only train scheduled to depart, according to a blackboard leaning against a column, was headed to York and London King's Cross from platform 1, shortly before nine o'clock one unnamed early morning. The only train scheduled to arrive was the same train from Edinburgh, nine minutes earlier.

Gerald passed unchallenged to the station proper. There was no train or ragged army trying to leave from platform 1.

A train stood silently by platform 3, on which were large flat trolleys with leather bags and suitcases. The train might've been unrelated to the dusty blackboard message. It might've brought people with nowhere else to go from other towns and villages. Engines and carriages needed somewhere to lie rusting. The train's carriages were dark.

Gerald stopped walking. An insect twitched. Gerald could have called out for anyone to answer, but everybody else had long departed. What remained was tired breathing from his chest.

The muffled space around him was its greatest in the centre of that mammoth empty place. Conspicuously alone among the dormant splendour, Gerald studied the iron columns holding up three long arched iron roofs high above him, admitting daylight and the wind. For the first time, he saw the patterns of past glories: the ornate flourishes high in every column, the very fact of railway stations.

On their way to or from the trains, travellers had stopped noticing the pictures of steam age locomotives with their careful engineering. The history that once made Darlington proud had been confined to railway museums and monuments few people understood. Historic merchant buildings around the town offered similarly intricate decoration, similarly neglected.

Gerald might've had no reason or every reason to feel small beneath the arcs, but every sense of antiquated grandeur strengthened him: his forebears' legacy. The dulcet dreams of long-lost empire were like the ghosts of heaven overhead, but ghosts for only him.

Before the train on platform 3 departed, the engine driver might've died. Dead crew and passengers might be lying in the corridors or seats.

Close enough to look warily through the eerie windows into the first dark carriage, Gerald could not see anybody there. He stepped up from the platform. The air was thickest in the carriage corridor, from which he opened the door to a compartment. On the two couches were shopping bags, handbags, and a book, but no passengers. The people might've been too old to take their last possessions with them when they left. They might've died in their seats, and people taking away their bodies left things they didn't want. They didn't need more merchandise to sell, among the excess goods to barter.

Bags, briefcases, and books rested on the seats in most compartments of the carriage, along with music players and tiny headphones. Hats and overcoats hung from hooks and rested neatly on the seats. Suitcases and cardboard boxes dwelt in racks overhead. Umbrellas leant against the walls.

Opening the door from one carriage of compartments to the next, Gerald's pace quickened as he walked along the corridor. A carton of flavoured milk, from which protruded a plastic straw, stood on a small shelf below a window. Black spots of mould were forming around the opening by the straw. In another compartment were two open paper bags. Vacant moments of past lives taught Gerald nothing of what happened the day the train stopped at the station.

Gerald proceeded through every carriage empty of people and their bodies, until he reached the sealed doors to goods for cartage. Stepping onto the far end of the platform, the open air was cold. Gerald hurried back along the platform. Nobody was there to meet the only traveller coming home that day.

Affixed to a closed W H Smith window was a too-familiar poster, picturing the predominantly green plumage of a yellow-eared parrot. Beside the poster in the glass was the reflection of a pink man staring dumbstruck at himself.

Gerald stopped. In the solitude in which he stood, he was taller than the parrot and much more worthy, at least to him, of long survival, but no caption implored anyone to save the pink reflected man.

His legs a short space apart, his limbs and body taut and fists clenched hard, Gerald punched at nothing in the space, wanting to punch something. "Well done the lot of you!" he screamed.

Gerald kicked an iron column. He only hurt his foot.

With more energy to kill and nowhere left to spend it, he stomped back through the concourse towards the open entranceway. "You idiots!" he screamed into the streets.

An old man continued walking. He left the fighting to younger people.

A woman stopped. She watched Gerald, with the lazy gaze of a disengaged spectator.

"You ignorant morons!" yelled Gerald.

She walked away, as if accustomed to the lunatics. Other people's deaths had made her weary.

Gerald could've screamed those agonies and angers at all the people who gave themselves away, murdering themselves, except that nobody would listen. His anger fired him and it tired him, as he slumped back against a wall. "We did it to ourselves," he wept in his contrition, watching the people walk away to die. "We did it to us."

Anywhere away from there was better than remaining there, amidst the roving remnants of a dying stupid people. Billions of other people meant nothing if none of them was with him. The only people left alive were people he could see.

Soon poised before his car's controls in the parking bays behind the building in which he lived, Gerald's hands gripped the steering wheel, against which his fingers bounced. Unworn clothes and cans of food lay on the front passenger seat beside him, where they'd lain since last he drove. The car windows were closed, so air wouldn't blow against his face. The white clouds high in the sky were unlikely to bring rain.

Stuttering back to life, the car engine beat better than could an old man's heart. Powering his car as fast and far he could, Gerald bundled across the pavement to the street. The clothes and cans fell among themselves, and Gerald hastily brushed them onto the floor where they would not distract him.

An old woman turned to see the car moving more quickly than ambulances and hearses normally drove. Gerald sailed past her, as he sailed past everyone. He headed eastward, towards Middlesbrough and the sea, before a sign to the Durham Tees Valley airport beckoned his mind furthest from everything he knew. His foot pressed a little harder on the accelerator pedal.

Scores of cars in coats of dust stood in the airport car park, abandoned when departing passengers boarded their flights to leave. The bays for buses were empty. No taxis stood in rank. Gerald stopped his car at the kerb outside the departure terminal entrance, beneath the repetitious railings he was too old to try to climb. There should've been space for pending passengers with luggage to alight.

If a flight that day were destined for anywhere on earth then Gerald would take it, for the chance the destination was better than the empty place he left behind or for the chance to board another aeroplane to another chance and place. He would board an aeroplane with anyone to any place she wanted them to go, to build their lives anew.

Gerald lowered his car windows and listened. Aside from contented mooing, the airport was as poor and lifeless as the county would become. He raised his windows.

Driving too fast for better times along the airport precinct roadways, no person or car obstructed him. He swung his car around a corner, through a bend, and near a high wire security fence. Beyond the fence was the airport tarmac, a wide-open plain of concrete grounds and boundary grasses much too long. Gerald slowed his car, turning until he faced the wire mesh. With the engine idling and brakes applied, his car stopped moving. The engine torque continued.

The runways were long and wide enough for aeroplanes to slow down upon arrival, before being taxied for direction to the gates. Aircraft from many countries once stood by the walkways protruding from the terminal. Airport trucks once streamed between them, towing trolleys of passenger bags and metal carts of airline food. Departing aircraft taxied to those runways, long and wide enough for them to revive their giant engines powering them upwards. They'd flown away and not returned.

Nothing moved along the tarmac. The gates were markers in the graveyard of his time.

The closed hangars at the far sides of the airport might've contained aircraft, if they'd not been sold for food or power to Asian and Arab airlines. Automatic pilots weren't enough for Gerald in his ignorance to fly.

Boats could sail the English Channel, but Gerald couldn't sail. Cruise ships needed crews and not disoriented old men.

The tarmac was Gerald's available universe. The only places he could reach were those to which he flew inside his car.

His car engine turning under him, Gerald stared into the fence that safety and security no longer warranted. He could drive faster along those runways than he could drive anywhere else, as fast perhaps as aeroplanes taking off. Anyone observing him would see his vehicle running amok across the tarmac more easily than he or she would see it running amok elsewhere. Any officers in the tall control tower would see a violating car and activate alarms to summon security guards and police.

Gerald's fist on the lever changed gears and his foot thrust onto the accelerator pedal, firing his car forward. It crashed over the kerb onto the grass, bouncing him in his seat before bringing down the fence. The instant of a danger passed as the fence broke into pieces under wheels. Sirens would once have blazed at his transgression, but the only sounds Gerald heard were those he made. Only he could save himself.

He in his car barrelled across more grass onto the smoother tarmac. He turned lengthways along the massive runway, as aeroplanes had done. The rows of unlit beacons would guide him skyward in the day.

Exhilarated as he'd not been for a long time, Gerald propelled his car still faster along the runway. He wanted to fly, to see Darlington from above: the streets, paths, and peaceful parks. He would see everybody left, anyone worth seeing, before flying above the countryside: refuges for people hiding from the solitude. He would fly until he found his people, where the sun was surely shining. He didn't dream of flying to places new to him as much as he dreamed of simply flying away.

The runway along which he barrelled would soon end, where aircraft would've risen to the air or slowed sufficiently to turn towards a terminal. Gerald slowed his vehicle, steering it to the side of the runway and back through a great half-circle. The car became light inside the arc, when he leant against the door beside him to weigh the car back down to earth. He slowed and stopped his car, facing back along the full-length centre of the runway.

His car was stationary, but the engine continued mustering power. Only the gears disengaged and Gerald's foot fighting the brake pedal kept the wheels in check.

The sprawling space from which aircraft flew lay long before him, never bigger than it was for Gerald then, stretching endlessly into the clouded sky. Leaning forward to look up through the glass windscreen, he satisfied himself no aircraft was arriving. Inside his mind, his car was already rising through the sky.

Gerald engaged the gears and thrust his feet into the accelerator pedal and car floor. The tyres screeched against the ground, as the heat and fire of hurting wheels blasted his screaming car away. His mind flew like a mammoth aeroplane as his car hurtled along the centre of the runway. He was alive, vibrant, breathing the air as his vehicle breathed it, invigorated for the world becoming nearer. If there were a chance that he would die then that chance was only small, too small to be a reason for him to stop. It might've been his reason to proceed.

The ride was pulsing with a passion and nothing left to fear. Gerald was crazy, careless, but nobody disturbed him. Nobody told him how to drive.

From the people who should've reprimanded him came infuriating silence. Nobody told him he would die. Nobody knew.

Glancing at the speedometer, Gerald's foot mustered another gasp of force against the pedal. He pushed his car past two hundred miles per hour. Spurring him onward was the futility of being him.

His feet pressed hard, his car lightened. Almost gliding above the ground, it seemed ready to rise: a bullet rocket surging to the heavens. The speedometer flickered when the car couldn't drive any faster. Gerald ached so hard to make it fly, willing the car upward into space, but the chassis wavered in the air and wheels couldn't leave the ground. Gerald couldn't fly.

The car started to veer to one side. Gerald quickly turned the steering wheel correcting it, but the car at high speed swerved across the runway. Grappling with the beast, Gerald pulled his foot from the accelerator and pressed it onto the brake pedal, trying not to press too hard, but the car spun screaming into a spreading arc, beyond his lost control.

The squealing car tried tossing him away, but Gerald's hands fastened to the steering wheel kept him in his seat. Smoke sprayed from the tyres as the car turned, wailing and burning. Beginning to roll over, one side of the car rose from the ground. Gerald leant against the height of it trying desperately to force it down, while his foot pressed further on the brake struggling to survive.

The car spun into nowhere, grinding a track into the ground. The tarmac friction that slowed jet engines and their tyres gradually restrained the car, becoming heavier again. Finally it stopped, with smoke still rising from the tyres and tread burning in the ground. Gerald switched off the car engine so it wouldn't writhe again.

Inside his trembling car, Gerald panted for some breath. His heart and frayed nerves within his brain tried their best to settle. An old man breath's recuperated slowly.

His life had become more fragile than had been a young man's health. His body could easily have been broken, slashed, trapped inside a crumpled, upturned car alight in flames. No ambulance officers were there to rescue him. No doctors or nurses were there to tend to him. Illnesses that hadn't harmed him when modern medicine survived were already killing men and women in the aged market town. Injuries from which people once recovered could be fatal.

Gerald might never have pulled himself free from the battered wreckage. Unable to recover from the pain, he would've lain there as he died: his blood-spattered face gazing at empty ground, his body interred in his car.

The slowly cooling engine murmured to him. He wasn't ready yet to die.

In spite of every reason not to, Gerald felt relieved to be alive. His loneliness could crush him and he dreaded his coming anguish, but the cessation of so many lives made Gerald cherish his small life. He needed himself and his resources too much to test them all for nothing, and would already suffer bad experiences not wanting any more. He could not afford the luxury of recklessness; no man alone could keep himself. He was mortal as were other men and women, and would try not to die before he became too old. If Gerald were still useful then he was useful to himself.

He could still drive along roads, over bridges, and perhaps head through the Channel Tunnel, but his was no time for Marco Polo: a novelty to new lands. Other peoples' rules and chaos would condemn him. Gerald wanted to eat the food he liked with beer and wine, listen to music and see movies, rest peacefully on a bench in a green park. Empty English towns were safer than other people's cities neglecting or accursing him. Gerald would be more alone in foreign parts than he was in his apartment.

His thoughts and feelings, he wanted to think and feel in gentle conversation, without the failings that had brought them all asunder. Any journey far away would be more daunting and uncertain than remaining close to home, in tranquil company of his kind, however few of them remained.

In the life in which Gerald came too late to want, aircraft would have stood before him, accepting and discharging passengers and crew. His world of people could have flown him and his wife to distant holidays with their children. They might all have lived forever.

Bound to earth, only his car could take him anywhere. It couldn't take him very far.

Gerald stepped outside. Alone amidst so wide an open ground

stretched out around him, only he and his car interrupted the long flatness, rambling into the ends of runways, taxiing areas, and abandoned terminals and hangars. Beyond them were darkening clouds above abandoned buildings.

He was in space, completely alone, and never felt more insignificant. The world was silent, as it would be every day. That silence was as men and women a generation earlier had not known silence could be. He was abjectly lonely, and would be every day. The bones in his old knees were becoming sore.

Gerald retreated to his car; he had no more ideas left. Petrol had become too precious for him to exhaust again as much as he'd exhausted that day, although he had no better use for it. Befitting his old age, he drove cautiously around the tarmac until he found the portion of the fence already broken; he wouldn't break anything he didn't need to break. His land without his people offered him so little, but still more than did any other domicile.

16

THE END OF EDUCATION

More and more aging men and women became too sick to work. New faces on the same people sat in the Darlington Memorial Hospital reception area, while staff becoming tired sat in rooms reserved to them, before taking beds to die. Enduring the extremes of every season became a feat that exhausted their last energy.

People near their solitary deaths couldn't bear the fear of watching vehicles ply past, knowing what they were, but Brandon watched them for the momentary movement. Ambulances did not break the silence with sirens, taking sick people to the hospital. Hearses took bodies to be buried, not hurrying to be anywhere. The last petrol in underground tanks was reserved for them.

Drivers conserved their fuel for moments they would need it, without knowing when they would. Their only certain journeys would be their final ones. The untold count of idle cars contained too little fuel to scrounge; the handprints in the window dust were those of people pausing to rest as they walked past. Desolation made them all seem very small.

Brandon's last class at Polam Hall was part way through its last year of education when the dwindling businesses and stores in County Durham became too few to sustain each other, with insufficient working people to earn salaries and too little left to buy. The businesses of death, burials, and cremations were the last businesses to stumble, but the tail of the economy finally collapsed. The men who'd built careers being coffin makers, gravediggers, and undertakers saved their final products for themselves. People worked when they'd not have worked in other circumstances, but could not preserve the power to the county.

The once fluorescent offices where men and women worked too hard were long-dead floors of blinded, dirty windows between nowhere. The failed fluorescent neon lights and words in coloured glass, which once shone variant colours into the day and night, idled in the dark.

The marks of fallen raindrops dried too slowly in the dust dotted the glass and fading brickwork in the high streets. Faces smiled from torn advertisements on rotting and rusted billboards, but the tones once pink were waning into tones of grey, much as they waned in faces of people stumbling past. Only a few men and women wore their gold and silver wristwatches, to measure how long to spend outside before nightfall.

What remained in Darlington were the nineteenth-century indoor markets below the most prominent clock tower, more important than they'd been for generations. They accommodated farmers, market gardeners, and everyone with a little excess food or beverage, or just wanting some variety in whatever they consumed. Lay fishermen brought fish they'd caught that morning from the river. Other people brought their biscuits, cakes, and hand-rolled loaves of bread. They traded books, batteries, and homespun medicines and candles. Everything to sell was sold at the persevering markets.

The markets were shelters on a rainy day, in which people wanting to congregate outside their homes could loiter. Men dragged from vacant restaurants the tables, chairs, and small refrigerators that had become public property. Others sat on ragged rugs around the floor, to set up their new stalls. Some people cleaned the floors, splashing their fraying mops in battered round steel buckets. People without anything worthwhile to sell, sold wares they'd bought a day or two beforehand. They traded them for wares they'd tried to sell the next day, in a routine trading circle like their lives so long ago.

The plastic cards, coins, and notes that founded the old economy languished lost somewhere. They were meaningless without exchange for goods or services, for other cards and coins and notes. Some men held their thick leather wallets and women their best purses, imagining they would come again to use them. Nobody remained to pay them a new fortune for their brilliant work or innovation. They couldn't win a lottery and buy those things they once pursued. They could loot empty homes, no one remained to care, but could take only what they found. They could occupy the rooms and suites of abandoned good hotels.

Aged people looked alike; paupers hobbled with the rich. Their lives and wealth had come to nothing.

Beyond an abandoned newsagent's doorway, the last unsold publications littered the shelves. Suspended in their final composed editions were discontinued magazines no longer glossy, catering to interests once commonplace and those not: trout fishing and basket weaving, haberdashery and needlecraft. Feature story captions around the covers almost obscured the photographs, begging people to browse and buy. The news in cancelled newspapers was no longer new. What had been current and important had become less than trivial.

Some people tried to read the torn and crumbling pages they'd already read a dozen times. If they remembered to forget the words and photographs they'd seen, they could look at them again and see each of them afresh.

Fading notices in closed shop doors and windows could seem like something new, but few things that anybody said had been unique. People who'd read them too many times did not read them again; the few men and women walking past no longer saw them. Any hapless fool who paused to do so could only cry. Impending exhibitions had moved along.

Their expectations of things to come had been so wrong. There were no more games at Blackwell Meadows, no more London Stock Exchange share trades. There were no more elections, nor grandiose summits. The only truthful forecasts might've been one or two about the tides and phases of the moon, except that everyone was dying. Too little of the news that anyone read foreshadowed what would happen. Opinion and commentary hadn't taught them anything.

Behind the street-front glass of a closed pet shop were several cats and dogs, their ribs and other bones pushed through their fur and hair. Confined to their small cages, their eyes pleaded with Alec and Hollie studying them.

Alec looked around the street, but saw only an old woman carrying twigs and sticks of wood. The time was late morning. The shopkeeper might've already come that day or might be coming soon, continuing to care compassionately for his charges, or might've passed away.

"We can't leave them," said Hollie.

Alec stepped towards the shop door, placed his hand on the knob, and tried to turn it. He couldn't.

Nothing around them would help him break into the shop. Alec removed his left shoe, exposing his left foot and sock to the cool air. Keeping that foot above the ground and using that shoe as a small hammer, he struck the shoe's heel against the window by the door. The window cracked, while the dogs inside barked excitedly and cats scooted to the far sides of their cages. The woman carrying twigs and wood watched Alec as she walked, without interrupting her slow gait.

More carefully, he used the shoe's heel to punch away the glass, breaking into it a hole. When the hole was big enough, he reached his arm inside and unlocked the door. The dogs continued barking as Alec, his left shoe back on his foot, and then Hollie entered the store.

The raw smell of fur and animal bodies was striking for people who'd never kept pets inside their home. There might've also been a hint of waste from the straw spread about the cages, but Alec wasn't sure. The straw seemed somewhat aged.

If the store contained cans or plastic bags of food to feed the cats and dogs then Alec and Hollie would've given it to them, but the shelves were empty. Less fortunate than birds in open air, the birds in cages depended upon sesame seed dispensers and water-troughs. The fish in water tanks had plants.

The shopkeeper's arrival would've saved Alec from deciding what to do. Nobody came.

"They need a chance," said Hollie, opening the small gate from a cage for several cats. The cats remained in their far corners of the cage.

Alec released the gates to other cages, but the pets remained fearful in their places. Leaving the door wide open, Hollie led Alec out of the store and across the street. From there, they watched, until a single green canary walked outside. It stopped on the pavement, looked around, and flew into the air.

In their late dying lives, people took whatever wasting goods they wanted from dark abandoned stores. They took clothes before the clothes they'd already taken became dirty. Shining small torches, they filled their aged arms with their sizes of garments and undergarments: flannelette pyjamas and packets of socks and underpants fitting their feet and waists. There were no fashions without people who believed them, and most men and women wore whatever apparel kept them warm on colder days and nights and cool on warmer ones. The once enticing clothes and hats lay in cracks of rocks among the shadows.

Men and women closed the doors when they left each shop because other people did, and for the next time they went there to replenish their supplies. Wrapped in unnecessary packaging, the unworn clothes lay piled on bedroom floors, beside the cupboards and chests of drawers already filled.

They died without regard to the change of business circumstance. Without anything else to do, the less disabled men drifted from other trades to digging graves. People called them "bury-men."

When ambulances and hearses were unavailable, small groups of men brought bodies of the dead on blanket stretchers out of homes to the nearest open soil. Formalised cemeteries had filled or were too far away to reach. The graves of people who died in houses with dirt gardens were in those gardens. The graves of people dead in other places were in parks or street-side lines of grass. Several bodies often shared a grave; strangers in their lives lay close together in the ground.

The aged society with too many people dying dispensed with forms to fill and paperwork, with rituals and services. Most of the dead were buried without mourners or ceremony, dropped into soil wrapped in the clothes and sheets in which they died. Passers-by turned their heads away, determined not to see.

Men who wanted to be carpenters cut and nailed together wooden crosses to stand in dirt above the dead. People who knew the names of the deceased wrote them on the crosses, and perhaps the dates they died, although few people read inscriptions.

The creed for a dying people allowed those burying a corpse to take whatever last possessions they desired from the dead's deserted home, without heirs or heiresses and with government too weak to intervene. They freed pets to live and die outside. They took food and wine they could consume, and dropped rotting food outside for birds, animals, and proliferating rats. They pushed long plastic tubes into car petrol tanks to extract what they could into cans, or drove those cars until they exhausted the fuel in them. They took the types of things they could buy and sell at markets, which other people would take from them when they too died. Custody, for however brief a time, was ownership in the postscript to their society.

With no use for them, bury-men rarely touched the grand possessions that dead owners prized more than they'd prized eternity. Collections of old coins and stamps, the senseless compilations and lesser arts and crafts that amateur enthusiasts gathered, lay neglected in the dust. They'd made the earth their bounty, with cultural relics and neat artefacts from poor corners of the world, but the bounty didn't matter. Nothing material enriched people left to die.

Bury-men didn't bother tidying beds or rooms, although some closed curtains across windows to protect furniture fabrics from seasons of the sun. Soon, the custom of drawing curtains across the windows of the dead replaced all other notices of death, letting neighbours think the dead had ducked away on holidays and would eventually return. People still alive kept their curtains open, but if they feared their life abating too close to death, they left their doors ajar. Curtains were slowly becoming closed across the windows of all the people's homes.

The bury-men departed with all the doors and windows shut, but never locked. Passing wanderers were free to take remaining refuse.

All the bury-men really wanted were rituals to make others responsible for burying them when they too died, instead of leaving them to lie among the rats. Without pretence, they had no delusions that anything they did was significant, except it was significant to them.

The last schoolteachers, working without pay but with the gratuities of parents, ran out of things to say. Their last students had no need for numbers without society. The lines and columns of long division and multiplication were obsolete. Science was important, but they would need to learn far more than the curiosities inside their student books. Their knowledge of geography would not impinge upon their lives. With little cause to study waning disciplines at nights, they didn't know enough to save themselves.

The teachers brought forward the graduation ceremony for the last young men and women at Polam Hall, who sat with their parents and the last staff in a room of the oldest part of the school; the more recent Liddiard Theatre would be too dark if the electricity failed again. There, they listened to another speech Brandon did not believe. He was seventeen years of age, an age where past generations of Englishmen and women prepared to study, work, and travel the world.

Beside him, Alec looked around the school in which he wouldn't sit again. Standing by the door was the last school caretaker. Rarely had the pupils or their parents noticed him, dressed in a ruffled smoke-coloured hat atop matching shirts and trousers, but that day he'd dressed into a suit, tie, and jacket. Abandoning his other memories, Alec slowly recognised him.

The caretaker was Tarpin Hobbs, dressed for that final graduation day as he'd once dressed for the most formal of office meetings. Tarpin's laboured limbs and body no longer stood so easily in those business clothes, but that day he stood like every other person.

Tarpin turned towards Alec studying him. Alec smiled. Tarpin turned slowly back to watch the ceremony.

Alec continued studying him. Cutting back the trees and shrubs or sweeping the long paths, Tarpin must've overheard the student classes and children's conversations. He must've known them all by name. He knew far more than anybody realised, without ever telling Brandon he'd known his father. They'd never so much as spoken to each other, not that Brandon ever mentioned.

The ceremony finished, Alec walked up to Tarpin. "What will happen to you without the school?" asked Alec.

"Why do you stay in Darlington?"

"Our home's in Hummersknott."

"Does that make you feel safe?"

"It makes us feel free."

Tarpin laughed, before stepping out through the door. Alec watched him in the last years of a life walk away.

Dressed back in his ruffled hat and clothes, Tarpin returned the next morning to sweep the floors of the last rooms utilised. He removed the last of the school notices and erased the last tuition. He took away anything left behind, closed the windows, and locked the doors. He left the keys for storage on an empty counter in the town hall offices, in an envelope addressed to the conservation officer no longer there.

The graduating class with whom Brandon sat at school returned to their disparate homes. They shared the chores, food, and warmth better than could anyone alone. People together cooked meals and sauces that solitary people were too tired to set.

In Hummersknott, Brandon ate the vegetables his family grew in the garden behind their home and the fruit they picked from trees outside empty houses. He tried his best to make a life where lives were no longer made, exchanging messages along intermittent media with friends trying just as hard.

Boys and girls who'd fallen easily into love and slowly out of it at school, when love mattered less, struggled to keep relationships when their hometowns were collapsing. Messages between them became rare and gatherings between them rarer still. They and their families soon travelled south-west, to Cornwall, trying to find wherever Englishmen and women were, leaving Brandon's family behind.

To warm them when gas failed to come, Alec and Brandon collected dead branches and trees for their fireplace. Better able to wield blows of an axe and strokes of a saw, Brandon chopped or cut them for their roughly hewn woodpile.

A few miles out of Darlington, north of Sadberge village along rural Hillhouse Lane, Alec, Hollie, and Brandon found the Dogs Trust: several blocks of kennels behind a tall wire fence and gate locked shut. Comforting anyone who read his notice announcing its recent closure, the last borough council dog warden had undertaken to find accommodation in other kennels for the last two dogs, although other kennels were also trying to find accommodation for their unkempt animals since the centre at Langley Moor had closed.

Hiding beside a row of bushes was the warden: the last custodian of animals he'd confined. His hat and uniform, embroidered with the council crest, had thinned and torn with wear, but he'd cleaned and ironed them as well as any person could. In his bony hands was a large brass ring, from which hung a wad of keys. On the ground beside him was a bag of dog biscuits, almost empty.

"I worry," he told Alec and his family.

"About the dogs?" asked Alec.

"About me."

Strutting along the grass and across the paths beyond the gate appeared two black dogs, their bodies lean. One dog noticing Alec's family barked and bounced towards them. The other barked with the first, and also ran towards them.

Hollie and Brandon stepped backwards; the dogs' feisty teeth and nails could kill them. Alec wrapped his arms around them.

The dogs leapt at the gate. They tried to push it open or climb it.

Alec, Hollie, and Brandon edged further backwards, Alec

closer to them. Their feet pressed against the ground were ready to run away.

Their presence might've provoked them. "They might be playing," said Brandon.

"They might be hungry," said Hollie.

The warden looked around the bushes; the dogs had no regard for uniforms. He should've been the people's comfort, but his hands were shaking. "I've tried my best to help them since they were puppies," he said, "but don't recognise them now."

The first dog dropped back down the fence to its place inside the compound. The other retreated with it. They barked, thrusting about their heads and agitated jaws.

The four human beings continued watching those exotic creatures they should not encounter elsewhere. If they moved around the encircling fence to another space without the bushes, then the wanton dogs would move along their side with him.

The warden might've been their enemy or plaything, their feeder or their foil. "Do *you* want to feed them?" he asked. "Do you want to *free* them?"

Alec imagined mean dogs someday prowling the county unchallenged, imprisoning people in their homes. "There's a park in Cumbria," he said, "with wild animals much fiercer than dogs." Those animals could reduce English towns to squealing jungles.

"Do you want to take the dogs there?" asked the warden.

Alec thought of killing those fidgeting two dogs, but he was neither hunter nor prey. It risked his life too much.

The warden stepped slowly backwards. The dogs fell silent.

Alec, Hollie, and Brandon stepped backwards too. Alec didn't want to move too quickly for fear the dogs might try again to climb the fence and harm themselves. Keeping the dogs secure from people and people secure from dogs, their enclosure was their habitat, to feed on birds or little animals wandering inside.

The last of the bag of dog biscuits, Alec picked up and hurled over the fence. It crashed on the grass, where the two dogs tore it apart, devouring their food.

17

THE SINGLE FAMILY HOME

The night of his sixty-sixth birthday, Zane Entwist stood alone among the pastel-painted walls of his two-bedroom terraced home. Silver tips dotted his groomed grey hair and he secretly wore spectacles to read. In his hands were a long flute glass and his second last bottle of Champagne. On the table was food for guests who still remembered. His front door left open, Zane listened for the sound of footsteps not his own.

He walked back and forth through every room, waiting for the guests to come, until finally Ingrid came. She stayed the night and soon made his home hers as well, because waking up to anyone was better than waking up alone.

Nothing else bound them after thirty years not quite together. Alec and Hollie had forgotten Zane's parties altogether.

On warmer days, people sat at the tables of cafeterias open and closed, beneath the antique pictures. They ate the bread and cheese they'd brought with their uncertain steps from home or from the indoor markets. They drank the last varieties of tea. Some prepared soups of refuse vegetables and bones with little meat in round steel tubs, proffering them in chipped mugs and breaking bowls to anybody there. People accustomed to their solitude could not find points of conversation with other solitary people. They eked out too little of the lives they once recalled.

Bicycles stowed for nights long past remained chained to iron racks and fences or were covered under shelter, for the few people still able to ride them. Weary men and women shuffling along pavements paused to gawk at people not so old, on days without too gruelling a fall of rain, but those slightly younger people were also getting old.

Brandon checked the faces, but never saw anyone near his age. Where everything else was slow or still, Brandon attracted their listless gaze. His thick locks of lush blond hair flowed indifferently towards his tall, broad shoulders when he strode. When he rode his bicycle, those locks caught the breeze he made. They flaunted his youthfulness to people whose hair was receding to types of white behind their hats and scarves, with matching beards on a growing proportion of men.

Some of those old people gritted their teeth at him, who'd not concede his every day to them. Sometimes, Brandon thought he should try to alleviate their final years, those people he'd someday be, but there were too many of them. He'd help people who'd help him, but couldn't help the masses of infirm. They were people who'd proudly said when they were young they didn't need anyone, before they struggled to carry bags of radishes from the markets to the parks.

Using his father's hammer and screwdriver, Brandon broke into a long-abandoned sports goods shop. Crowd playthings in some counties were rarities in his: old stock on the furthest corners of the shelves that had been more trouble to discard than it had been to ignore. Brandon brushed away the dust from anything he wanted to examine, and learnt to play the sports for one. He kicked a football from the street against a building wall trying not to hit a window. When the ball bounced back, he ran until his feet trapped it and dribbled it across the streets and paths. He kicked it back against a wall, in a recurrent game of declining skill called exercise.

Interrupting him was the small noise of hands in kind applause. Brandon stopped, leaving the ball to roll across the street while he looked up. An audience might play with him instead of wanting just his labour, but the only person watching him from the windows was an old man. His face was like a pallid bust on a museum display, but his aged hands were softly clapping.

"Do you want to come down?" Brandon called out.

The old man stopped clapping. He shook his head.

Brandon strode to where the ball had stopped and kicked it back against the wall. Like a performing circus animal, he continued kicking the ball against walls and running to kick it back again, staying within the old man's sight. The contest between a player and a ball was Brandon's chance to boast within his brain what he had done. Missing the ball, or it crashing against glass, wouldn't concern his one spectator.

Bored with that game, Brandon began dribbling the ball back towards the store. The old man softly clapped his hands again. Brandon turned around to face him and he bowed. The old man smiled, and clapped his hands a little louder.

The applause was reason for Brandon to return with a stick of white chalk and mark the outside building wall with the height of a tennis net: one racquet length and width. On the street and path beside it, he marked the lines of one side of a tennis court. Brandon served and struck a tennis ball against the wall, above the net and bouncing back into the court, scoring a match game with himself. The complimentary viewer at his window watched him in the rhythm of the ball, developing his skills. Brandon practiced until he could've been a champion, if he ever had anyone with whom to play.

The lonely round of show finally tired him. Brandon looked up at the building window, but the old man had gone.

Taking tools from broken stores, Brandon and his parents performed the household chores that remained undone in homes around them. They oiled door hinges that began to squeak. They sealed the leaks around windowpanes. Without fuel to power the lawn mower, Alec and Brandon clipped the grass with shears. They raked the cutback strands of grass and swept them into the gutters of the street. Their small suburban home, which had once been like most other homes along the street, became the prettiest, but not as pretty as it had been when they were young.

Too long a time had passed since anyone rang the bells or knocked on doors around the neighbourhood. A large dog lay waiting outside its fallen mistress' home, becoming thin and weak. It watched anything that moved. The waters of a creek flowed somewhere near.

Trees, shrubs, and grass could make empty houses seem less destitute than other empty homes. The windows Brandon saw from his home were closed, with curtains drawn across them, although that might've been because the air was cold in falling rain.

The rain cleared. The curtains remained drawn.

"How could we have done this?" he asked his parents. "What could anybody like more than being alive?"

Drinking from a long mug of lemon juice gave his father time to contemplate an answer, much as drinking from long mugs of beer once had, before resting his mug back on the table. "Don't search for reason where there was none," he told him. "People age without children."

Brandon stood quietly, still yearning to understand. He tried to think of anything to say about a future that had become too hard to find.

His mother looked at him, unwilling to reveal what she was thinking. His father raised his mug in a sad, sardonic toast. "To Barrenville," he said, the only time he used so mean a moniker, "but how can we revive her?"

Whenever Brandon and his parents walked or rode their bicycles far enough along the street, an old man living alone watched them from his lounge room window. His wife, who Brandon best recalled from her tightly fitting red dress, had passed away. Too tired to remove the weeds that flourished in the grass and too weak to drag away the branches of a tree fallen across the driveway he could no longer use, the old man's house looked much alike the empty ones around it.

Having seen him watching them, Hollie prepared him a warm mug of soup to drink. She knocked on his front door.

"It's not locked," he barked.

Hollie opened the door. She faced him sitting at his chair beside the window.

Gruffly, he glared at her. The whiskers of his unshaven face formed a scruffy white-grey beard. A woollen blanket covered his knees and legs. The room in which he sat was dark, darker than it needed to be. The television set and radio that could've played whenever power flowed were silent.

"I thought," said Hollie, "you might like some soup."

He grimaced without gratitude, but she walked towards him and he took the mug from her hands. "You could've brought this to me sooner," he snarled. "You're too wrapped up with that infernal son of yours."

"If you can leave the mug outside the door when you're finished," Hollie calmly told him, "then I won't need to come in again." She turned around to leave.

"You never think of anyone but yourselves," he muttered.

She left him alone. Her mug did not appear outside the door.

Eight days later, Alec and Brandon were among the bury-men carrying his corpse in its old clothes from the house. "We can dig his grave here," said Alec.

"We have a pit," one man replied.

They dumped the body in the rear of a small truck. "His name was Otis Hatchett," said Alec.

The man looked at Alec and the corpse, shrugged his shoulders, and climbed into his truck. He didn't want anything from the dead man's home.

Later, Alec pushed open the dead man's door. He found his kitchen crockery and retrieved Aunt Mimi's mug.

Public gardens once neatly tailored became unruly, without a gardener's touch, although weathered signs still forbid people walking. Scattered among the grassland were piles of upturned dirt, where skimpy wooden crosses marked clumsily dug graves. Most lawns for leisure and aesthetics had become amateur cemeteries in which, walking together as they did, Alec, Hollie, and Brandon paused to read the few inscriptions. They were often feeble writing, although sometimes artists keen to paint also inscribed careful script.

Outside one dark and empty house, where cats defaced the

wilting flowers in porcelain pots, was a grave before which Hollie stopped. Alec stopped with her, placing his hand upon her shoulder. Inscribed on the cross was a name they hadn't heard for years. "*Anna Smythe, Durham Constabulary, Aged 59.*"

"Fifty-nine could've been so young," lamented Hollie. "A name, a job, an age are very little to represent a life."

"Would her life mean more," asked Alec, "if a list of everything she did covered a mausoleum wall?"

Hollie shook her head.

"All I want my cross to say is '*Husband of Hollie...*'"

"Dearly beloved husband," Hollie corrected him, turning towards him.

"'*Dearly beloved and dearly loving husband of Hollie*'," smiled Alec, "'*Loving father of Brandon.*'"

"And your name," said Hollie.

"No need."

Hollie stepped closer to her husband, until they stood with their arms around each other. "I don't want that day to come," she said.

"Not as much as I don't."

Hollie chuckled, before turning back at the wooden cross. They did not approach the house.

Near their home lived a widow normally hiding from their sight. When Alec saw Mrs Cheevers one morning sitting in a wicker chair on the pavement outside his home, she'd aged far more than just the few months since last he'd seen her. Her age was no more than his, but she was very thin. Her face and cheeks had reduced to loose skin draping from her bones.

Leaning against her legs was a brown cane. She must have called upon every effort left inside her to push the chair from her home along the pavement to be there. Around her shoulders was a rainbow-coloured shawl, on what was already a warm day. Without intruding, she made Alec's family home a spectacle for an audience of one.

Alec couldn't help but see her there, as she must've known. "Good morning, Mrs Cheevers," he said, unable to recall her Christian name.

"Sorrell," she smiled, her voice faltering. "I hope you don't mind me being here, Alec."

"Not at all, Sorrell," replied Alec, walking from his home towards her.

"I've often watched your family," she said with a tinge of sorrow, looking up at Alec from her chair. "My husband, he watched you too."

"Can I get you anything?"

"I would like a cup of tea."

The gas and electricity supplies were again suspended that morning. "I can only give you cold tea, Sorrell."

"I won't stay for very long, I promise."

"Do you want to come into the house?"

"You were always very kind Alec, but you have a family. You don't want to lose your time to the ramblings of a geriatric woman."

"You don't think *I* ramble?" smiled Alec.

"I want to speak with you before, well, you know..."

Alec wouldn't say what she wouldn't say herself. The members of his family could speak of death among themselves as they wouldn't speak of it with other people.

"The mind in which I entrusted so much is failing me," she continued. "My hands can't do much; I spent an hour to drag this old chair here, to see you better. I can't keep my home as well as you keep yours, but isn't mine the second nicest you've seen?"

Alec politely nodded. He hadn't thought about it.

"I want to say that you were right in what you did: some things you did, the most vital thing, not like the things I used to think were so essential." Her weakening wavering fingers, once firm and precise, she rested on her belly. "This body," she confessed, as if it were something apart from her, "this hollow lifeless body, this awful wasted vestibule, hasn't served us well, certainly not me." The first moisture of her tears glazed across her eyes.

Her words were for Alec to pass onto people young enough to act upon them. Not that he quite knew when he should.

"I'll be going now," she said.

"You're welcome to stay."

"I've already taken up your time."

"I could help you walk," said Alec, stepping towards her to help her stand.

"No," she said. "Not now."

"Can I carry your chair?"

"I have too many chairs," she said. "Would you mind terribly if I left it here? You could use it if you want and some days, when I'm feeling strong enough, I'd like to come and sit here. Seeing all of you, it makes this not such a bad locale in which to...you know."

Something meaningful – kind words of his condolence or kinder lies that she was not about to die – could not raise themselves in Alec's mind. His thoughts were of her dying in that chair or of him not seeing her for several days and finding her body in her home, but he would not begrudge her wanting somebody to bury her. He would find the people to dig her grave in the soil behind her home.

"There are different kinds of aloneness," she told him. "Being alone isn't loneliness, when it's only for a while. The solitude we know will end is very different to the loneliness we know will not."

"You can sit here whenever you'd like, Sorrell," smiled Alec. "If you ever want to come into our home, you can do that, too."

"Thank you, Alec," she said, although he'd done very little. She took her cane in her right hand. In spite of her words, Alec held her left arm as she struggled to stand. "You let me go now." Her cane supported her as she turned away.

Alec watched her shoes inching along the pavement. Turning to wave would've been too difficult for her, he knew. Besides, she wouldn't have wanted him to think she mightn't see him there again.

Late that day, with the gas supply resumed, Alec took her a cup of tea. She'd left her front door a little open, and Alec gently knocked: a courteous, respectful breaching of the silence. When she didn't respond, he pushed the door further open. Resting in an armchair, with a cup of tea on the floor beside her almost empty, he found her dead.

Their final conversation might've been her final comfort. Whatever words she'd strained to utter with her parting breaths from life, perhaps laughing sadly at herself, weren't profound for people who weren't there. Nobody remained to hear her die.

At her wooden table lay a sharp knife and hundreds of tiny white wooden matches in a partially completed image of a spring lamb, standing at a fence. She must have sat for hours concentrating on her intricate work, cutting the matches and laying them in the picture she was making.

Covering a tall cabinet was a white sheet that Alec pulled away, revealing a glass display case filled with dainty dolls and figurines: the first crowd he'd seen for a long time. There were long-limbed ladies with shining gowns draped behind them. Some held flower posies in lattice baskets. Others held parasols. There were also smiling babies and little children. Theirs might have been the faces Mrs Cheevers wanted to conceal while she died. Alec gently placed the white sheet over her, out of the gaze of imitation eyes.

He could've asked Brandon to help but, instead, Alec stepped out the rear door of her home to find a shovel. There, among the trees and plants for food, he saw several weathered planks of wood, a pile of dirt, and a grave already dug, in preparation for him coming there. Some dirt had been there long enough to sprout budding tufts of grass. Standing at the far end of the grave was a thick and sturdy wooden cross. Painted on the cross was the inscription "*Doctor Sorrell Cheevers*." A thick black line had subsequently been struck through her title.

The grave was damp, with a small puddle of water along it. If she'd dug the grave then she'd have expended her next to last energy to do so, before expending her last to talk with him that morning.

The door to a small shed was open, where Alec saw a wheelbarrow. Leaning against the door was a black shovel. The shovel was dry, without rust. Mrs Cheevers had placed it there that day.

Her wheelbarrow in the house, beside her armchair, wasn't as strange as it would once have been. Alec wrapped her pliant body in the sheet and placed her in the barrow; some people, their shrinking bones calcified and muscles wasted, could be light to carry. He pushed her clumsy chariot to the garden.

Trying to be delicate couldn't keep her body in the sheets, as they tumbled into the hole that she'd prepared. He shovelled the dirt over her, sometimes resting as he did, until the dirt with all its tufts of grass was in the ground again. Alec returned the barrow and shovel to the shed. He closed the door. Inside the house, her cabinet of ornaments, her nothingness in a glass funeral box, remained intact.

Above her grave, Hollie and Brandon stood with Alec. Graves made age immaterial, the very old no more or less deceased than the very young. The dead lay among equals.

All Alec knew was what he'd heard in funeral services, in old films and television that came to mind. "Earth to earth," he said, gazing into the grave, "ashes to ashes, dust to dust." Those words seemed inopportune. "Thank you, Sorrell, for wanting us to know."

Hollie stepped closer to her son. She placed her arm around his waist.

Alec understood the prayer Sorrell Cheevers might've needed, lying snugly in the soil, peacefully at rest. "Please God," he whispered, "bring her home."

Alec, Hollie, and Brandon stood silently, as mourners normally stood in requiem, before Alec stepped away. Hollie followed him.

Brandon remained beside the grave. If standing there he mourned, he mourned what he'd never know. More than a service for the dead, he wanted life, something left, before growing old not dying alone. Burying the deceased kept the county clean for people still alive, but didn't bring them back to life. "I know what I need to do," he told his parents, turning towards them.

They turned back to face him. Alec took Hollie's hand.

"I don't know what else to do."

18

THE PEOPLE NO LONGER THERE

With antique equipment to print photographs in the dark rooms of his home, the old man in a red cap continued scouting Darlington, carrying a camera around his neck. Instead of photographing people as he once did, he turned away from the few people so they wouldn't impose upon his photographs of trees without their leaves and paths without their people. He called them art, but images of empty streets weren't art when so many streets were empty.

The oldest men and women crept on their walking canes and sticks. They looked through other aged faces, without speaking to each other. Conversations between experts in all things had fallen silent. They had no call to speak aloud inside their land so nearly passed.

Getting older in their tiny lonely lives, they'd long ceased to be community. Rich men and women had turned to vagrancy, knowing no one else would help. The people who wouldn't help a stranger had learned not to exhaust themselves by asking strangers to help them.

They rested at the chairs and tables of what had been street-side cafeterias and on seats left for them along the pavements, until gusts of wind blew them over. Rain and morning dew dampened them, until moments of the sun dried them again.

Men and women pottered, looking for things to do. What they did was never clear, as it had never been.

The people dying each day disappeared from view, leaving their small possessions in the ruin. Animals scavenged everything they could, prospering better than Gerald was. They had each other for their company and were Gerald's sense of company, watching his country dying from his downcast window.

Gerald once desired the riches snug within the stores but, in conversations with himself, he wondered why he'd bothered. Within dead homes were people's picture prize ornaments. The curios stood inviolate, until squirrels brushing past knocked them to the floor. Birds, they'd come to seem so loud, made their nests among the scarves and hats.

A fantasy from Gerald's childhood drifted back into his head; old age was better than any other age to recall and contemplate childhood. He, the small boy, was lucky enough to be locked in Sainsbury's Supermarket at night. He ate all the sweet things that he wanted, knowing nobody would punish a child trapped inadvertently.

That fantasy had been realised. He could take anything he wanted from the stores, but no staff would find him in the morning.

The world of change had dissipated, had itself changed, without new things at which to marvel. Each day would be the same as the last had been, and as tomorrow would become. Only the dates of death would change.

Without a present or a future, only the past survived. Reminiscences were something more beyond Gerald's lost control: constructs playing again inside his head. His mind and time were more of him having nothing left to lose, leaving him alone in his soliloquy.

Gerald pondered his myriad of memories from the eras of his youth, trying his best to fathom where his great life had gone. England had been as great as she had ever been until her penultimate long time, when her people neglected her for narrow lives and other peoples. Gerald spent his life being only him, no longer certain what being him could mean. For what had they been striving in their campaigns and their causes, their erudite opinions over wine and roasted coffee? He'd learned the insignificance of most that modern man had done.

Expectations of the coming years had passed without history to show for them. Gerald didn't understand the passing of his life.

The circumstances of their demise were clearer than any reason he could gauge, the causes of their travesty obscure. Gerald didn't know the truth of anything, except the presumptions by which he'd once lived so well were wrong. The truth had surely been there, but the people who might've seen it were too certain in their stupidity to notice. Gerald tried to think but couldn't know how they let themselves grow old, trying to comprehend the incomprehensible.

He'd cared more about goods and services than the people with whom he traded, more about ideas inside his head than the people he believed, more about his work than about himself performing it. His life had fallen far away, while he slept through his imperfection and catastrophe.

In his apartment, Gerald's failure was absolute. Rather than sit without his senses in a never-changing home, he preferred to anguish outside.

His idle car asleep between abandoned cars, he walked without a pattern or a purpose about the silent streets and paths of parks. A woollen coat kept his body warm. Brown mittens sealed his hands. A thick hat sheltered his grey head. A melancholy man meandering in slow motion, nowhere obvious remained as a place for him to be.

Gerald passed a stranger and watched her eyes, hoping she would smile at him. Before their eyes could meet, she turned her face away.

Men and women who'd grown old had once been young. The faces wrinkled with their age had once been smooth.

A woman sat alone on a wooden bench in South Park, without looking at the small white-painted crosses in the dirt. The unkempt plants and shrubs fed only animals. A cat had come to scrounge for scraps that only it could see.

Water no longer flowed through the placid fountain pond, its decorations long aged and nearly dead. A pack of dogs drank from the stagnant bath and basin, their sipping splashes breaking the silence.

The water over darkness reflected Gerald's face worn harsh. He removed a mitten, braving the frost, to touch the shivering ice-cold water. Ripples spread away from his reflection of a life.

Gerald had everything to miss, but he missed people most of all. The people dead had been the friends and acquaintances of people left to die. If strangers in long-closed bars and restaurants or passengers beside him on discontinued transport services were among the people languishing on benches in the parks, then Gerald didn't recognise them. They'd been worthy of his greeting, as he'd been for them, but few of them got to know. They should've paid attention.

He couldn't bring himself to miss the people he never knew as much as he missed people he had known, but still he missed them. There was no greater beauty lost than men and women no longer there. Gerald loved them, although they'd lived so far apart.

All he retained were faint impressions of the people they had been and things he once believed. Gerald grappled for understanding as people grappled to understand the deaths of people that they loved, in the times that people loved. That understanding was most difficult to reach when the dead had let themselves expire. He didn't know what he would do without them.

Feeling was easier than understanding. People resting in their little homes might've been more content in their long solitude than was Gerald to be alone. Those vanguards of the world gone past sat lonely in the cold, with thoughts that made them weak. There'd been a time his busyness for other things had let him leave them be, but no more. He would expend time with them just to expend that time in company. People he didn't like had come to be the friends he'd gladly make if he could be with them again, even if all they wanted was somebody to help them up the stairs to die.

Prebend Row was almost empty, but for long-surviving birds pecking for specks of food in cracks between the stones. Old buildings high around were the same they'd always been, but without the merchant class to justify them. The borough council had ceased its business and sealed shut the town hall doors. If the rusting hands of the tower clock still turned, they did so surreptitiously.

There were no festivals without people to participate. Where once there'd been outdoor markets, fairs, and sometimes a tall Ferris wheel, the only sounds were Gerald's slow steps treading through the silence of the square. They left nothing in their place but the fading recollections of people who were dying.

The bleak bronze-age figure of Joseph Pease in his suit and coat remained upon his pedestal on High Row. So soiled with time, Gerald could not interpret the panels in the plinth.

Trapped in statue, Pease was Gerald's last companion, not quite able to discern if the effigy watched him too. Conspicuous around the lonely town with so few left around, the dead man stood in silent homily. If Pease was dismayed at the end-time games he'd seen his sublime descendants play, he did not confide his wisdom to people hard of hearing.

Around England, there must've been a thousand or more statues of such men and women from ancient days. In their gesticulating poses from the past, they still rode their great horses, stood in salute, and feted their fellow God in heaven. Their antiquities could've kept their people young, in the midst of all they'd seen, but their inheritors hadn't realised the reasons those legacies were there. Gerald's forebears worked hard to build the treasures left to him, living with less than had the modern-day impoverished, without leaving themselves to die.

His people could've lived, but lost themselves so that only infrastructure survived. Artefacts of art and grand technology might yet endure, but they could be so facile. The great world of engineering and accomplishment they'd only inherited; Gerald was no accomplice in their creation. The things they were had not survived, except for the few of them remaining. The last people left alone could not sustain the heirlooms passed to no one.

The dry steps along High Row were much too cold for Gerald

to sit upon them. If he did, he mightn't be able to stand up from them again.

He tried to think, but remembered better when he didn't try. The itinerants who once loitered around the town and outside restaurants had moved along. Working men and women who'd refused to feed or even notice them would've thrown everything they owned into the air if doing so would lure them back again, but beggars were among the men and women no longer there. Without the chance to earn and spend, money was less meaningful than ever.

Gerald trod slowly where he and Vanessa strolled, in the lives they used to lead. She still dogged his crazy thoughts; he missed her more than any other person. In a township rife with friends, he could've talked about her; he thought less of missing her when he was missing everyone. Vividly imagining people he'd left behind was not insanity, but keeping his mind from doing so might have been. His former friends and lovers were no longer his.

Thirty-one years earlier, they'd held each other's hands, with reason to live forever. (In Gerald's most cloistered moments of calculation, he knew how many years earlier he'd done most things in life.) Their confidence had been misplaced, their hopes null and void. If she were to see him as he'd become, he wondered what she'd make of him. He wouldn't care if she had aged as he had aged but, without sight to wreck his memories, she remained as he remembered. The days since then, the dying days of earth, he'd lost everything, except her youth and beauty.

His love endured without time and them together, as no other sense he'd known endured. His love would not abate because he'd not see her again. Love was better than the misery left in him to feel; misery was better than feeling nothing. Life's only consequence was love and sorrow.

Time alone convinced Gerald she could've saved them. He gave Vanessa up to keep his life intact, but withheld from her a life that died without her. The life he'd wanted to preserve was dead, that lifetime lost ago. She was the aspect of his life he could've kept. He would sacrifice everything he didn't have to be with her again, at the ages they had been or the age he had become. He survived instead with much too little, in the bungled life he undertook.

If Gerald knew the future waiting for them when last he saw her, he'd have shared his knowledge with her. He could've done no more to please her with his touch, but the years inspired the words that he the shining knight would say. He would rescue them and keep her home with him, if she wanted him to save her. She'd been younger than she thought she was, but he never told her so. A premonition of their lives might've saved them both. If by grace or misadventure he had the chance to live again, his only priority would be people he could touch.

England would never again be as it once was. The society they'd made had passed away. He loved but failed to save her.

Desolation drove imagination from his mind. Only two years older than Gerald, Vanessa should still have been alive. He might've been among the last people to see her, if the night she left him she was injured and lay comatose in the hospital, without anybody telling him. She might've lain dead in a morgue or been buried in a cemetery. She was too young to die, but everybody was.

She might have been safely holed up anywhere, whatever power flowed to people in that place. She could've been exiled far away, struggling over sea and land towards her aging home; she would find him on High Row. Hers could've been a paradise in hell, from which she could no longer come back home. She might simply pass away in another place to die.

If a part of her was still an entity somewhere, then Gerald didn't know. He knew nothing more about her than he knew the final time he saw her. The conversation he longed to have, they never shared. If she was exiled far from her home, then he was exiled within his.

The ghosts they'd left behind might still be there, in never-changing patterns on High Row. Rain had long washed away the pictures drawn in chalk, but Gerald thought he saw the last lines of a single hopscotch court. Perhaps her ghost walked there alone, while he walked in his biology.

Suddenly, he thought he saw her, standing close to a light pole no longer functioning and watching him. Gerald might not have been sane enough to keep his imagination whole. He could no longer hold her hand.

Gerald missed most Vanessa, but she necessitated so much else to miss. He could be disappointed with the abstract of society as he could not be disappointed with someone real to touch. They'd lived their lives to make them old without the wisdom age could've brought. At sixty long years of age, Gerald was finally trying to find some wisdom. Vanessa's hand was almost touching his, as they walked together on the stones.

His thoughts were tiring him. The muscles in his neck were sore. The time would come when Gerald could no longer count the years since everything had changed. He felt too young to have finished the best years of his life and too old to remember them. Too many years remained.

Gerald rested on a bench, his melancholy face slipping closer to his rounding shoulders. The cold against his coat and aged self might make him ill, but he would not be there very long. His hands tried to warm his face, gazing through the fading light of day.

Apparitions of thinning crowds walked in clouded light, in their poise and pace of everything all right, not knowing Gerald saw them. Those apparitions slowly aged, becoming frail and free to die, treading carefully not to fall. Only he remained to think of them, recalling they were there.

Hope was worse than grieving with the certainty of death. Gerald could dream too much to think that dreams alone could comfort. He wanted Vanessa with him more than he wanted to revive and prolong any other facet of his life, but wanting something was not enough to make it happen. He would desecrate everything around him for one more moment with her, but couldn't.

Too much alike other people he had known, no better and no worse, his only grace had been Vanessa. The other lonely people were no more stupid than he'd been, but she'd been better than they'd been: a goddess for the ungodly. She could no longer save him.

If she were proud of anything then she should be proud for having tried to move him, but Gerald had nothing of which he could be proud. She was more alive in memories than he'd ever been with her. Longing to be where she went, he couldn't see a face still smiling and know it smiled because of him. The errors he made when he was young, he made in perpetuity.

Someone should've warned him, through the last years of their land. Nobody told him why.

His loneliness was reason to abhor the dying and dead who left him getting cold, but Gerald missed his people too much to hate them. The world wasting away had lost the presence of his compatriots; England was everything to him. They were a people, just a people, and always were.

Their ruin lay more in what they should've done, than what they did. They'd expended lives for less than nothing, and acquiesced. They rotted, but they rotted at the core so no one noticed.

The only wealth they ever needed, the only cause worth pursuing, the only leisure ever gratifying, had been their people. Their thoughts of life had never reached too far, but they could've born the children who would've been their future. Their flesh and blood would die of their old age without having matured. They'd left behind England, and left behind poor Gerald.

An old man getting older among the last of his small kind, Gerald no longer just wanted to be amused. He was already much too old. Holding Vanessa in his arms might not suffice, if they couldn't make the love he felt into fruition. He might've lived with her sixty years but died without their issue, leaving her the working widow, murdering her no less than him.

Night and rain would both soon fall. Struggling to collect himself, Gerald gripped an armrest, levered his arm and mitten-covered hand and pressed his other hand against the bench. He pulled and pushed himself upright. Drawing his coat close to his body, he trekked on Tubwell Row.

St Cuthbert's Church nabbed his last attention. The churchyard's worn grey headstones remained conspicuous between the wooden crosses in the long grass ground. The men and women who'd made Darlington were never more obviously dead and passed away.

Never before had Gerald studied the inscriptions in the stone, where a sculpted soldier statue still fought a bygone war, the Boer War, so very far from home. The epitaph, that constant eulogy not just for the dead from Darlington but for what English people were, was cold. They'd been bloody stupid heroes so much greater than Gerald was. There'd be no monuments or memorials to him.

He'd once thought wars were the only means by which Europeans died. Wars were just one means of a people dying too soon.

If he gained knowledge from his loneliness and were to learn all the wisdom of the world because he had nothing else to do but think, then he was no less killing time by doing so. He would still be going nowhere with nothing left to see or hear, without reason, unable to recoup. No one would know about him, his new-found knowledge would be pointless, when he passed away alone. His scholarship was no less mortal than his stupidity, his learning no less terminal than his ignorance.

St Cuthbert's timber doors were locked. Man, not God, had sealed them. Perhaps only He survived.

19

NIGHTFALL

Leaves fell in autumn unison; there were only the passing seasons. Small winds spilled pale brown leaves that no one swept away, changing the seasons of the streets. The multiplying leaves littered the carriageways and pavements, where cars and people would once have stirred them into gutters and against walls. They fluttered in the air, until a shower of rain impressed them in the ground, creating meagre streams. The rain matted the rotting leaves into a pale brown cloak across the ground, obscuring all the kerbs. Through it, black worn steppingstones weaved a feeble path.

Windows to boastful buildings became forlorn. The magnificent crumbled to be meek, too brittle without people in them.

Nobody knew how many Englishmen and women remained alive in County Durham: a thousand perhaps, a hundred maybe; too few to be society. In a world they once complained had been congested, nobody still counted their small number. Dystopia had supposed to be too many people in the world. It became too few Europeans.

Sometimes, when the town was its most quiet and a wind headed in the right direction, Gerald thought he heard the sounds of trains headed south to London or returning north. It didn't matter what he heard. They were like the rare aeroplanes still slipping through English sky, too far away to touch. The last of the cabin lights to shine at night were the furthest away.

Power plants might've exploded or melted down without scientists and technicians to manage them. Their safety mechanisms might've failed without reserves. They were thus carefully extinguished. Engineering that conquered ground and sky had stalled.

The electricity supply to Darlington ceased sometime late September. Electronic display clocks ceased illuminating numerals, but older clocks of revolving hands immortalised that last instant of the time: fifteen minutes past nine o'clock. The time once blazing from all sides became reticent to speak.

Battery-powered clocks continued displaying the time, but progressively they stopped. A battery-powered old wristwatch reminded Gerald of the time whenever he wanted to be reminded, but he rarely wanted to be reminded. Antique clocks fell still when human hands became too frail to wind the keys. Clocks could continue turning after human beings had died, but without anyone to see, there wasn't time of day.

Computer terminals and telephone networks lay dead, starved of any means of communicating with each other. A lonely person's words typed into a keyboard remained unread. Tears into a telephone remained unheard. Silicon chip memories lost their wisdom without power to revive them. The last of the old movies stopped playing on television sets. Idle toys and other ornaments in silver, glass, and metalwork were useless to people waiting for the night.

Only the sun still shone, while places that electricity made bright were dark. The world was its most desolate and sky furthest away in the shadowy caverns of what had been commercial premises. The ceilings that once cast beams across the floors cast only shadows from the sun. They made the lifeless buildings starker than were the streets of air. The caves for ghosts were ominous.

In his apartment, Gerald's refrigerator door opened without the sounds of rubber seals breaking their little vacuum. Without refrigeration, cow's milk quickly soured. Gerald drank it before allowing it to waste. The powerlessness of the people was his.

His teeth crunched through broccoli eaten raw, without the tenderness cooking provided. Vegetables tasted as they'd grown, unchanged from their existence embedded in the ground. Gerald's weak tongue and cracking lips pushed away subsisting dirt. They suffered by comparison with the savouries he could no longer find.

He chewed some chocolate from a bar to remove the remnants of dirt broccoli from his mouth, and put the rest of the bar into his pocket. For dessert, he ate uninteresting sliced peaches from a can. The food still left him hungry.

In the half-light of an almost vacant building, Gerald trekked down the stairs, his hands resting on the banisters. Each lower floor was darker than any floor above, until glass panels in the building doors admitted daylight to the entrance hallway. It refracted around Gerald and seeped along deep passages, to light a little more the building burrows. No longer was there light that once assured him, but just the vestiges of daytime through the glass.

The air was cold when Gerald laid his bowl and spoon upon the ground outside; bugs and ants would gorge upon the film of sweet peach syrup. The next fall of rain would wash clean the bowl and spoon.

Prepared as he'd been prepared for too little in his life, Gerald lay near them pots and pans from his kitchen cupboards. They would catch the falling rain for him to drink and use to wash himself. His clothes and most cutlery and crockery he'd wash, before leaving them out to dry. Doing the things he did each day saved him from feeling tired.

Seepage into soil and storm waters replaced the sewerage system. Behind the shrubs, Gerald shielded himself from other unclean people. So vulnerable, the sordid sense affirmed his poor depravity. He quickly covered himself again and slunk away. Private garden holders kept their modesty lost to others. Gerald only had the night.

He could've taken an empty house to use its fireplace, but houses were normally colder than middle-storey apartments.

Besides, all but one of the empty houses hadn't been his home. His parents' home was too far away.

An amateur aged gas fitter, Gerald sealed the building valve from the pointless public pipes. Using a blunted hacksaw he'd taken from a dead person's abode, he slowly cut the tarnished pipe into the building.

In each new step of his rustic life and death, he'd undertake more chores that he'd never before done. They weren't pleasures to perform, as he'd once expected work to be. They weren't comfortable careers, chances to meet people and talk with them between and after work. The product of a once glorious career, Gerald's toil was far removed from office days and coming home to his easy-life apartment. His only motivation was survival, but there'd never been any better.

His chore routine unfolding would feed and keep him in his subdued subsistence. Those self-sufficient chores demanded more physical exertion than had his desk career and tiny tasks around his home.

The pipe cut, Gerald set up the bulky welding equipment he'd taken from a store. With protective covering across his eyes, the flames ignited. Taking tongs in his other hand, Gerald tried affixing a valve to the cut pipe to which he could attach a gas bottle, but he couldn't make it stick. Whatever he needed to do, he couldn't. Finally he conceded, with plans to try again later.

Gerald sealed his home from every opening to outside cold. He'd already closed every double-glazed window. He closed the curtains in every room whenever he didn't need the light.

His apartment door locked, Gerald walked the streets of fallen leaves, past dark and sombre buildings like the one in which he lived. He might've walked so somebody looking from a window would know that he was there. He might've walked for the chance of meeting someone to become his friend.

Hugging the edges of a building was a solitary brown dog, a mongrel in a county once of pedigrees. Its curiosity piqued by the stranger whose kind once filled the land, the dog started walking with him. There'd been a time Gerald would have fed the last of his chocolate bar concealed within his pocket to wandering animals, which walked with him until they knew they'd get no more, but he could no longer afford dependency. An animal was something to feed when he wasn't certain what he'd eat. Animals were becoming fewer in the cold. A dog's inquisitiveness in Gerald was nothing left for him.

From a distance not to frighten them, Gerald watched two little squirrels nibbling at food inedible for people. The dog kicked away towards the feast without regard for diners already there, sending them a scarpering. Finished there, it returned to Gerald and stared at him. Gerald shook his head, and began to walk away.

The dog followed him, until it again raced away. Hidden safe from view, Gerald took and ate more of his chocolate bar. The last few squares he dropped on the ground where the dog would find them. He walked far enough away for the dog not to know he'd left them.

The building in which Gerald lived alone comprised a realm of empty dark apartments in which a dog could live, but animals would soil them. Gerald kept the dog behind him as he walked from the pavement up the steps, past the useless electronic buttons no longer ringing inside apartments, and unlocked the street-front door. He closed the door with the dog outside watching him. When next he looked, the dog had gone.

Rather than remembering what he couldn't do, Gerald tried to think of what he could. Playing cards did not require power, but required more than patience. Games of solitaire were games to play with fools. Battery-powered disc players could play old recorded movies and old recorded music, but Gerald saved the batteries for torches. The harmonies to which he listened were the harmonies in his head, from the times when he was young. Songs he'd already heard too often could make him tired.

Before modern amenities for leisure, people talked with other people, but those people had gone. Anything Gerald would've done among his population was more than he could do alone. His retiring mind had only books to read and only during daylight.

Sitting in his sofa, in the little lounge room he'd already seen too often, Gerald watched the shadows of the setting sun drift across the floor. Other solitary men and women might, perhaps, have been thinking about him. Nobody knocked on anybody's door. He listened to the quiet.

Daylight became meeker by the minute. The natural light remaining was not enough to brighten his old furniture or the pictures on the wall. Hand-held torches drained mortal batteries, and Gerald used them only when he needed to see something. He rarely did.

The encroaching darkness was little duller than daytime had become. The last of the muting light in his apartment abated, abandoning him. Night fell at dusk, without illumination to stave it off until Gerald chose to sleep.

He'd never before seen night so overwhelming. There'd been dark nights before, through the intermittent blackouts, but none so deep as night that wouldn't end. The streets that human lights once filled were empty spaces in the black, as if the lights had never been there. Once luminous lights lay buried in the night, the darkness of his life, as every night would be. No one but he was there.

Without the last dim light of day, the air against Gerald's face cooled. It was colder than Gerald remembered dusk being one day earlier, understanding something more of the new life in which he lived.

He should have already been in bed, but had no mood to sleep too soon and wake too early. Waking would only be worthwhile if he could wake and realise that everything he thought that he recalled had been a long destructive dream; Gerald would live his life better a second time. He would be glad for people he hadn't noticed his first time.

If he knew that God would answer then Gerald would ask Him for that chance. His old man's life had come upon him much too soon.

Gerald could not imagine purpose in his living without people he could know. In the life for which he wished, in the land that should've been, he would have been under lights with his wife and sons and daughters. He would bounce their children and grandchildren on his knees. Nothing else about that life was so important.

He yearned to form that image, but didn't know enough about

the lives that never were. He couldn't picture any woman to be the daughter never born. A son might've been like him, when he would implore his son to learn sooner than he'd learnt from his stupidity. If any woman hurt him, or he hurt her, then he should let his heart tear apart for however long he needed to feel miserable, until the pain abated. He should cry and try again.

Through the framed silhouette of his lounge room windowpane shone long beams from the high-beam headlights of a silent passing ambulance, spreading shadows across the ceiling. Soon the space in which Gerald sat was dark again, his eyes adjusting to the naturally black night. Silent hearses carted the dying and dead away: withered native bodies, as old as Gerald would become. The passing eons of his life afforded him too much time to think and so regret, wondering whether anyone again would want to know him.

With no one to hear his wisdom, Gerald sat alone. His name was unimportant, without anyone to use it. He recalled it only when he recalled the person he had been, in the life no longer there. Remorse remained his company.

The dated darkness gave the night an unfamiliar taste and odour. Gerald could have been anywhere, in any time, in the darkness that engulfed him. Only his sofa cradling him and soft rug through his slippers assured him he was there, not dead, inside the dark that could have been his home.

Inside his mouth, a tooth was tender in the cold, touching a little nerve behind it. Gerald mightn't have noticed it when he was young, but in his age he might find a dentist's surgery and chair without finding a dentist to save him from the pain.

The town-scape outside, if it still existed in the night, was no less dark than Gerald's home. Old people were vulnerable to nights concealing threats they couldn't see. Gerald's vulnerability would let him know if he was old.

Reaching through the darkness, Gerald's fingers groped about the coffee table, until he found his battery-powered torch. His torch shone through the room and what would have been the black; Gerald was at home. Unnatural light was comforting to see again, in a little vestige of what England had achieved. It was his chance to breach a corner of the night, and maybe see his way.

Holding that torch in one hand and using his other hand to push himself, Gerald rose slowly from the sofa. His torchlight lit the rug and lowest edges of the furniture he was careful not to trip, as he followed the cautious light across the floor. The window was a place from which to look, and he stepped into the patch of light. Finally, he stood before the glass, placing the torch against it so less reflection obscured his view.

His left hand touched the window. The glass was cold, much colder than his home.

The picture of a blackened space became larger as Gerald's face moved closer to the window, gazing through it into night. Other people's homes reflected splinters from his light, simulating strangers watching from the windows. A floor lamp and shade were something like a figure of a person. In any blackened room a person might've sat or stood.

For Gerald to feel alive, he couldn't merely see the night through panes of glass. He should feel fresh air on his face.

Starting toward the street, he turned around. The spot of little light from his small torch swept across the room and hallway until, several steps into Gerald's journey, it shone on the closed door of his apartment.

Age had brought him caution from which loneliness could not absolve him. Fear might've been all that remained in him to feel, but what might lurk beyond that door? No longer was he young enough to walk outside without reluctance. The glass-panelled door secured the building from the street, unless someone broke the glass and manipulated loose the lock. Another door sealed the building from the rear, which a man taking Gerald's tools from the bricked bin stores might break. A fire could burn in that back door fireplace.

Only his apartment door might still defend Gerald from anything outside. His solitude made him more afraid.

Gerald had nothing more to do that night and end of day, in the apartment in which he was confined. His little beam of torchlight led him to his bedroom.

As secure in his small space as Gerald could be, his torch

lay on his bedside table. It shone a beam of light past him, creating his shadow against the wall, as wearily he removed his clothes and slippers. Gerald dressed into his thickest flannelette pyjamas and climbed into the sanctity of bed, without the light of an unnecessary electric clock beside him. When once he would've extinguished an abundance of bright lights, he extinguished his solitary torch.

In bed, he could pretend the nights were still as they once were. The darkness let him see what he couldn't see in light. He pulled his sheets and woollen blankets close until they touched his face. Gerald wouldn't leave his bed before the morning. He mightn't leave his bed again.

20

WINTER

Sunrise became later and crisper every morning. The damp sky turned to dusk earlier each evening. The air was cooler each night than the last. It was never cooler than in the moments before morning, when the lights of sunrise slowly pushed aside the shadows on the streets.

The last late-autumn eaves hung precariously from baring trees, before falling. Autumn waned into winter bare.

With every turn to colder weather, old people became more prone to influenza and pneumonia. Linked by their looming deaths, neighbours began watching after one another, just a little. They pushed vases along windowsills each alternate day. If one day a vase didn't move, then a watchful neighbour came to see if somebody had died.

If neighbours couldn't bury the deceased, then they hung white sheets from closed windows and tops of doors like flags of their surrender, quite unlike simple washing hanging from old lines. Passers-by helped carry corpses to the nearest plots of soil and dig holes in the dirt, or notified the bury-men loitering at the hospital hospice and the markets. The bodies buried, they left the sheets inside the empty homes, among the items surplus to their needs.

Waking to each morning, Gerald contemplated the coming

lonely day and same chores he'd undertaken yesterday. He dressed into brown clothes, because they never looked too dirty. The arch across his weary shoulders was what his long life had become. His fingers were becoming thin and joints pronounced, more difficult to straighten. The aching in his bones might've been arthritis. He gently clasped those hands together, and hoped they would endure.

The water taps were closed so that nothing would gush out if the supply resumed, although Gerald knew it never would. Pretending that it might, he sometimes turned the taps above the kitchen sink. One day, a single drop of waterfall slipped from the spout into his open hand. The tip of his old tongue tasted the cold dampness on the skin of his soft palm. It was everything to him.

Bottled water contained more minerals than did water from the sky, but would soon exhaust. The last of the lukewarm soft drinks and fruit juices were sweeter sustenance. Fearful of tooth decay without fluoride in the water, Gerald cut apart the tubes of toothpaste for every trace he could extract. He wiped his teeth with his tongue to feel his teeth were clean.

While whiskers grew unchecked on other men's faces, Gerald shaved before his bothered him. Squeezing the last white shaving cream from rusting aerosol cans, he groomed himself as he'd done throughout his adult life. As best he could, he cut his hair in its reflection to keep it short and neat, but the silver strands proliferated and his pale and speckled scalp became more exposed. He was doing well each time he did anything he once did.

Reflected in his bathroom mirror, Gerald's face was forever tired. His once full features had become lean, his body slowing with his age. Creases lengthened and deepened each time he looked. Whether his cheekbones were becoming more pronounced was hard to tell when he saw so much of them. Becoming uneasy in their sockets, the eyes once his exuded tiny senses of the man he used to be. The part light of day reflected from moisture forming there.

Along some pavements stood large steel drums, their covers cut away, in which people lit public fires. (Gerald's contribution to the fuel included Doris' notices.) Rubbing their hands against the warmth while they waited for their meals to burn, strangers stood like solitary moths around their final flames. The eyes of one old woman inadvertently connected with Gerald's across the sparks.

"Hello," said Gerald.

"Hello."

"Can you weld a gas valve to a pipe?"

She shook her head. They continued looking at each other, not really congregating.

When they finished eating, they took away their plates and cutlery to leave outside their homes. Gerald disposed of refuse where nobody could see it, keeping clean his corner of a drab and docile town. The markets became smaller in the encroaching winter dusk, without people saying where they were going.

Winter finally seized the county. Cold houses, from which sparsely set weak palls of smoke rose into the darkening cloudy sky, and the dens of best and worst apartments were the last hives of dwindling life. Retreated to their scattered homes, shrivelling faces took what warmth they could from little flames. Their aged teeth yellowing, they rested in old armchairs where nobody could see them, in the last years of their lives: parting images from a morbid dying people.

Standing at the open door behind the building, too cold to step out further, Gerald spilled wastewater onto the winter ice. It drained towards the frozen grass.

Wearing his thickest coat and hat, and with a long scarf wrapped around his face and neck, Gerald braved the weather to fulfil the fewest chores required. The ice in pots and saucepans he'd left outside slowly melted when he brought them into his less-cold building hallways. He washed the clothes he'd worn too many despondent days, and hung them from apartment door handles in corridors and from bannisters. He dabbed the middling water on his skin to clean himself.

Gerald dwelt in silent solitude in his dark and dusty home, there needing light and power less than he needed them elsewhere. Days and weeks were like months and years had been, when people doused their brains with leisure in the lights.

The thoughts he made a hundred times he soon forgot and made again: of women he met and never knew. Concocting new thoughts became more difficult the longer he was alone. His thoughts resounded and exhausted him as his activities once had. Choosing his memories helped him fall to sleep each night, but without the peace and comfort that lies had once accorded.

His dreams were fantasies far removed from his experience, desperate for distractions from time alone. Gerald often dreamed of meeting by strange chance his long-passed love again, conversing with Vanessa about the changes since last they were together. He tried to kiss her, but she remained aloof, unaffected by the feelings that still afflicted him. Sometimes, she let him kiss her, when they talked of love and longing.

Gerald was profoundly glad for that companion, until he woke back into the night. Dreaming hope was easy, when believing anything had become difficult.

He missed her soft touch close to him, before he'd become old. He missed her lips warm against his, before his lips became chafed. Bed sheets against his skin were coarse aside his memories of her. His was the only heart still beating.

His aloneness was loneliness in the senses he still felt. He'd come to feel his solitude, himself in the oblivion. Gerald wanted to talk with anyone, to hear a voice not his voice inside his head. He wanted somebody to listen to him thinking. He alone still dreamt about them being together.

Sleep no longer came too readily, but the mornings were too cold for him to leave his bed too soon. His blankets and pyjamas kept his body warm, but they couldn't warm his fragile face. Sunlight on a cloudy day slipped around brick barricades and staggered meekly through the windows towards him. Gerald studied every moment growing into day.

No sounds came from anywhere in his apartment, apartments around it, or Marlborough Drive outside. They were completely silent, as they always seemed to be. The silence made the days seem like a sound, more daunting each new morning than it had been the last. The silence every day confirmed that he would always be alone.

Most days Gerald lay long in his bed. He read books when daylight was bright enough and his arm bold enough to leave the warmth within his blankets to reach his bedside table. His bed could make him weary.

From the comfort of his pillow around his head, his mind succumbed to the speckles in the ceiling and the walls. Emerging in them were patterns becoming familiar: human faces, lush trees, and aeroplanes taking him away. Gerald closed his eyes to see what he couldn't see with his eyes open. He'd wish that everything would become again what it had been when he was young.

Slowly, his eyes opened. Nothing changed because he wished it would.

Moving sluggishly as aged bodies did, Gerald climbed from his bed into the cold air of his room. A shiver ran through his arms and shoulders. The chest of drawers near his bed contained clean undergarments into which he quickly dressed, before pulling on his warmest winter clothes. He turned the tap above the bathroom washbasin, but no water dripped from it. He turned it back again each day.

He hadn't realised how cold and dark winter could be: the first for him without utilities on which he still depended. His circumstances made an ordinary winter much worse than it would otherwise have been.

One early morning Gerald woke to darkness, after falling asleep under two blankets in his lounge room sofa. The day was, he guessed, his birthday, although he wasn't really sure. If sometimes he struggled to recall his age then it was because, in another life, he'd have expected to live for twenty more years and hoped for ten beyond. In the life of a dying town, Gerald couldn't expect anything. He could hope for little more.

Birthdays becoming older could've been the best days of the year, when lives were going well and people acknowledged age without regret. They were the worst days in poor lives going badly: the days when the lonely in their homes were loneliest.

If birthdays were still important, they were the only days that were.

In another fate for his rapidly dying country, Gerald might've celebrated with family and friends. He might've drunk good beer and wine, eaten decorated meals, and danced to music playing alive from young musicians, instead of nibbling doctored food from tin cans remembering songs no longer played. The only party underway was a long funeral, with only Gerald left to mourn.

He could've made a cake with icing from rudimentary ingredients, but there was no purpose in a cake too big to eat. Grocery stores long ago stopped proffering packets of colourful wax candles; customers didn't want anything to remind them of their ages.

No candles burnt in recognition of a day Gerald didn't want. "Happy birthday," he whispered to himself, through the clothes around his face. "I wish that everything was what it was...," he started to say, before daring to wish a little more. "I wish that everything were better."

Gerald drew his breath and blew. He couldn't blow out candles not there.

Being sixty-one years old had never seemed more aged than it seemed to Gerald to be old, but he'd felt much older than his years for quite a time. His solitude more than his age condemned him, too quickly getting older. Had his life continued as it was, before England died, Gerald would've felt younger than he'd come to feel. He hadn't understood when he was young what he could feel when he was old. "I wish my life had been a dream that morning wipes away." The morning remained unchanged.

Sitting again in a chair of four at the dining table at which he ate his meals, Gerald opened a tin can of herrings and packet of water biscuits. With him was a partly drunk wine bottle with the cork slightly in it. Small fish in a can and glasses of grape water were the best cuisine available, in the muted light of his apartment.

Gerald's imagination tried to sit Vanessa in the chair where last she ate a meal with him. Her clothes were those she'd worn when last he saw her, but he could not recall her well enough to see her face. She was a spirit, in which he couldn't quite discern her eyes.

He ate a fresh biscuit, picked away at a wet herring, and sipped a glass of wine, studying the sediment in the bottle. Gazing across the table at the space in which she sat, his shoes could almost touch her feet under the table. "How are you, today?" he asked aloud.

Gerald gave her time to answer, while he wondered what next to say. If she told him she was well, then she was faring better than he fared. He didn't know her well enough to give her words he couldn't hear.

He struggled to say very much at all. Gerald wanted to tell her that he loved her but, so many years since last he saw her, he wasn't sure he did. He could've asked her if she loved him, but the question sounded much too miserable to ask. He didn't want to be a tragedy.

Gerald supposed he should be sadder for having lost his parents than for having lost Vanessa; he had so much for which he could be sad. Choosing between the people of his past and the person who might've been a future was a foolish, stupid choice. The hypothetical election was cruel to each of them and crueller still to him. He wanted anyone to be with, in anybody's home, and dreamt of nothing less. Nobody at the dining table spoke to him that day.

Gently, he resealed the cork in the wine bottle, before returning it to the cupboard. He replaced the last of the water biscuits in the lukewarm refrigerator and carefully placed the empty can and last of the fish juices outside. He would remain bored, without amusement, until the men and women dead came back to find him. He was waiting for a people to return, knowing they never would.

Preserved foods and beverage in his pantry became rows of empty bottles and piles of empty plastic packets outside the building rear, for pungent animals to clean. When the last Englishman and woman had passed away and last tin cans licked dry, even the rats might leave.

No people looked out from any windows, not that Gerald

saw. The homes without curtains drawn across them might have been empty for a while. The fallen leaves were fragments of a rotting rug without a pattern on the ground. Studying twists of light and shadows for other remnants of his people, Gerald hoped to see some stragglers and survivors, doing what he was doing. If he dared hope then he would hope that Vanessa was among them, but he knew that she was not. No one would hear his desperate beckoning for company if he screamed it to the streets. Besides, he was too old to scream.

Without reason to venture from his home, Gerald stood in the centre of his lounge room where he stood with her so young. The room and life had fallen dark since then, but her sweet form survived as his mirage for a long night. The air had fallen cold, but they could've kept each other warm. Longing to hold her there again, Gerald's tender hands reached where they once held her. His fingers slowly opened, and held the space of air in which she stood. They almost sensed her warmth still with him.

His face moved towards hers. Eyes dipped, he kissed her lips in the still air. Pained in his passion, he bid her well into the nothingness into which he too was headed, if he wasn't there already.

Christmas Day was overcast. The snow of recent days lay frozen on the ground. It could've been another frame of Gerald's story of the lives that never were, with him beside the soulful wife of his imaginings, whoever she was. Their grandchildren unimaginable could've bounced upon his crumbled knee. Instead, he ate his tired meals and drank his drink alone.

Cooped up in a building he despised, Gerald imagined opening the lounge room window and setting his curtains alight; he no longer feared the flames of fire engulfing him. His funeral pyre would surely attract anybody left alive, if anybody was, but he couldn't wreck that grand memorial he'd spent his life to keep unchanged. He wouldn't murder his mausoleum.

Mere dusk wasn't reason to succumb to his cold bed that evening, waiting for his grandchildren to visit. Gerald dressed into his thickest coat, hat, and gloves and picked up a hand torch he rarely used. Standing on the steps outside the building, his scarf around his head covered most of his face, to keep the bracing air from sealing his mouth and lips. His arms held close to him, Gerald surveyed the wintry night of Christmas town. Any fire or human light would suffice, but he saw only his weak torch beam in the bleakness.

Listening for a voice calling out to him, Gerald wondered why his grandchildren took so long to come. The only sounds were of the wind and a single distant dog ensconced within its shelter, howling like a wolf. The owls and other birds were sleeping.

His torchlight cast through dark across the spaces of the street, onto trees and long-familiar buildings, homes, and fences. The slights of light were just the light from his small torch reflected in the ice. If it reflected in a pair of eyes lurking in the darkness then Gerald would not be frightened. An Englishman would be too old or sick to harm him. A rogue coming from the shadows would make him glad that anyone was there.

Gerald waved about his little beacon, trying to draw attention from anybody there. The cone of shining light was small, the trail of light becoming lost before it reached the clouds. He held the torch above his head and dragged it back and forth across the darkness. He must've been conspicuous, standing at one end of the only light at night, but even market towns were large enough for people to be unaware that someone else was near.

Another bout of snow would've been a lovely spectacle in another setting and a story, but not for an old man standing senselessly in such a lonely space. Nobody could see him, against the dark and damp. Nobody could hear him if he tried to speak aloud. The coming year would be no better than the last, in ritual hell of eternal repetition. Gerald let the torchlight fall.

Much too far away to have seen Gerald's lonesome torch, Alec was with Hollie and Brandon in their home in Hummersknott. Their fireplace cast a warm, dancing light upon Brandon's hair becoming long. Alec recognised in his son the young man he had been, before his hair had tinged to hints of grey and cheeks became a little thin. Grey also began staining Hollie's hair, which she kept shorter as she aged.

The Christmas gifts they'd exchanged were idle banter: books they'd taken from empty bookstores many months earlier and hidden in neighbours' empty houses. The cards they'd written to each other could've been written any Christmas, wishing them all good fortune, striving for some hope: *"Merry Christmas"*, *"Good luck in the new year"*, *"With all my love."*

They'd played games of canasta with well-worn playing cards, keeping score within each game but not a tally of the games that anybody won, until the night became dark. Their skills had grown enough for any one of them to win.

Warm steam rose from rainwater boiling in a saucepan on the stove Alec had erected over the fire. A kettle boiled the water they drank as tea, each clasping their mugs with both their hands. Teabags soaked too many times were tasteless.

Alec had repainted walls and stained the timber trimmings throughout their home that year, without painting over the marks outside Brandon's bedroom door. Those pencil marks denoted his height each childhood year until his sixteenth birthday, two and a half years earlier. "Son," smiled Alec, reminiscing as they did each Christmas night. "Do you remember that birthday you became so mature, you wouldn't let me measure your height?"

Brandon grinned. "When you and mum weren't looking, I'd already placed a book on my head and held it there."

Alec was perplexed. Hollie moved a little closer.

"The book was on the line you'd marked a year earlier."

Alec laughed. "I never knew."

"I didn't want marks on a wall to be a meter to the birthdays when you and mum aren't with me anymore."

Alec stared at the firelight and shadows across his son's newly adult face; Brandon didn't need to plead to be believed. Slowly Alec fathomed Brandon's fear of a future more alone than his and Hollie's would be. "This coming year," said Alec, "we might all need to leave, for Cornwall."

21

THE OLD MAN IN THE PARK

Weeks of seven days were minor keepsakes from the past, measuring lives still passing and all they'd left behind. They were like months and years had been, when people doused their brains with leisure in the lights. Dates were something for societies, reference points that people set among themselves. Rarely troubling to recall them, Gerald had no fortune left to care.

The calendar Gerald marked with pencil on damp paper was for cycles of the seasons. They'd warned him of nights becoming long and cold. Holed up lonely in his home, they assured him days would again be warm.

The worst of winter finally passed when Gerald most needed spring to come; every brighter sun in bluer sky consoled him. More light in longer days gave him time to read again the books he'd already read.

The hearses became fewer. The people left unsaved were almost dead. Perhaps only Gerald remained to die.

The first spring sun in a morning sky was unseasonably warm, while melting snow lingered in the shade. Not yet rising to the spring, grass lay flat and lifeless by the pavements, without people to sweep away the rotten melded leaves of seasons past.

The curtains behind most windows into darkened homes were closed.

Wearing another of his usual woollen shirts and trousers, without needing a coat that day, Gerald stood outside his building door. The world was silent, without the birds not yet returned. The winter might have killed the cats and dogs, or they might've been asleep.

"Hello," Gerald called out, hurting his aged throat. He'd forgotten the sound of an old man's voice.

No voice called back. No hand waved. The people to befriend another stranger eluded him. They might've watched him from behind glass but, committed to their isolation, refused to show their faces. They might've fled the town, while only foolish he remained.

"Hello," said Gerald, less loudly, more deeply. Only someone nearby could've heard. He mightn't see anyone again.

Taking a corkscrew he'd left in the building entrance hallway, Gerald carved a short message in a glass panel in the doors, enticing any passer-by to find him. "*I am alive.*"

Gerald rested on a chair he kept there, staring to the sky through the mirror image of his written words. Any people left in Darlington needed to find each other, to share lives they'd never before exchanged, before the weather again became too cold or wet. They might be more survivors of the end, or people coming into town from other empty places. Gerald hadn't seen them through the winter, staring from his windows. They mightn't have seen him.

He contemplated where they could be: the indoor markets, the railway station. The only place to find them Gerald wouldn't check was the hospital hospice. He wouldn't befriend a person dying too soon.

Gerald's arms and legs mustered the strength to stand and step outside again. Marlborough Drive was empty but for Gerald, as was Grange Road.

Along Parkside and beyond the gates into South Park were plots of upturned soil among the little bits of snow. The few birds resting on bare tree branches didn't rest on wooden crosses starting to lean. Others pecked away at graves of dirt.

The nineteenth-century Clock Tower Lodge remained a brighter shade of white than time alone deserved.

If the silent swans of the lake remained, they hid. If they'd sung their swan song before they died as legend had it, then Gerald hadn't heard them.

Just as old and once as elegant as the Clock Tower Lodge was the iron bandstand: a raised octagonal white pagoda with railings around most sides and columns supporting a pointed roof for shelter. It reminded Gerald against a foolish thought of the last days of society.

In the bandstand was a bench, on which Gerald slowly realised sat a figure of a person, the first he'd seen for much too long a time. Facing away from Gerald towards the lake, it wore a thick grey coat below a dark brown hat, as old men sometimes wore.

"Hello," called Gerald, before the cold air in his throat forced him to cough. "Hello!" he said more carefully.

The figure didn't move. The person Gerald presumed to be a man might've been deaf or asleep.

Gerald left the winding paths and strode across the flat long grass towards the figure, moving like a man much younger than he'd felt for years. Moisture dampening his shoes and trouser cuffs, his pace quickened with every enthusiastic stride. He would've run, excited and impatient, but he was too old to run. Gerald didn't think about the figure but about himself in company. "Good morning," said Gerald. "Thank goodness, I found you."

Gerald bundled up the steps into the bandstand. Relieved to reach him, Gerald pressed his hand on the figure's shoulder. The coat was slightly damp from early dew.

The figure fell forward onto the bandstand floor. His hat fell from his head. His thick white hair was long, with a white beard above his cheeks and chin.

Gerald hurried around the bench to where the old man fell, crouched down, and grabbed his shoulders to help him up. "Come on," said Gerald, shaking the old man's shoulders.

The old man's head fell backward, forward, and around. His eyes remained closed.

"Wake up!" said Gerald, shaking him more frantically. "I'm here." He needed the old man to see him, hear his voice, and tell him he was sane. "Damn you!" His hands shook the old man a final time, before releasing the old man's shoulders and letting him fall back.

Panting heavily, his lungs and frame aching, Gerald slumped backwards. The old man's still eyes were slightly open, revealing the cream peripheries around his irises. Gerald slapped the old man's belly, trying to provoke him to lash out. He should know that Gerald hated him.

Lying back along the floor, his eyes closed exhausted, dampness moistened the back of Gerald's shirt. Motionless, but for his heavy breathing and heartbeat racing, Gerald's arms and legs ached. The old man was dead.

Gerald's eyes slowly opened, to the bandstand ceiling overhead. The corpse was the first he'd seen but for images, real and contrived, on picture-playing screens. A hundred thousand corpses in digital relief had not prepared him for one real dumped beside him.

Pulling himself to his side and with his damp shirt clinging to his back, Gerald pushed himself upright and sat beside the body. The old man's face was pallid more than white, his crumbled skin not yet yellowing. Gerald didn't know what a dead man's colours ought to be.

He wanted to talk about what happened, but the old man wouldn't listen. Gerald wanted them to share their knowledge and plans for something new. They could talk about the food they ate for breakfast; Gerald had become accustomed to canned tomatoes.

The old man wouldn't answer. He had nothing more to say.

The old man might've been another person barricaded in his home through recent months. For many years, he might have come to walk around the lake or rose garden whenever the weather allowed. He might've seen the fountain waters play, and watched the birds and trees change every season while the town around him died, without noticing that anything had changed. He might've walked defiantly through the snow and ice before that day to die on that cold bench, or he might've died that morning. His might be the first of many bodies Gerald found.

Gently, Gerald touched the back of his fingers against the old man's cheek. His skin was cooler than the air, neither warm nor cold.

No cuts or marks were on the old man's face or hands; nobody had hurt him. He'd surely died of natural causes, brought upon him by his age; old people finally die. The birds pecking away at most things hadn't pecked away at him. His hat and coat might've protected his face from animals that could've scratched his skin. He appeared much as any man who'd become so old and died.

The air had been cold when the old man sat, but had warmed since then. Gerald had missed talking with him by however many minutes, hours, or days had passed since he died. The old man's thoughts in the last moments of his life intrigued him, as did those throughout his final days alive. If Gerald had come sooner upon that park that day or any prior day, braving the ice and snow, then he could've given two dying men some company.

A corpse was company when Gerald had no other. He turned his better ear towards the old man lying down, hoping to hear him say why he was dead and Gerald was alive. The old man seemed indifferent. Gerald couldn't hear his muttering.

Gerald had failed to find another lonely person not willing to be lonely. He could do nothing more than he was doing.

The old man might not have been alone. Gerald pushed himself upright, his hand and feet almost sliding on the floor. Standing uneasily, Gerald looked around the park to see anybody coming. None did. Outside the park were streets upon streets of houses, flats, and apartments. Among them could've been the old man's home.

The bandstand was the highest place around, from which once people spoke and concerts played. "Hello," Gerald cried out, too old to call too loud.

Nobody answered. Nothing moved.

"Hello," Gerald whispered.

In the bandstand stood several shovels, hammers, and screwdrivers, along with a single white cross. Dried brushes lay atop tin cans of paint: some black, some white. They were tools for burying bodies and the old man might've buried other bodies in the park, leaving one cross for himself. Perhaps only Gerald remained to bury him, while the bandstand's white paint was peeling off in cracks.

Without thought of doing anything else, Gerald knelt behind the dead man's back, uncertain how to move a corpse. He pushed his hands under the dead man's arms and around his chest, holding him as if hugging him. Clumsily, he lifted the dead man's torso, but the body was very heavy, much heavier than any living person. Gerald let it fall back to the bandstand floor.

Carefully balancing his weight upon his aging knees and legs, Gerald held the sleeve of the old man's coat. Struggling with the unwieldy body collapsing back onto the ground, Gerald finally pulled the sleeve from the old man's arm. Walking around the corpse and struggling almost as much again, Gerald pulled the sleeve from his other arm. He tugged and dragged the coat under the old man, until he held it in his hands. He then draped the coat across the old man's face, protecting him a little from the birds and animals.

Already tired, Gerald slumped onto the bench. He sat where the old man died.

The old man lying dead below the coat had been a human life Gerald tried imagining. He might've been famous, once. Gerald didn't know his name, residence, or favourite soup. He didn't know if he'd enjoyed companionship in recent months or ever. Old friends or new ones might've sat with him on the bench, but those friends had died and winter had been cold. The old man might've been somebody's husband. He was, at the least, a man and woman's son.

Wanting at least to know the old man's name, Gerald crouched again beside the body. His hands searched through the deep pockets of the old man's coat, until he found a ring of four time-browned keys and a silver pen, like scores of other keys and pens in abandoned stores and homes. Like Gerald, the old man had no reason to produce a testament to his name. He hadn't carried a wallet. Gerald slipped the keys and pen into a pocket of his shirt.

Holding the old man under his shoulders so his feet, not his head, crashed down each next step, Gerald dragged the body from the bandstand towards the grass. The coat fell from the old man's face, but Gerald did not replace it. If the old man opened his eyes then he should see where he'd been.

Gerald dragged him to where the long grass cradled the old man. There, he straightened the old man's legs and body on the ground. A grave needn't be longer than a man was tall.

Using the largest shovel from the bandstand, holding the timber handle and staff less cold than was the steel, Gerald strained to dig through the moist grass beside which the old man lay. The frozen soil was tough to pierce, but Gerald soon dropped a portion onto the beginnings of a pile. The old man remained motionless inside his burial clothes, facing his unfolding grave.

Gerald hadn't broken dirt since he was young, and his breath soon became shorter. The muscles of his arms and shoulders became sore; his hands were old but soft. Repeatedly, he wiped his fingers across the salted sweat dripping from his brow. The bones of his back and joints between them once unknown to him began to ache, becoming an independent twisted entity apart from him. The dirt evicted from the ground stained the cuffs of his long trousers.

Manual labour exhausted him, as work had rarely done. Gerald paused to return to the bandstand and rest on the bench, almost convalescing. He was the old man in the park.

The dirt that Gerald dug was slow to leave a hole, while the old man lay undisturbed. Gerald's only reasons to believe he was not alone were the dead eyes of a corpse he was burying in an aged public park, the first grave he'd ever dug. He was an old man burying the body of another dead before him. Hundreds more bodies dead could be wasting in sealed homes and dark apartments without anybody finding them.

Returning to his chore, shovelling and discarding the deepening dirt became rhythmical. Digging more holes for graves would become harder than the first. His rhythm would slow and fatigue would interrupt him as he aged. Dying would be easier than trying to stay alive.

Aged people would bury the dead, and other aging people bury them when they too died. The only task Gerald imagined performing for his people was burying them. It was his dire premonition of the future, his destiny foreboding, but he alone could not bury all the solitary dead in city parks of graves. Finally, one last man or woman, who'd already buried the next to last, would rest unburied on the ground. One person did not constitute a people, and English people were then dead.

Digging as he was, delusion could be easy, as it was when Gerald caught a weary glimpse of a bicycle approaching, along the path around the lake. Gerald stopped digging, stood upright, and watched, becoming transfixed by the sight. His eyes and vision might've been starting to fail, and his mind might've failed him long ago, but the blonde man riding the bicycle seemed young, much younger than any man or woman Gerald had seen for a long time. Gerald was too tired to call out to someone who'd ignore him, too old to cry out to his hallucination of a man he once had been.

The rider stopped pedalling, veering his bicycle towards him. Gerald stood still, watching the young man stop beside the bandstand, against which he rested his bicycle. Taller than Gerald, with eyes that homed upon him, the young man strode towards him. Gerald released the shovel, letting it fall to the grass. He stepped forward to the young man and wrapped his arms around him.

Gerald continued hugging him, holding him. He tried to hide his little tears where he thought the young man couldn't see them, fearful they might frighten him away. "I'm sorry," said Gerald, wiping his eyes dry and stepping back. "You're very young."

The young man stepped aside. He picked up the shovel and thrust it into the open soil.

"I'm Gerald Keaton."

The young man continued digging, his thoughts in silence. The dirt moved easily with the strength of two young arms, but the task was a travesty for someone never quite alive.

Never quite alive too, perhaps, was Gerald standing by him. "Do you live in Darlington?" Gerald asked.

"All my life."

The young man spoke as if that time was long, but his life was short to Gerald. "Me, too," said Gerald, struggling for more words in conversation. "Do you know *him*?"

The young man stopped digging, studying the dead man's face. "No." He resumed digging, quickly deepening the grave.

Gerald looked at the body and the hole, embarrassed for being useless. He was tired enough to sit on the bench and rest, but dared not let his laziness frighten the young man away. Instead, he hurried to the bandstand and brought back another shovel. Trying not to obstruct the young man working, Gerald stood away from him. Unable to force the shovel too far into the ground, Gerald dug little scoops of dirt. The grave grew and piles of dirt on the grass rose quickly, while the young man dug and Gerald did the best he could. The body lying on the grass was both their burden.

"I'm Brandon Frewer."

Gerald stopped digging to hold out his hand. "Pleased to meet you," he said.

Brandon saw the outstretched hand. He looked at Gerald, surprised at the formal greeting after the older man had hugged him, but he reached out his hand and shook it. Gerald smiled, shaking his hand keenly, before Brandon pulled his hand away.

The two men dug together, Gerald profusely sweating. "I have to rest," he said. Carrying his shovel so Brandon knew he wasn't abandoning the chore, Gerald staggered back to the bandstand and up the steps, where he collapsed onto the bench. He wiped the worst of his sweat from his face, while Brandon continued digging.

"What do you know about him?" asked Brandon.

After collecting his breath a little longer, Gerald reached into his shirt pocket. In his open palm, he tendered towards Brandon four brass keys on a ring and a silver pen.

Brandon paused from digging to glance at them. "Not much to show for being alive."

The dead man might've left more to show for his time on

earth, but he'd needed strangers in a park to lay him in the soil. Gerald placed the pen and keys beside him on the bench.

Brandon dug until the hole was a couple of feet deep and slightly longer than the dead man had been tall. "That'll be enough," he said, letting his shovel fall to the grass.

"Allow me," said Gerald, slowly standing up again. Preparing him to be interred, he straightened a little more the dead man's arms so they would not obstruct his movement forward.

He and Brandon crouched behind the dead man's midriff. They prepared themselves, holding their hands and arms rehearsing what they were about to do. "Are you ready?" asked Brandon.

In tandem, they pushed their arms under the dead man's back and bottom. Gerald struggled longer than Brandon to grip his share of deadweight. "I've got him now."

They rolled the body forward, until the dead man tumbled face down on the grass, his head and shoulders close to the top end of what soon would be his grave. Brandon lifted his legs and pulled them towards the other end, while Gerald again knelt behind the dead man's sides. To match Gerald's stance, Brandon knelt behind the dead man's waist. "Are you ready?" Brandon asked a second time.

Gerald struggled for every spurt of effort. The dead man's turning face appeared in front of him, briefly looking at him, before he and Brandon rolled the cumbersome corpse further and he fell over the rim into the broken ground. The most arduous of his labour finished, Gerald fell back on the damp grass and sighed. He wiped more of the recurrent sweat from his face and neck.

The dead man landed facing upwards from the earth, although his limbs and body lay crooked in the soil. Brandon knelt down beside the grave and reached his right hand low into the hole. He straightened the dead man's arms and legs as much as he could, so he lay deepest in the dirt.

"Not yet," said Gerald, his breath and pulse settling down. He ducked back into the grandstand and retrieved the dead man's silver pen, useful only to people with something left to write. Leaning low into the ground, careful not to fall there with him,

Gerald placed the silver pen in the dead man's hand. He lay the dead man's coat over his chest so that only his face was visible, his eyes not quite closed. Gerald set the dead man's hat on his head, although it slipped onto the dirt. They owed him their respect for having come so far.

22

SEARCHING FOR A LIFE

Clouds encroached upon the sky above Gerald and Brandon, standing guard beside the grave they'd made. If the old man were to flinch, then he should do so soon.

Gerald was the more sombre, without knowing for whom he mourned. He wasn't going anywhere; he could afford the time. He wanted to say something kind about the man who'd given him a small semblance of companionship, albeit briefly, without knowing he was there.

The old man was any person lying dead, his burial for all the people who had died. He was the man that Gerald and Brandon would become. They were two, perhaps three, almost ordinary men.

The dead man might've gone somewhere different to the place other people went, which might be the place to which Gerald was also headed. Gerald wondered where that place could be, if he was not already there. He yearned to reach the day when he'd finished all but the last of his long mourning, for all he'd lost since he was young. He thought of envying the old man, but didn't know enough about him. He wondered what he knew, if he knew anything.

Gerald turned to face his new-found friend, who might've already forgotten Gerald's name but was too polite to say so.

The young man's youth let him stand more upright, less tired from his labour.

Looking back at the open grave, Gerald whispered to the dead. "Who are we, after all?"

The service finished, Brandon turned towards the older man. Gerald shrugged his shoulders much as young boys did, but with the despondency of false youth in a lie. He remembered too much the boy and man he no longer was.

Brandon was the first to shovel loose soil from the pile onto the body in the grave. Gerald dumped his slower, smaller scoops of dirt into the ground. The comparison was unimportant, for sharing any task was better than suffering it alone. The splashing specks and pools of earth obscured the dead man's face, hiding him away.

They shovelled the soil until the last of it covered the old man underground. Higher than the surrounding ground by more than the size of him, Brandon pounded the loose soil down with his shovel. The mound of dirt was obvious that day, but grass would grow on it and the weather would erode it until it disappeared. Grass had already begun to grow upon other graves. Wind, rain, and snow had already begun to level them. They would do the same for all the graves.

Gerald wanted the old man to be remembered, at least by him, each time he walked into the park. Returning to the bandstand, he took a hammer and the last cross painted white. Brandon watched him kneel by the padded-down mound of earth. Gerald dug a small hole above the place in which lay the old man's head, where he mounted the white cross. He used the hammer to pound the cross a short way further down, to mark the ground and record the old man's life and death.

Brandon took the hammer from Gerald's hand and struck the cross deeper into earth. Gerald used his hands to push the soil around it.

Gerald struggled to stand, until Brandon offered him his hand. Brandon pulled the older man upright, and again they stood together before the grave they'd laid in the dead man's park and place. Gerald's only legacy: the cross was straight and neat, but might not remain erect through the coming years and seasons.

Brandon turned back towards the bandstand, where stood the cans of paint and screwdrivers to open them. "Do you know if he died today?" he asked.

Gerald shook his head. A blank white cross in the ground shouldn't be the only marker of a life, but they couldn't paint the date the old man died, his name, or age. They couldn't write an epitaph for a man they didn't know.

Again in the bandstand, Gerald took a can of white paint, screwdriver, and thin brush. On the wooden bench, he wrote in large letters and numbers the address of his apartment on Marlborough Drive. His invitation to anybody coming into the park to meet the man who'd died was also his invitation to Brandon. When he'd finished, Gerald offered him the brush.

Brandon shook his head. "My parents and I are leaving Darlington."

"Where are you going?" perked up Gerald, placing the brush on the can of paint. "Can I come with you?"

Brandon hesitated. "I need to check with my parents."

"I'm sure I'd like them," said Gerald, trying not to seem to plead. "They might like me." Gerald feared imposing too much upon him. "I could help?"

Brandon reached down to the bench. He picked up the dead man's keys.

"You can have everything he owned," said Gerald. "I don't want it."

"Don't you want to know his name?" asked Brandon.

They examined each key for insignia of what it might've secured. The only markings were of long-closed companies that manufactured keys, as Gerald was better placed to recognise. "They're keys to locks on building doors," said Gerald, "not cars." The only bicycle near them was Brandon's, leaning against the bandstand. The dead man must've walked there.

"One key has to be his home," said Brandon, "at least one."

Brandon led them walking past the Clock Tower Lodge and stone-boxed fountain out of the park. Curtains were closed in the front windows of the houses across Parkside, but still he strode to the nearest driveway and short steps to a front door, on which he knocked.

Gerald struggled to keep pace behind him, but he needed the young man to know he wasn't any trouble. If the dead man had left someone at home, then he or she would have come to find him.

Brandon turned the door handle. It didn't open. Nothing suggested that anyone had recently been there, although nothing suggested no one had.

He pushed a key into the keyhole, but couldn't turn it. Every lock into which he slipped a key was a better chance to find the dead man's home: a moment closer to entering it. Brandon tried to force the key to turn but couldn't.

The profile of a second key didn't match the hole. Brandon couldn't press the key into it.

A third key was of a different type altogether. Brandon didn't need to try.

The fourth key fitted into the hole. It turned slightly, but didn't turn full circle. Brandon could not unlock the door.

Gerald followed Brandon back to the street-side pavement. "Your parents must be very proud," said Gerald, "very happy."

"People who care about people nowadays find being happy hard."

Gerald slowed his pace, allowing Brandon to slip ahead. The old man's home could've been anywhere. Gerald watched Brandon persevere.

At the adjoining house, Brandon again knocked without reply. He again tried to place each of the four keys in the lock and turn it, but couldn't open the door. His disappointment with every door he couldn't open was also a sense of eliminating every wrong hope, until finally only a right one would remain.

Spinning around, he confronted Gerald. Brandon stepped around him back towards the pavement. Gerald hurriedly walked beside him.

"Are you a parent?" asked Brandon.

"I loved a woman once." Talking was difficult while Gerald was trying to walk so fast. "I shouldn't have let her go. I never really did."

The pattern quickly became familiar, but still none of the doors answered and none of the keys opened any locks. Brandon slowed his pace enough for Gerald to walk easily beside him. He led them across Loraine Crescent, determined to try every home facing the park from which they'd come.

"I should have tried more to find someone I liked enough maybe to love," continued Gerald, "and loved enough maybe to marry."

Brandon stopped and faced him. "Is that your advice to me?"

"Never being two of us, I never had the chance to contemplate being three or more."

Saying solitary lives could satisfy would've been kind, but lies had already condemned too many people. Brandon resumed walking. "It's half the story of what could've been a life."

Their pace slowed with every empty home: the next and the next along Parkside. Gerald watched Brandon try to slip each key into each lock. None turned very far, if at all. Brandon led them along Heslop Drive and back again, while Gerald waited each time Brandon tried, and failed. The profiles of the keys became sufficiently familiar for Brandon to know the first to try each time he confronted a new lock. Keys akin to keyholes encouraged him, his body rose, before they failed to turn. Every key was worth trying to insert into each lock, until it failed to turn.

Brandon flexed his fingers. If they were Gerald's fingers, they'd have long become sore with the repetition of his failure. If Brandon were to remain ignorant, he would know he'd tried. He might've been too stupid to abandon his quest. Gerald should've been so stupid.

Gerald's legs were tired of exercise and his aged mind was weary with routine, but he relished the young man's company too much to care. "What made your parents have you?" he asked, as Brandon stepped back onto the pavement.

Brandon continued walking. "What made yours?"

The bandstand where the old man died was becoming far behind them when they reached the other end of Loraine Crescent. Brandon stopped.

Gerald stood beside him, letting him decide what they should do. Brandon slowly turned around, walking back towards the park without stopping at doors he'd already tried and failed to open.

"I envy your parents," said Gerald. "I envy you."

Brandon crossed Parkside. He led them back into South Park. The stone drinking fountain was dry.

"What about the Clock Tower Lodge?" asked Gerald, to prolong their time together.

"It's a council building," replied Brandon, "with offices and meeting rooms." Curtains were drawn across the windows. The clock had stopped at its own time of day or night.

On the porch outside the lodge were several benches. Gerald stopped at one to rest. Sitting there might keep the young man with him.

Brandon faced him. Thousands of people weren't asking Brandon for his company. One man was. That man would take the scraps of life that Brandon threw with rudeness and indifference, and still be glad to have them. "If you want to come with my parents and me," smiled Brandon, "I'm sure you can."

Gerald stood quickly up and took the younger man's right hand with his to shake it, his left hand wrapped around them. "Thank you, Brandon Frewer, thank you."

Brandon turned away but hesitated, looking at the keyhole in the lodge door and the brass keys in his hand. "The council stopped needing so many offices," he said.

Gerald watched Brandon step onto the porch and slip a key into a keyhole. It didn't turn.

Brandon slipped a second into the hole, and turned it. It turned full circle. The moment startled Gerald, but he heard and Brandon felt the bolt draw back.

Brandon turned the knob. He opened the lodge door.

Looking back to Gerald, Brandon smiled, vindicated. Brandon wiped the soles of his shoes on the doormat, before proceeding through the door.

Gerald imagined being that old man, as Brandon couldn't quite imagine. Through the open doorway was a hallway to closed doors. Gerald brushed the dirt from his hands and trouser cuffs, although small amounts remained. He checked his other clothes were clean, wiped his shoes on the mat, and followed Brandon in.

Lying on the hallway floor was a small screwed up ball of coloured paper. Brandon leant down and picked it up. He unwound it, glanced at it, and passed it to Gerald. It was a notice campaigning to protect a mahogany tree in the Cape Verde Islands in which purple herons nested.

Gerald screwed it up again. He threw it back towards the open door.

Brandon stood back for every chance for daylight through the front door to illuminate the closed door beside him. His hand began to reach towards the knob.

"Wait," interrupted Gerald, his thoughts not clear to him. He reached his hand into his pocket and showed Brandon his apartment key. "I don't want a stranger in my home after I die." He might have also been afraid of learning something about the dead man that taught him too much about himself.

"I want to know if he had children," said Brandon, "grandchildren."

"So you can find them?"

"I want to know they exist."

Searching for a path towards an answer couldn't leave them knowing less than the little they knew already. Gerald returned his key to his pocket, while Brandon watched him. The older man nodded, before together they stood facing the grains in the old timber door. Gerald stood where his shadow wouldn't shade the knob.

The dead man might've lived where he'd lived since he was young. He might not have lived alone. Gerald became curious to browse through the old man's life for a reason why the old man had died and he was still alive. He wondered many things about him.

In a moment of his doubt, Gerald wondered whether the dead man's home had been the Clock Tower Lodge. He might've carried in his pocket a key to a building other than one in which he lived; the lodge might just have been a place to which the old man had a key, to which he would've come had he not died one day, that day most likely, while resting in the park. In a cruel twist of chance among a finite choice of keys, a key to another door might have opened the lodge front door. There'd been no woodpile on the porch, no trace of fuel for fires.

The young man turned the knob. In the last, he pushed open the door.

23

RELICS OF AN AGED LIFE

The room before which Gerald and Brandon stood was dark, but for the light from the hallway behind them. That little light around their shadows reflected from scattered polished surfaces. The room was a little warmer than the hallway had been; a scattering of tiny embers glowed from a fireplace. Around the walls were shapes of chairs, sideboards and cabinets. If the old man drew the thick curtains closed across the windows before he left, he might've left to die.

Brandon stepped through the open doorway. Moving cautiously through meagre light, he proceeded around a table towards the nearest window. There, he carefully drew the curtains open.

The light of day through glass revealed to Gerald at the door the room, which seemed to shine more than merely reflecting sunlight through the window. Gerald stepped forward in his awe, beholding everything before him. Brandon at the window turned around.

The two men stared astounded at the room to which a dead man's keys had led them. Scores of perfectly preserved artworks decorated walls, cabinets, and sideboards. Beside Gerald, two marble busts of human heads stood on marble columns: Aristotle, Socrates.

Slowly, the two men explored. From the wall above a sculpture by Rodin hung several engravings. Rembrandt's sketch was of a man embracing his prodigal son. Norman Lindsay's pirates held their captives. They were tastes that people no longer held, but were tastes nevertheless.

Gerald and Brandon moved among the menagerie of fallen splendour and people who'd been splendid, inspecting the treasury for all it spoke to them. Men and women, boys and girls murmured, their murmuring becoming louder. Generations past were again alive: talking, playing, and laughing. They were optimistic and anxious, confident and concerned. They became visible, if only to Gerald and Brandon, dressed in new clothes for the season and yesterday's worst cloth.

Life surviving was around them in the biography of relics. Colourful oil paintings were as diverse as those by Bruegel, Gainsborough, and Rubens. Painted glories sprawled across the canvases: romantic heroes draped across artists' clouds. Smaller enamels were of men and women in Madrid. More intimate framed oil portraits included faces of Byron, Havel, and the Curies.

Gerald stood before the styles, contemplating paintings he reached out his hand to touch. The strokes of artists with their oils were gentle on his fingertips.

None of the civilisations left alive had produced the arts Europeans had produced. Each work could educate a thousand men and women and instil something fresh into each one. The visions of an eye could inspire the meek. The lines and colours of a hand could subdue the angry.

Standing in a glass-front cabinet were plaster models of the Coliseum and Parthenon intact. Beside them were the Brandenburg Gate and chariot. Without obvious reason from the life he'd led, Gerald recognised the face of Christ divine watching over Lisbon. In miniature, it stood as tall as the Alexander Nevski Cathedral. From more modern times were two colourful resin steeples of Gaudi's unfinished cathedral. Gerald basked in the brilliant and beautiful, exhorting and exalting them.

In another cabinet, the crystal bowl was Bohemian. On

another crystal were Viking symbols, as the Viking head woodcarving testified. The silver lady with fluttering robes was from the radiator of an old Rolls Royce motor car.

Gerald led them into another room, where he opened the curtains across another window. The window glass was old and watery, with little bubble imperfections.

Dominating one wall was a framed fine tapestry of coloured woollen thread in the image of a woman in a garden. Hanging from another wall was a cuckoo clock, which required human touch to pull down the pine cone weights that turned the hour and minute hands. The finite, recurrent ticking of the clock became the only sound they heard. The time was almost twelve thirty.

Brandon might've been too quick to pass the replica Little Mermaid near the door. "Enjoy the exquisite as much as the expansive," Gerald told him, "the intricate as much as the impressive."

Brandon paused, stepped back, and saw the beauty of a fairy tale. The cuckoo popped from the clock and softly cuckooed.

The lodge was something of a life in miniature. A museum as much a home, the rooms were a pan-European pantheon, which didn't clutter as fewer possessions had cluttered larger homes. A single figure in a park, a senseless body in the ground, became a man who'd surely sat in the red leather-clad armchairs in every room. The mansion, a park-keeper's home, seemed suddenly to befit the old man in the earth. It befitted Gerald and Brandon, too.

They were greater than Gerald had been great, in his isolated life. They made each other greater still. They made Gerald and Brandon greater than any man alone could be.

If European peoples weren't represented elsewhere then they were represented in the libraries, in homage to their lives. The library of movies included *Das Boot*, *Les Diaboliques*, and *The Man Who Would Be King*.

The music library filled a massive cabinet, including not just Abba and the Beatles but also Chopin, Liszt, Mozart, and Tchaikovsky. Gerald could almost hear Peter and the Wolf.

The most expansive of the libraries were the tall glass-front cabinets of cloth-bound books. The embossed names of writers and their writings down the spines included only some Gerald recognised and too few he'd read: Austen, Burns, the Brontes, Schiller, Shaw, Thomas, and Verne.

In each cabinet door was a keyhole, but not a key. Gerald pulled at a door, but it was locked. "May I see those keys?" he asked Brandon.

Brandon gave Gerald the ring of keys. Only one might turn the lock in front of him. It did. Gerald opened the cabinet door only to know it opened, before closing it again.

In another room, Brandon stood before a colourful military banner and standard on a mounted pole, but Gerald stepped between them and the young man. "Europeans should never kill Europeans," Gerald told him.

"Heraldry is much more than war," Brandon replied.

Gerald thought carefully about his words and stepped aside. Facing the banner and standard, he dipped his head. The symbols represented nobility and honour, of which he'd seen so little and practiced even less.

Too many faces of the brave peppered the walls for Gerald and Brandon to contemplate two mortal men drifting in the flow. Imageries of splendour lost swelled around the lodge. The dead man's heritage was also the living men's rights of birth, to savour as he'd savoured. Far from diminishing their memories and supplanting their knowledge of modern attributes, the past enhanced every sense of what they were and might've been. The wonders of those rooms and their achievements across the world were for the glory of the world, and no less so for having been Europe's birthright. The last Europeans could revel in the objects of their wake.

Hanging from a wall near them was a copy, Gerald presumed, of Munch's painting *The Scream*. It beckoned him and Brandon nearer. The colourfully pained face in the painting was incongruous among the classical, fine lines and gentle form of other paintings in the lodge. The man imperilled, mouth wide open and hands covering his ears, might've been screaming or hearing other people's screams.

The dead man might've known. He too might've screamed for

what he lost, or cared and felt enough to scream for what the world was losing. He might've heard the orchestrated screams outside.

"Is this wonder or tragedy?" asked Brandon.

Impressions of their antiquity abated. Gerald wouldn't lie as other men and women had gladly been deceived. The glories thriving in the lodge were of countries dying outside the windows. Their lives and blood had been their good history and fortune, which fools had failed to keep. Generations surrendering them were almost too miserable to bear, not just because the people dying were theirs: Europe's imminent demise. The vigour of the lodge was wasted in two men's single bones.

Brandon spun around and stormed from the room and through the hallway out the front door. "What have you done?" he screamed to open air.

Old men and women hearing him would've shielded their deaf ears. In their homes, they would've stepped behind their batten walls.

"You could've stayed so great!" Brandon screamed again, as the dead man might've screamed. "You could've stayed the greatest!"

Gerald watched him from the front door, too tired to scream. If he could hear the thoughts inside the young man's head then he imagined hearing thoughts like those that he once made, but he'd become too old to make them anymore. If he was angry then he was angry with himself as he had been, young enough to choose his future and not choosing very wisely.

Brandon dropped his head. The younger man reminded Gerald he was old, much as Gerald must have reminded Brandon he was young.

"Everything could have been so good for you," lamented Gerald. "Our solitude weakened us. The solitude of so many weakened us too much."

Brandon looked at him, then past him. He came towards and past him back into the lodge.

Gerald turned and followed him through the hallway to a flight of stairs rising into darkness, up which Brandon bound, his hand sliding up the banister. There, Brandon opened more doors to rooms and drew more curtains from the windows.

The litany of small white crosses sprinkled about the park of graves was more conspicuous from the upstairs windows than it had been walking on the ground. Gerald saw again the bandstand and the grave that he and Brandon dug. If the dead man saw anything from the place in which he lay, then he saw Gerald at the window.

Gerald and Brandon were in a master bedroom, dominated by a huge four-poster bed with sheets, blankets, and thick pillows neatly set. Near it was a mantelpiece on which stood a single photograph inside a golden frame. Brandon walked across the room until he stood before it. Gerald followed him, until again they stood together.

The photograph was of a middle-aged man and woman standing behind seven children. The man might've been the old man buried in the park, making the photograph half a century old. They were smiling faces in a town that lost its smile, posing for the camera and for them. It recorded a moment left unchanged, when everything else had changed.

The woman and children gave the dead man's life further context. Gerald's life had no context, beyond England's art and glory.

Gerald imagined a stranger walking upon his home in muted light, and was ashamed at the little there to see. His only photograph lay hidden in an old drawer and envelope that only he had opened. He alone knew whom he loved, and no one still loved him. He didn't own a clock that needed him to wind, but only battery-powered torches that would expire in spite of everything he did.

Around the photograph before them stood seven coloured cards, each of which Brandon picked up and he and Gerald read. The greetings were all addressed to "*Dad*," any other name unimportant. They were seven different adult handwritings and Christian name signatures.

The woman in the photograph might have died. The man might've sent their sons and daughters away to do more than wade through aged lives with him. They might still be alive, if the man's longevity had been his genes.

Lying near them was a red leather-bound book, the cover of which was inscribed in gold lettering: "*HOLY BIBLE*." Without picking it up, Gerald opened the front cover; the lush leather warmed his fingers. The fountain pen inscription, confident and intimate, was "*From a Father to his Son*." Gerald closed the cover as he'd found it, in deference.

Occupying the other rooms upstairs were neatly blanketed beds and classical oak furniture. "Are they for his children coming home?" asked Brandon, "or have they already left?"

The rooms connoted something too personal to the man who'd passed away for Gerald and Brandon to intrude. Brandon returned to the master bedroom, where he took the ring and four brass keys from his pocket. He removed the front door key and cabinet key from the ring and gently placed the ring and last two keys on the mantelpiece beside the family photograph. The dead man's children might know what the last two keys opened. "We still don't know his name," said Gerald.

"We don't need to know."

Brandon drew closed the curtains across the upstairs windows. He closed the bedroom doors.

Gerald gazed at the young man with health and strength with time to resurrect the nearly dead. They were each other's lives, one man behind and one ahead, but Gerald's life was trite; it would end with him. He would've cherished any chance to take the young man's burden and try again in life anew, but he could have no mortal life anew. The dead man's home had made life seem long, but the journey was too short. Gerald's unwavering shame for what he'd done with his past life kept him estranged from his young confidant.

Brandon walked back through the downstairs rooms as if he'd been there a thousand times but would soon leave forever. The last of the fireplace embers shone from blackened wood, although only Gerald standing near could see them. They would soon stop shining.

"There's no shame in being old," Gerald told Brandon, while Brandon revisited the relics, "but there is shame in being old without a future left behind." The glories of their past could've been reason to celebrate a future founded upon their finest attributes, aspiring to something better, but the future would not be better if Brandon died alone. "The future is the important place to be, whatever you make of it." Brandon was a future beyond the wasting lives around, a reason for Gerald to continue being alive.

Gerald pulled down the pine cone weights on the cuckoo clock. The hands would turn a short time longer.

He saw in himself a tiresome old man, with little to offer the young man's family. Brandon's parents had a son and no reason to interrupt their lives to be with Gerald. Their conversations would be strained; the words aloud enthusing Gerald would soon bore them.

Brandon left the cabinet door key in that keyhole. He closed the curtains across the windows.

"This dying land we bequeathed you was my making, not yours," Gerald continued, "for what I did, didn't do, and could've done." Gerald dared not mention his dire loneliness, for the conflict in his wills might keep a man like Brandon with him. "People who don't yet understand the mistakes we made don't warrant your assistance or, for that matter, your forgiveness. We who understand our errors don't want to lose our final chance."

When Brandon returned to the hallway, Gerald pulled shut that next-to-final door. Brandon pulled the front door closed.

They were leaving the lodge as they found it, aside from that ring and keys. In the custom of the dying, Brandon left the front door key resting in the lock, unturned.

"Don't let old men enslave you tying cords on our pyjama pants," Gerald told him. "We were young, without helping the elderly we became. If you let us think we need you, you make us lazier than we already are. We didn't help ourselves."

While Brandon stood listening, Gerald was a sage imparting wisdom that only age had brought. Without Brandon to hear him, that wisdom would have festered in Gerald's head.

"When you get the chance to be sensible without making mistakes we made," continued Gerald, "then take that chance.

You don't need stragglers imposing upon your family. We'll burden you. We'll waste your time. One day you'll tire of us and so you should. You need a wife to sustain us. My best hope for you restoring our longevity is you going to Cornwall without me."

Brandon studied him, more closely than he'd studied anything inside the lodge. "What will you do?" he asked.

"Go back inside," guessed Gerald, "read among the artefacts, keep the cuckoo ticking." The relics of their civilities were valueless if nobody enjoyed them. The wonders of a world were meaningless without the people who made them.

Brandon slowly walked away. Gerald followed far behind him.

From a distance, Gerald watched Brandon in the bandstand strike the lid of the can of paint with a hammer, sealing it from drying. Brandon wiped the brush on the long grass. He rinsed it in the lake. The bristles might yet harden but would be there to use again, by someone who might know enough to write the old man's name.

Gerald knew he'd just been a brief distraction, which the young man might mention to his parents. If Brandon never returned, if the dead man's children never came, then Gerald's dying breaths might be exerted struggling to write his name, a signature waving life away, on a cross beneath which he lay to die. That cross would weather every year, until finally it slipped and fell against the ground.

He imagined Brandon in time inscribing a grave with the names of every Englishman and woman ever born. That single cross would reach into the sky, with perhaps only Brandon left to see it. A throng of smaller crosses each dedicated to one person could stretch across England, with perhaps only Brandon left to walk between them.

Having returned everything they'd taken to the bandstand, Brandon mounted his bicycle. Instead of riding far away, he rode back to Gerald watching him. "Will you be all right?" asked Brandon.

Gerald considered many possible responses and considered not saying anything, before finally replying. "No," he smiled, in a silly little joke upon himself. "I need you to be my happy ending."

Brandon hesitated, before riding away. Gerald watched the young man go, until he and his bicycle passed through the gates and out of view.

Gerald staggered backwards. He slumped against a tree.

If the sound he almost heard was not the wind, then it might have been a singing swan. Looking back up at the clock tower above the lodge, he thought the hands so slightly turned.

24

THE NAKED CHIMPANZEE

Rain clouds swelled overhead, threatening to break, as Gerald
drifted back to Marlborough Drive; he had nowhere left to go.
The last people left alive hid amidst the rambling catacombs,
where Gerald couldn't see them. They remained as distant as
they'd always been.

No stranger waited for him when he returned to the building
in which he lived, standing in the thin shelter outside the door.
In a glass panel was the message Gerald carved that morning: "*I
am alive.*" He didn't still believe it.

Gerald was among the next to die, the next to last of them
to die. He might die asleep and never notice his quick passing,
or die awake with time to feel the age that death imposed upon
him. Words in a glass-panelled door and on a park bench near
a grave were cravings made to no one. Hopes of dreams for life
didn't cease being fantasies for being made so desperately.

The most tragic thing a man could do, no matter how much
wealth or fame he'd gathered through his life, was die alone.
Gerald had lived long enough to die alone, in a rotting small
apartment. Hope was nothing noble without reason to believe.

The clouds began to spit at him. From his pocket, Gerald
pulled his pair of keys and removed the key for the building
door. After opening the door, he left the key in the lock, where

he need not remember where it was. Security to safeguard him from the street had become superfluous, as it had for the old man, although Gerald had no reason to suppose that anyone would come for him.

The building entrance hallway remained as it had been that morning. In a corner of the empty noticeboard remained Doris' drawing pins, where Gerald had collected them. His last key, he left in his apartment door.

Inside Gerald's barren walled apartment, heavy rain streaked against the windows and splashed on the sills. Standing still, the sweat he'd spilled burying the old man gripped his shirt to his skin.

Unwashed for several days, Gerald could use the saucepan of past rainwater in his kitchen sink to dapple a moist towel on his skin, as he'd done to bathe himself for all so many months. He could pour more rainwater on him in his shower recess, but it wouldn't rinse away the dirt and perspiration of digging a dead man's grave.

The rain against the windows reminded him too much of water that once poured from his bathroom shower. Feeling dirty among the dead, in a town entombing him, Gerald yearned for the refreshing wash he'd been too long denied.

The air that afternoon was warmer than it had been for months, cool but not too cold. Walking briskly, Gerald took from his bathroom a bar of soap, plastic bottle of shampoo, and towel. That briskness denied his age, however briefly he could muster it. He hurried from his apartment into the corridor, down the stairs, and into the building entrance hallway. He set his towel on the convenient chair and popped his toiletries outside the building door, before retreating back into the building.

Without believing what he was doing, Gerald unbuttoned his sweated shirt. Exposing his ugly wrinkled drooping chest flouted every past convention of public place apparel. He was defying the dead, although without an audience he was more indifferent than bold or brash. Doris Poedecker could no longer compose a notice asking residents not to undress in communal areas.

Gerald's thin pale skin began to shiver. If anyone could see him then he might've been embarrassed, but he'd made too many choices in his life for which he felt ashamed to care what someone thought about him then. His shirt dropped to the floor, leaving him half naked.

He loosened his laces and pulled his leather shoes from his feet. He removed his cotton socks and dropped them on his shoes. The cold mattered less the more of him became so cold. He removed his trousers, before finally dropping his soft underpants. Close to the glass-panelled door from an almost empty building, Gerald stood bare before the rain-soaked street.

Gerald's hands crossed in front of him, concealing his tawdry self from nobody to see. The doors and windows across the street didn't reveal anybody watching, even if birds cowered in dry corners. Skywards were only clouds and rain. The day would soon be dark. Water overflowed from pots and saucepans he'd left on the pavement, but Gerald couldn't experience water on his body better than under falling rain.

Slowly opening the building door, only his left hand defending his modesty, Gerald dared the worsening cold. His shivers became frantic. His teeth began to clatter. Rainwater splashed his legs and arms, although the little roof above the door sheltered the rest of him. Gerald's foot held open the coarsely cut door behind him, as he stood naked in the air.

There were no other pedestrians or moving vehicles, as there might not be on so wet and dying a day. He listened for the sounds of anybody calling him, but the rain made too much noise. People in their homes might've thought that he was taunting them, but still they hid away. Closed windows sneered at him.

His left hand still protecting him, Gerald braved the world too cold and stepped forward to where the uppermost step stressed the tender soles of his old feet, letting the building door close behind him. He shuddered, standing meekly in a private shower on a once public street.

Gerald wanted somebody to see him, standing like virgin man in destitution below a sprawling waterfall. That somebody could shout at him and tell him he was mad. He or she could laugh if

Gerald heard the laughter, and be Gerald's great relief that the world remained as it had been.

Being there might've satisfied some strange new curiosity, to stand nude before the naked streets and buildings. He stood as primitive man had stood, where everything around him was no longer primitive but would become primitive again. He'd thought that he was special and when enough of them were special, being special became ordinary. Theirs had been civilisation, but they'd never really changed.

"Hello," screamed Gerald, although it hurt his creaking voice. If anyone were glancing from a window to the street, then Gerald wanted his or her attention. He wanted the attention of people not looking out at all. "Hello!" he screamed still louder, begging them to come outside.

Secret eyes could've been viewing him, but did not confess their gaze. The thundering rain impaired his eyes and ears, as they impaired those of anybody there.

No longer covering his modesty, Gerald picked up his shampoo bottle and soap. He stepped down to the pavement, where the heavy rain fell hard upon his head and shoulders. His arms swaying loosely back and forth, he proceeded across the kerb and into the middle of Marlborough Drive, in full sight of windows from all sides.

There he stopped. The rain bombarded him, soaking his hair and flesh. Rooms of homes stared over him, the only feature made from pink for them to see. People could snigger or could mock him, but they should let him know that they were there. Somebody should wave to him from a window or step out from a doorway, if only to deride him.

Holding his soap and shampoo bottle, Gerald lifted his right hand to his face. The back of his hand wiped the water from his forehead and eyes, but the falling rain swept it back again.

Leaving his shampoo bottle on the road, Gerald rubbed the warm soap across his skin, cleaning away the dirt and life he had accumulated. The rain dribbled soap bubbles towards the kerbs and gutters of his sprawling bath in bitumen and brick. When he finished, Gerald laid the bar of soap on the road, where the rain inched it away.

Gerald poured a small amount of shampoo from the bottle into his hand. He forced the lotion through his hair, rubbing it into lather he pressed and squeezed into his scalp. White bubbles tumbled atop the water flowing from him. He rubbed his hand against his hair. It was clean enough to squeak.

The shampoo bottle slipped and fell. The rain also inched it away.

The rainwater became lukewarm the longer Gerald stood in it; the last nerves in his flesh had become stoic in the cold. His eyes closed and he lifted up his face, into which crashed his public shower. The water flowed into his open mouth where he drank it, while his hands and arms relaxed fell down beside him.

For the rain to wash away all soap and shampoo from him, Gerald spread his arms out wide. His eyes closed and face upturned, the rain doused and cleaned him well. His hands fell loose at the wrists of his outstretched arms. He shook his head and hair to rush the water over and throughout him, before his head fell low, relaxed, submitting.

Gerald was clean, but stayed standing in the centre of the street. His eyes remained closed, feeling heavy rain upon him and languishing in the cold. His two good eyes would fail in time to one and then to none. At his death, he could stand where he wanted to stand, without sanction from anyone. The world had ended and the few people left alone ought to be naked, as had been their infant ancestors.

The brains of people sometimes failed them, tormenting them and freeing them with episodes of their dementia. Sixty-one years of age had sometimes been so old as to suffer those curses and those comforts. If Gerald was hallucinating what he thought he saw and didn't see, then he might also have been deluded about the extent of his old age.

Perhaps he was, in fact, already senile: an incarcerated patient crouching in a corner of a cushion-clad asylum. High above him might have been a steel-barred window. Gerald swung his head back and forth to bash his skull against the concrete linoleum floor, but couldn't reach beyond the near side of his brain.

He might've been a patient bound to a white-sheet gurney

bed, with tight leather straps across his torso, arms, and legs. His outstretched arms sensed rain falling onto his weary limbs, but a crazy man could not be certain of his senses. Gerald opened his wet eyes and saw the falling rain he felt. Closing his eyes again but leaving his arms outstretched, he tried to feel the straps against his flesh. They might've already made him numb.

Gerald would've sacrificed his sanity to save the lifeblood of his people. He smiled, imagining his grandchildren and great grandchildren watching him in his senility from behind a hospital observation window.

He might have always been insane, and his memories of a time in which he lived a life and great career might have been more of his delusions. Being a lunatic had become a socially acceptable thing to be. He might've only become insane since he came so close to dying.

The rain continued to fall upon Gerald's head, shoulders, and outstretched arms. Slowly, he believed it. His craziness consoling him as he prepared to die was not a pardon from what he'd done. He needed to be careful, less he let himself become insane. He didn't want to be a mad thing left alone.

Holding his old arms aloft was taxing him. Becoming heavy, Gerald's arms and hands fell to his sides. His eyes opened. Cars or trucks would once have blasted him with horns demanding that he move, before a police officer took him into custody. One speeding vehicle could kill him there, but Gerald would gladly die if by doing so he knew that he was not alone.

Gerald checked his thoughts. He didn't want to die, although he had no reason not to want to. Being old made his situation worse than a younger man would have suffered, but any age to be alone was worse than any age with people there.

Beckoning the people not wanting to be involved to notice him, Gerald walked about. His people had been the light, the heroes and the heroines, the saviours of the world, but hadn't saved themselves. They'd worked hard for everything and presumed they deserved something more for doing so. They'd earned good money to take everything for granted and gave away more money than they could ever earn, but failed completely in everything they did. The naked solitary man walked between the brick and concrete edifices of his inhumanity to himself.

His reflection in cold glass abruptly caught him. Gerald stopped and saw himself, the introverted man without his urban clothes, under falling rain. His skin was faintly white and very little, his creviced body hollow and absurd, among the red ground walls climbing large around him.

That sight of him, naked and alone, convicted Gerald of all his unimportance. Without a family, without a people, he had no call to prime himself and never had. He was just a hairless chimpanzee, who'd thought his suits and office space could make him something more.

Gerald hugged his arms close to his chest, but his bare feet slid against the rain. His legs buckled under him, and he stumbled to the street. His hands reached out and broke the fall, until only his palms and hard-boned knees held him above the bitumen. His hurt left hand was agony and he couldn't dull the pain, while rainwater lashed his naked back, flowing over him into the river street.

The street was near his face as he crouched there, a broken man inside a broken land. Dizziness blurred his vision and he couldn't think or feel too clearly, but his sore brain strove to resurrect the instincts he once knew. Gerald wouldn't cry, although nobody but he would know if he did. The water through his hair across his forehead came too close to his wet eyes.

In incremental staggering movements, Gerald lifted the palm of his left hand to look at it. From the graze eked out a speckle of red blood.

Gerald's head dropped downward, not quite touching the wet ground. Were the world around him, Gerald would not have walked naked in the street. He would not have slipped and fallen. If England and the market town survived but still he fell, then he would quickly have picked himself upright. Instead, he crouched there naked in a torrent. Nobody was there to help him stand.

Tears gripped his eyes, closing into deeper darkness. Gerald wept, no longer for a woman, nor for him losing sweet poor her, but for what he'd come to be. Gerald wept for his regrets, for anything that might've kept their lives secure instead of condemning him the dunce to be alone. They had no reason to have died, but never understood. His anguish was his eulogy, but it was hopelessly inadequate. His life was pointless, embarking upon pursuits in which he could only fail, so weak without a people. He was acutely vulnerable, precariously not coping, without anyone upon which he could depend.

Gerald knew he was pathetic, bumbling through the late hours of his life. He was pathetic to himself and to the ghosts of men and women watching him, but had too much to fear to care about their thoughts. He had himself to try to save, and did not know if he could.

Without security of tenure being alive, he couldn't move too far away. The death to which he was so close was his, that slow-grown suicide. The future was oblivion in grey, dying in the land of his inheritance, with only God to hold his bleeding hand.

ABOUT THE AUTHOR

Simon Lennon has lived, worked, and travelled throughout Europe, America, Australasia, Asia, and the South Pacific. He is married with six children. He is the author of the following books.

Fiction
The King of a Vacant City
Swansong of a Childless People

Non-Fiction
Western Individualism
The End of Natural Selection
The Need for Nations
People's Identity
Of Whom We're Born
Biological Us
A Land to Belong
The Failure of Multiculturalism
Reclaiming Western Cultures
Christendom Lost
Aiding Islam

www.ingramcontent.com/pod-product-compliance
Lightning Source LLC
Chambersburg PA
CBHW030257200626
46816CB00002BA/673